A **Red Dust** Novel

SPLINTERED HEART

LINDA DOWLING

New South Wales, Australia

A catalogue record for this book is available from the National Library of Australia

Splintered heart: A Red Dust Novel/ Linda Dowling. — 1st ed.
ISBN 978-0-6487148-0-4

'and in the end we are all just stories.'

For my brother Marco and our Aboriginal people, particularly the
Wailwan/Weil tribe of the Carinda–Walgett area.

Author's Note

This is a work of fiction set in Australia around the 1960s and '70s. The attitudes towards Indigenous people were different back then compared to the codes of conduct and morals of today, and particularly our more recent anti-discrimination laws. The Indigenous peoples of Australia had lived in Australia for at least 65,000+ years before the arrival of British settlers in 1788. They were dispossessed from their land in 1788 by Britain, which claimed eastern Australia as its own on the basis of the now discredited doctrine of *terra nullius*. Initially, Indigenous Australians were in most states deprived of the rights of full citizenship of the new nation on grounds of their race, and restrictive immigration laws were introduced, giving preference to white European immigrants into Australia.

Discriminatory laws against Indigenous people and multi-ethnic immigration were dismantled in the early decades of the postwar period. A 1967 Referendum regarding Aboriginal rights was carried with over 90% approval by the electorate. Legal reforms from the 1970s won by Aboriginal and Torres Strait Islander people have re-established Aboriginal land rights under Australian law, 200 years after the arrival of the First Fleet.

Parramatta Girls Home has also been known as Parramatta Industrial School for Girls, Girls Training School Parramatta and Girls Training Home. First built by convicts in 1841, Parramatta Training School was a brutal and cruel institution for the incarceration of young women for more than 125 years.

These were not schools as we know them but prisons where harsh and oppressive conditions were concealed under the guise of child welfare philosophies to justify their creation. In 1946, Parramatta Training School for Girls was re-established for the reception, detention, maintenance, discipline, education and training of young women. It then became known as Parramatta Girls Home, but the name belied its function: it was no home. In reality, it was a prison where young girls were stripped of their dignity and liberties and were punished frequently with physical force and threatened with imprisonment.

The Forgotten Australians are the survivors of neglectful and often cruel institutional care in Australia between 1930 and 1970. Roughly 500,000 children who were put into orphanages or so-called homes and institutions suffered at the hands of callous institutional staff. These children suffered deep and lasting feelings of abandonment and many were physically and psychologically scarred.

Although this novel does make reference to the Parramatta Girls Home, this is for fictional purposes only, and the content and characters do not depict any person, either living or dead, who was connected with the institution.

CONTENTS

PART ONE

SPLINTERED

ONE

THE FIBRO MAJESTIC

The summers in the western suburbs of Sydney were stifling. It was 1968 and a particularly fierce summer, where the heat bounced off the walls in the tiny two-bedroom fibro cottage in Fairfield, and the heat haze on the tar roads shimmered in the distance, distorting the road. Lisa O'Connor's father called their cottage the Fibro Majestic, where the cicadas screeched and the mosquitoes were out in full force, all welcoming the approaching night air. The summer seemed to go on forever. Hot days turned into hot nights until relief came with the southerly winds.

The cottage sat on a long and dusty road. When the cars travelled past, the dust clouds would settle over the cottage and then penetrate every crack in the Fibro Majestic's doors and windows. The dust would cover everything in the home. It was choking. Lisa's mother never stopped dusting. Her mother never stopped complaining. Misery was like a river that flowed through their home.

Lisa O'Connor entered the world kicking and screaming in 1955, premature at six weeks. The first born, she was thin as a rake, her father would say. She was followed three years later in 1958 by her brother, Mark, who was chubby but with skin that glowed golden. He won every baby competition their mother entered him in.

Lisa's father, Desmond O'Connor, had decided to settle in Fairfield, in the western suburbs of Sydney, although he had been a farrier since the age of thirteen in the rural area of Mittagong, in the southern highlands of New South Wales. Fairfield, however, was more affordable and quiet. As a returned soldier after World War Two, he was given the choice of Fairfield or inner city Glebe by the War Service Homes Commission, which provided opportunities for the soldiers to settle into civilian life. The commission was first established in 1918 to enable ex-members of the forces who saw active service outside Australia to secure loans for the provision of homes.

Glebe had looked grim and was full of cramped terraces, being an inner city suburb of Sydney, and there was not a blade of grass to be seen. Desmond had recoiled with distaste. 'I'm not bringing my kids up here, Agnes,' he had complained to his wife. 'Where would they play? There's nothing but tar and cement. It's like a bloody rabbit warren. Nothing but burrow after burrow. Even a ferret wouldn't live here!'

When he drove out to look at Fairfield, the other suburb recommended by the War Service Homes, he smiled when he saw small- to medium-sized farms. Market gardens, vineyards and orchards flourished in the low-lying area, benefiting from the alluvial soil near the five creeks that ran through the Fairfield area. There were also dairy and poultry farms.

Desmond had heard that an Aboriginal tribe known as the Cabrogal people wandered the area. In the last quarter of the nineteenth century and the first part of the twentieth century, significant numbers of migrants from Germany, Italy and the Baltic states had also established farms in the area. They were all hard workers.

'This is it,' he had exclaimed to Agnes. 'I can't be a farrier here as there's not much work, but I'll start in the boilermaker trade.' Because of the rural feel, Fairfield felt like home. This is where he would raise his children.

Agnes was the homemaker and Desmond the breadwinner. Like all Irish, he was a hard worker, but he loved a drink. He had married an unhappy lady who never let up with complaints. She would repeat things over and over like a budgie that had learned a new phrase, until her nagging made him leave for the pub. He drank too much but it eased the sound of her voice and the painful memories of war. Abuse was everpresent in the family, physically and verbally, always alcohol driven. He would bellow like a bull when he was on the drink, his behaviour often violent and erratic, turning him into a different person.

Lisa, at thirteen years old in 1968, was scrawny for her height and on the verge of saying goodbye to her childhood. Her thick jet black hair fell to her waist, and her long brown legs drew many stares in her shorts, drawing a natural curiosity from the male population. Although shy, her smile was engaging and there was a twinkle in her green eyes, which glowed like emeralds under her thick lashes. She was very athletic at school, and her passion was sports. This was her outlet.

Lisa's mother Agnes had been previously married to a much older man and had needed to marry because of falling pregnant at sixteen. Janine, Lisa's half-sister, was the product of that brief and disastrous marriage, due to Agnes' ex-husband's drinking and gambling. He died in a car accident when Janine was only two years old, but by that stage, Agnes had moved back in with her mother. Agnes never discussed or made mention of him. It seemed taboo.

Agnes later remarried the tall, handsome Irishman, Desmond O'Connor. She had met him in the local pub when working part-time as a barmaid.

Janine, a secretary, was twenty-five and recently engaged. She was their mother's favourite daughter and physically resembled Agnes, whereas Lisa took after her father. Janine was always worrying about her appearance. Her unruly hair was the bane of her life. It sprung out of her head like a coir mat, just like their mother's. Janine would often stare intensely at Lisa' long jet black mane, which did not go unnoticed.

Janine had met her future husband Lenny Wilkinson at a party. Janine said Lenny was instantly attracted to her because she resembled his own mother. When Janine mentioned this to Agnes, she thought it odd but dismissed it when she met him. Agnes thought Lenny was charming. He was a surveyor by day and a boxer by night. He continually trained and boasted that he had won twelve amateur fights. Lenny came from a very comfortable family—as Agnes put it, 'My girl has hit the jackpot.'

Everyone seemed to like Lenny. Everyone except Lisa. His eyes never left her and followed her every movement. 'He creeps me out,' she would say to Mark. 'I don't trust him, but I don't care, I'm not marrying him.' Lenny's personality took over the room, and he would ooze with charm. He had an army crewcut and always wore shirts that emphasised his muscle development. He was aware of his physical presence. Even Agnes was flirty when he was around.

So wedding plans were in the air for Janine as well as Lisa's favourite aunt, Zena, who was her father's only sister. The family had seen numerous boyfriends of Zena's come and go over the years, but her latest, Alan, a wealthy grazier, would make it to the altar.

Lisa's mother had scoffed and ridiculed when Zena had broken off her two previous engagements. 'That tart is gathering a collection of rings; she could open her own jewellery store,' Agnes would say, never bothering to hide her hostility towards her sister-in-law. 'She is a middle-aged floozy who just flaunts herself amongst the men, and always has done. Her third engagement. Probably offers them things . . . physically. That's how she draws them in,' Agnes would snarl to her husband. 'I only welcome her in our house for you, Des; otherwise, I wouldn't bother. She's a promiscuous cow.'

On those days, Des really took an ear battering and Agnes would whinge long after Zena had left. Des had stopped trying years ago to make the relationship with Agnes and his sister work. They were poles apart. Maybe that was the difference. Agnes pregnant at sixteen, her life changed forever. She never spoke of regret and never let on any dreams she had lost because of the pregnancy. However, her bitterness seemed to escalate over the years.

Zena was the total opposite. She was formally educated and well-travelled. She somehow knew life in suburbia was not the right fit for her. After completing her Teacher's Certificate, Zena saved and then packed her bags. She headed overseas and travelled through London and Europe. Full of life, a raven-haired beauty and almost Rubenesque in her curvy shape, she loved the company of men. Her legs were long and well-muscled from dancing and riding horses all her life. The men were drawn to her like bees to the honey pot.

Lisa adored her Aunt Zena, who was in her early thirties. Zena was an engaging and vivacious woman who laughed easily. Lisa couldn't understand why Agnes didn't like her aunt, and she never wanted her aunt to leave when she came to visit. Zena just seemed oblivious to her mother's cruel mouth and penetrating eyes.

Lisa's half-sister Janine was visiting this weekend. Lisa had never warmed to her and the air had a frostiness when they were together. Janine had the same iciness as their mother and wished her aunt was visiting instead.

While waiting for Janine to arrive, Lisa watched her two best friends in the lounge room: Mark her younger brother and Cassius the blue heeler. Her father boasted again how he had gotten the dog for free. 'You never get cattle dog pups for free,' he said. 'But this one had a broken tail as a pup, which made it look like the letter 'L' sticking out, and he had battered ears that had a curly appearance at their tips, making them look like cauliflowers. That's why I called him Cassius . . . you know, after the famous boxer Cassius Clay, who changed his name that bloke to Mohammad Ali. Queer if you ask me.' Lisa spent hours with the dog. She had a special affinity with animals, more so than with people.

Agnes spotted Cassius inside and snarled, 'Get that dog out of here, Lisa! I don't want him in here, especially when we have food around. I have told you this before. We'll all end up with fleas.' Mark opened the door and let Cassius out, and Lisa followed. It was more peaceful outside with the dog anyway.

It was late afternoon when Janine arrived. Agnes and Janine quickly got under way discussing finances and the pending nuptials. 'Thanks, Mum,' said Janine. 'You know, as soon as you mention the word marriage, everything doubles in price.' Agnes began taking notes on Janine's wishes like a meticulous bookkeeper. Money was not in abundance, so they were working out the 'can afford' and 'cannot afford' details.

Two hours later, Agnes shuffled her notes together. 'We're done now. It was good to clear this and know exactly where we stand, Janine. Do you want to stay for Sunday dinner?'

'No, Mum, I'll be on my way. Where are Lisa and Mark?'

'Outside . . . with the dog. They never stop talking that pair, and they seem to think the bloody dog is human.'

Agnes went to the back door and hollered their names. Mark was the first to appear, shortly followed by Lisa. Cassius was right on her heels.

'Come inside, please. Janine is about to leave.'

Agnes opened the door, and Mark and Lisa trooped in. 'Not you.' Agnes kicked out at the dog.

Janine smiled and hugged Mark, but as Lisa approached, a coolness clipped her voice. 'Hi Lisa,' she said. Her expression soured and an awkwardness settled in the room. Janine fidgeted and her words came out in a rush. 'I should leave now.' She kissed her mother, and they walked to her car.

Lisa looked at Mark and shrugged. 'Boy, that was odd,' she murmured. 'Janine is so weird.' Leaving her brother to fill up with cookies, she went to the bedroom they shared and lay down on her top bunk. Late afternoon sun filtered through the house, and she tried to keep cool until the fierceness of the sun disappeared into the night. She had the top bunk as Mark was not as nimble due to his weight. He just loved food. His little rolls of belly fat cascaded over his shorts. As he grew, her mother was horrified when people would state the obvious. She would frequently tell them off publicly for criticising her son. Agnes was never afraid to speak her mind.

Later in the day, after Janine left, Lisa could hear her parents discussing the costs of the marriage. Zena's name was also mentioned. Her mother was being critical, and her harsh comments flew through the air.

'Honestly, Des, here we are budgeting for our daughter's wedding and making every penny squeak, while your sister seems to be flouting her fortunes and her future husband's wealth. All that talk of getting married abroad and honeymooning in Europe last week when she was here. Then I hear my own daughter trying to meet the cost of a simple wedding.' Lisa could hear her scoffing and clucking throughout the conversation.

Des remained silent. Agnes was on a bender. On days like these she was relentless in her criticism.

'Des, don't ignore me. I'm talking to you! Zena said they're travelling to Europe for their honeymoon,' Agnes snorted. 'She's just marrying Alan for his money. The ring on her finger looks almost fake it's so big. What a bloody show off! She must think she's marrying Rockefeller. Well, their marriage is not going to last; she hates isolation. She likes all the bright lights, your sister.'

'It's just the way it works, Agnes. Alan is a wealthy grazier. Zena has just been fortunate that he has the finances to do as he pleases. Stop nagging. I'm sick of listening to you harp on about this.' Des went back to reading his newspaper.

'It's not fair. The cow has had three cracks and she ends up with a bloke who's loaded.'

Lisa did not hear her father speak. Sometimes Lisa thought he just tuned out. Selective hearing. There was no doubt he could hear his wife's continual venomous spray against his own sister, but sometimes he didn't bother to retaliate. However, his responses were quicker off the mark and sharper when he was on the grog. Lisa knew her mother and Zena had never had a good relationship right from the outset. After Zena's visits, her mother would always bicker, no matter how hard Zena tried. But then her mother never seemed to have a kind word for anyone.

Des finally spoke, his voice raised. *Here we go*, Lisa thought, listening intently.

'For God's sake, Agnes, leave it alone! She's my sister, and I only wish her happiness. Yes, I agree, she may not like the isolation; however, Alan seems like a fairly decent bloke, a hardworking grazier. An honest man. We should only want their happiness going into the future. Third time lucky. And she is older now at thirty-three.'

'Age doesn't make anyone smarter,' retorted Agnes sharply. Des looked at his wife and spoke heatedly. 'That's for bloody sure! She should know her own mind by now, Agnes. Anyway, there will be no wedding in Australia; they want a very quiet wedding overseas. Zena made a lot of friends while living in London, so that's what they plan to do. She'll be Mrs Smith when she gets back home.'

Lisa could hear the dishes and pots clanging loudly as her mother washed up. Agnes did not like a difference of opinion, especially one involving her aunt. She clearly thought this engagement would not last, just like the others. 'That Alan must be a twit not to see through her vanity. Bloody gold digger.'

Lisa had only met Alan on two occasions. Zena had introduced him to Agnes and Desmond when it was clear they were serious about each other.

Alan Smith, her aunt's future husband, had a huge sheep station in western New South Wales, not far from a town called Walgett. It wasn't just a few paddocks; it really was the outback—red dust and wide plains. The station and homestead were called 'Woori'. It was fascinating for Lisa to hear the stories about the place, as well as about her aunt's earlier years.

Aunt Zena had finished her Primary School Teacher's Certificate and travelled abroad, obtaining teaching positions mostly at private schools in London. Zena was intelligent and articulate. When she returned to Sydney, she worked for private schools but then accepted a post to Walgett Primary School after reading an article about the lack of teachers in rural areas. She had a yearning, she had told her brother Des, to get back to the bush. It was there that she met Alan, the tall laconic grazier with piercing blue eyes, at a fund raiser for the Royal Flying Doctor Service. Zena said it was love at first sight. When they first came to the house when Zena announced her engagement, Alan's blue eyes danced when she spoke. He seemed to hang on to every word she said with an amused expression. Smitten. Love was written all over his face. He was awed.

Lisa liked Alan. He was comfortable in his own skin and had a relaxed confidence that people were drawn to. He loved Lisa's curious nature, especially all her questions about the bush.

'What does the name Woori mean?' she had asked him.

'Hey, you got the pronunciation right, kid. It rhymes with eye. Most people don't have a clue how to say it right! I recall my father told me that Woori means "Gift from God".'

On their last visit, Zena had asked Lisa to come and stay with them at Woori during the next Christmas holidays once they were married and settled. Lisa was thrilled with this suggestion.

Having no children, Zena regarded her niece Lisa as a daughter. She knew of the problems and turbulence in the family, as well as the strained relationship Lisa had with her mother. She had also told Alan of the fiery relationship her brother had with Agnes.

'They will keep fighting until they can't fight anymore. It's an Irish thing . . . and the grog doesn't help,' she would lament.

Lisa couldn't wait for the opportunity to escape the fibro cottage. She had her bag packed under the bottom bunk, ready to go when they were ready to have her. Zena had mentioned the following Christmas, when their renovations to the old homestead were complete. The old home had belonged to Alan's parents, and being an only child, it was on the small side. Lisa's mind was brought abruptly back to the present by her parents' raised voices.

'Well, mark my words, I'll bet that no wedding invitations are sent out. She'll change her mind at the last minute.' Agnes just had to get in the last word.

Fist clenched, Des barked. 'Cut it out, Agnes. We did grow up in Mittagong, remember. The southern highlands of New South Wales.'

'So,' Agnes smirked. 'What's that got to do with anything?' Lisa thought she was just asking for a beating. *Mum, you are really pushing your luck.*

'So . . . So! What a stupid thing to say,' Des shouted. 'Let me refresh your memory as the usual fog seems to have settled in your mind. It was bloody cold in winter and stinking hot in summer, and there were acres and acres of land. No bright lights and yes, only a couple of hours from Sydney, but Zena loved the lifestyle there. And she was the only girl in the family, growing up with five brothers. She loved the horses and the animals that Pop had. You're too harsh; you always are. You're being a right bitch. I've had a gutful of your moaning. You are always moaning.' Des stood up and advanced on Agnes, lifting a fist as though to strike her but then stormed out the front door, slamming the door so hard the windows in the kitchen shook.

Later that afternoon, Lisa was still dreaming about Woori and trying to keep cool in the bedroom when she heard her mother's unmistakable yell, 'Dinner's ready.' Her mother was just like a general. Dinner was always early on a Sunday. The whole neighbourhood would always know when it was time for dinner at the O'Connor residence. Lisa heard her father's Holden pull into the driveway. She wondered how many schooners he'd managed to tuck away.

Mark waddled through the back door as Lisa took her place at the table. Her father was already seated, and the smell of beer was obvious. 'By the way, keep that bloody dog out of your bedroom,' her mother snapped. 'I was vacuuming this morning and found dog hair all over the floor. Did you hear what I said, Lisa?' Agnes' voice rose in anger.

Lisa remained silent and her eyes were downcast. She always seemed to be subjected to her mother's tirades. Agnes used her unpleasantness as a tool to force her children to live their life how she wanted it. Lisa longed to break free of her mother's dictatorship.

'Answer me when I speak to you. The dog has to stay outside. I don't want that dog in here. And while you're at it, clean your room up. You live like a pig in there. I don't know how Mark tolerates it.'

Lisa's silence only infuriated Agnes, so she jabbed Lisa in the arm. 'Did you hear me? Answer me!'

'Oh, I wish you would just leave me alone,' Lisa muttered under her breath.

Mark rolled his eyes. He had heard it and knew his mother would have too. He knew Lisa should not have said that. Answering back was a cardinal sin.

'What did you say?' Her mother glared at her. 'Des, don't just sit there. Do something! Didn't you hear her answer back?'

'I didn't say anything,' Lisa said softly, shrinking deeper into her into her chair. For a moment, her mind went blank with fear.

'Des, I said do something!' Her mother's eyes were bulging, her voice shrill.

'Don't let her answer back, Des!' Agnes' hysterical symptoms were often successful in driving Des to strike out at Lisa.

Agnes grabbed Lisa's arm and started to drag her to the laundry tubs. Lisa tried to pull away.

'Help me, Des! I'm going to wash her mouth out. She is not going answer me back and think she can get away with it.'

Des finally exploded, a combination of alcohol and the constant nagging voice. Lisa's father strode forward and grabbed Lisa by the arms. 'Don't fight me,' he ordered as he and Agnes forced her head down and rammed the soap in her mouth.

'How do you like this, then?' Agnes yelled as she dragged the bar of soap in and out of her daughter's mouth like she was scrubbing a pot. 'Answer back and you'll get another dose. This behaviour won't be tolerated. My nerves cannot take this. You are never to speak back to me. You think I can't hear you? You can leave this house and go to a Girls Home. They take girls like you there.' For a heartbeat, Lisa thought it might be a better option, but she'd heard the stories about those 'homes' so she soon dismissed that idea.

Agnes stomped off, and Des followed, shaking his head. Lisa stood alone in the laundry. So much for a quiet Sunday dinner. She wiped her mouth and spat the soap out over the tubs, wondering if she would one day enjoy the taste of soap. And they were always threatening to send her that 'Girls Home'. More emotional blackmail.

'Come out here, Lisa. We haven't got all night.' Lisa drew a long breath. If she didn't move, there would be more trouble, but sitting down to an evening meal made her stomach churn. She sheepishly took her seat at the table. Mark looked terrified. The atmosphere was particularly tense and not conducive to eating.

Lisa hated the days like this. It felt like the house would erupt, like a snake uncoiling, ready to strike. Dinner was always a chore for her to eat. She would push her food away, and many arguments were had at the table. 'Why do you always have to be so bloody difficult, Lisa? Eat your food for God's sake,' Agnes, would snap. 'You can't leave the table until everything is finished.' Some nights, Lisa would sit for an hour at the table after everyone left. Her mother would say she was deliberately disruptive. But Lisa just did not like food, especially her mother's cooking. It tasted like cardboard.

A rubber cord from an old electric frying pan lay over the back of her father's chair as a reminder that poor behaviour or poor manners would not be tolerated. The cord stung more than a cane or ruler, and it had a permanent position at the table. Lisa almost preferred it to having her mouth washed out with soap.

As she ate, she pondered on how there were such double standards in their house. Lisa and Mark had to be good and not speak at the dinner table, and yet her father, when he had been drinking, used the worst language. This time, she kept her thoughts to herself, *Imagine if we washed his mouth out with soap!* Lisa also knew she would never be loved in her mother's eyes. She always appeared to be in the wrong. Her mother was always disapproving of anything she did. *I am worthless, stupid and ugly. Only Aunt Zena seems to care for me,* she thought miserably.

TWO

THE UNION STRIKE

The Christmas holidays were coming to an end, and the new school term was pending. Money was needed to purchase books and new uniforms. Lisa's mother looked horrified when Des came home and said he was on strike. Her father belonged to the Metal Trades Union, and they had called a strike wanting better conditions and more pay. This meant no money coming into the household as her father had stopped working to support the union. This infuriated Agnes as she needed money for the new school year, not to mention Janine's wedding.

'Bloody unions! Why don't you just work, Des, and not bother with them!' Agnes barked.

'Because I would be a bloody scab then, wouldn't I,' her father roared back.

Lisa didn't understand the word scab, but her father tried to explain that the union men stuck together. 'If we don't stick together, the bloody bosses win and we get nothing, no extra money, nothing. That's why we fight.'

With no money coming in, the tension in the home escalated. It was like a smouldering fire ready to burn the house down. Lisa had made a short list for school: exercise books, new uniforms for winter and summer. Mark had made his own list, similar to Lisa. She dared not ask her mother for money, and it looked like her father was not returning to his job for some time. The menu at home changed dramatically and seemed to be nothing but potato and stews. Roast on a Sunday was replaced with pancakes.

The only paper she could find for school was plain white butcher paper. 'We have to write on something, Mark,' Lisa said. 'This looks awful, but it will have to do. We'll catch up with money for books when Dad finally goes back to his job.'

When she started the new term, it was embarrassing in class to pull out the wad of paper held together with brown paper string. Miss Shaw, her teacher, questioned her about the paper. This only brought attention from the other pupils.

'It's . . . it's all I have Miss Shaw,' Lisa stammered, feeling her throat tighten as she struggled to get the words out, her face hot with humiliation. She began to sweat, then glanced around the room looking for an open door. She just wanted to run and hide.

Lisa was taunted by the girls at school, particularly Annette Gardner. If it was not about being scrawny or having second-hand uniforms, Annette would always find something else. Annette was a cute, perky blonde who always seemed to know the answer to every question. Her uniforms were neat and crisp, and her mother was always there to pick her up after school in the latest Holden. Annette enjoyed ridiculing Lisa and got particular joy when she blushed. Lisa just knew her lack of proper school books would be new fodder for even more teasing.

Lisa continued, trying to rescue the situation, even though her voice wavered with embarrassment. 'It's just temporary, Miss Shaw. My exercise books are coming.'

Miss Shaw felt sorry for the girl. She was aware of the taunts. Kids could be so cruel, and she noticed Lisa's discomfort. 'Hey, that's okay Lisa, don't fret. It's no problem. Let me see if there are any spare books you could use in the teachers' Mess Room.'

As Miss Shaw left the classroom, Annette snickered. Lisa felt a fluttering in her stomach.

'Stop staring, Annette. Please leave me alone,' Lisa muttered under her breath.

'You are a pathetic retard,' teased Annette.

Lisa kept her head down and tried to ignore her.

Annette pouted and made her way towards Lisa's desk. 'Why don't you speak? Why do you always keep your stupid head down?'

Annette suddenly lunged at Lisa, pulling her hair. Lisa tried desperately to defend herself as the other students started to shout, 'Fight, Fight,' when Miss Shaw quickly re-entered the room.

'What's going on here!' she exclaimed as she rushed to pull the girls apart. Lisa's mouth was bleeding.

'Detention for both of you. This is most unacceptable. You will report to this room at lunch time. No leisurely lunch break for either of you, and I will be calling your parents to tell them of your behaviour.' Annette smirked as she watched Lisa wipe the blood away.

◊

When Agnes put the phone down to Miss Shaw that afternoon, her blood pressure went through the roof. *Little cow,* she seethed, *disrupting the classroom now. Wait till she gets home. Wait till her father hears about this.* Her fingers drummed on the kitchen table, the anger mounting as she sat waiting for Lisa arrive home from school.

By the time Lisa finally arrived home with Mark, Agnes was ready to explode.

'There you two are,' she said coolly, her lips curling into a sneer.

'Mark, you go outside,' she ordered abruptly.

Looking frightened, Mark ventured, 'What's wrong, Mum?'

Agnes' eyes were locked onto Lisa. 'I said go outside!'

Mark took off down the back steps. The force of his mother's words sent him scrambling. He could sense trouble brewing.

Lisa leaned against the fridge, one hand fidgeting with her plait. She could feel her heart beating rapidly.

'I had a call from Miss Shaw today.' Agnes started advancing on Lisa, who only glanced at her mother. *She knows.*

Before Lisa could think another thought, Agnes was suddenly upon her, driving her head into the fridge. Lisa shook her head, momentarily stunned. The skin had broken and she felt a trickle of blood. In the space of a heartbeat, her mother's fury was like an inferno.

'Now get to your room and don't come out until I say so,' roared Agnes. 'We will wait till your father gets home to punish you for this.'

Lisa felt woozy as she made her way to her room. She lay on her bed and sobbed. *She wouldn't even let me explain. I didn't do anything, I was just trying to defend myself.*

Her father didn't come home until late. He must have headed to the pub and by the time he got home, he had drunk a skinful. Lisa could hear him lurching around the kitchen, staggering and hanging onto things so he would not fall. Agnes now had two people to deal with. At least because he was so pissed, Lisa would not get a belting tonight.

The union strike continued for a good four weeks, but her father seemed happy, despite the financial effect on the family, as his wage was going to be increased. He told them the union had been successful in holding out, so the working conditions, as well as a salary increase, were under negotiation.

Since her run-in with Annette in class, Lisa had priced the exercise books at the local newsagent while walking home from school. If she could get the money to buy just one, she would be happy and the maybe the relentless taunts at school would stop. It was bad enough having to deal with her mother continually, let alone deal with the girls at school. It was too much.

When Lisa came home from school that afternoon, she noticed her mother's handbag on the kitchen table. Her purse lay open, and she saw a pound note. Lisa stared at the money for a while and thought it was all the money she needed to buy more than one book. She breathed deeply. *Would her mother miss it?* She closed her eyes and could hear the taunts again.

The heat flushed through her body at the thought of being caught stealing and the repercussions. Her hands shook like she had palsy until she reached into her mother's purse and took the pound note. As she stuffed the money in her pocket, she felt light-headed. Her heart was beating faster. She took deep, controlled breaths and made her way to her bedroom to hide the note.

It was late afternoon when she sat on the back step with Mark and heard her mother speaking softly to her father. He was just home from work. Lisa craned her neck to try and hear the conversation through the screen door, but their conversation was inaudible. Lisa drifted in her thoughts. *Maybe they won't miss it.* Then she heard her father calling her into the kitchen.

'Stay here, Mark. I think this is going to be big trouble,' Lisa told her brother.

Moving with apprehension and fear, she bit down hard on the inside of her cheek. *I know what's coming. They know what I've done.* Her mouth felt dry and she moved so slowly it was as if her legs wouldn't work. As she approached her father, she rubbed her arms repetitively, as though she were cold. Raising her eyes to his, she saw his face was hard with anger. *Volcanic eyes,* she thought, *with the look of a mean fighting dog.*

'Sit down, Lisa,' her father bellowed as he walked towards the chair where the electric cord lay. She looked at her mother whose bitter mouth was firmly clenched, her eyes cold and flinty. Lisa slid into the chair and awaited the punishment. *I've really messed up big this time. They know I took that money.*

Des took a deep breath and stared at her, and although he spoke quietly, his words were laced with steel. His eyes were bulging and the veins in his neck stood out.

'Lisa, a pound note seems to have disappeared from your mother's purse. Do you have any idea what's happened or do you know why it's missing?'

Her back stiffened, bracing for the punishment, and her gaze dropped to the floor. Her hands rested in her lap, and she began to crack her knuckles. She knew there was no way out and she knew her guilt was showing. She looked at her mother for sympathy, but Agnes merely smoothed her hair as if she were getting ready for a social event.

Her father grabbed the electric cord. Lisa did not move but sat staring at her feet, willing a different ending to what she knew lay ahead. She felt her body shutting down, not speaking or responding. *Stay numb, Lisa. Block it out,* she ordered herself.

'Well, what do you have to say for yourself?' her mother questioned with a twisted smile. Lisa remained silent as the tears streamed down her face. She wished she were somewhere else as a wave of nausea engulfed her quivering body. A scream locked down in her throat and fear became a tangible living force, holding her captive.

Her father's voice grew stronger. 'I will ask you again. Do you know anything about the missing pound note?'

'Yes . . . I took the money! she sobbed. 'I needed it for school. I'm so sorry, please, please don't hit me.'

'Stand up,' her father commanded. 'This household will not tolerate theft!' The cord dangled in his right hand, and he moved his body into a position where he was clearly going to beat her with it. It wasn't the first time, so she knew the pain about to be inflicted.

When she stood up, her father's eyes remained wide and rounded with very few blinks as he dealt the punishment. He seemed to enjoy it. Lisa bit back a scream when she felt the first lash strike her legs.

'Stop. Please,' she whimpered as she tried to pull away. Her father was holding her right arm and was almost behind her. He didn't stop.

Lisa could see her mother's warped smile, her cheeks going a light pink with pleasure. Agnes lifted her chin while she watched the cord striking her daughter's legs.

Her father stopped on the sixth blow, his chest puffing out. 'Go to your room now and bring that money back to your mother. It's for food on our table. Next time you need money, just ask.' As Lisa limped past her mother, she felt the tears flow hot on her cheeks.

Lisa reappeared and handed the pound note to her mother. Agnes' eyes narrowed. 'You won't try that stunt again. I know every penny in that purse!'

'I only wanted to buy some books to write in for school,' Lisa sobbed, wiping the tears away. Her mother grunted scornfully, her eyes cold and flat as she turned away. No excuse would be accepted.

Lisa felt the welts forming on her legs. Returning to her room, she lay still on her bunk. 'Are you okay?' Mark asked gingerly, having snuck inside. Lisa was the person he loved most in the world.

'I'm fine, Mark.' Her voice sounded so frail.

'I just wanted money to buy some books. I don't know why I got beaten so badly.' She felt hollow and empty, her very being eroded by grief and misery.

Why couldn't her parents just be nice? Why was it so hard to get money for school essentials? What she would give to live with her Aunt Zena instead of them! She cried herself to sleep.

The following morning, there was an envelope on the table with her name scribbled on the front. There were some coins inside. She stuffed the envelope into the pocket of her school uniform. *Why couldn't you have just given me some money when you saw my school notes scribbled on butcher paper?* she thought miserably.

THREE

THE FIANCÉ

Janine was coming over later the next evening to follow up on her wedding arrangements with her mother. Agnes was happy now as Des had returned to work and there was more money in the pay packet.

'The unions do a bloody good job even though we all starve during the process,' Agnes said. Despite the extra money in Des' wage, things were still tight financially and there wasn't a great deal extra to splash out on a wedding. On top of this, Janine was not comfortable asking Des to pay for the wedding. Janine had confided in Agnes, 'I never feel he loves me, Mum, that's why I'm not comfortable asking for money. Maybe it's because I'm not his natural daughter. I always feel like an outsider, like the object he had to adopt.'

'Don't be silly, Janine. That's a stupid thought,' Agnes admonished. Deep inside though, Agnes knew Janine was right. Des did treat her differently. When they first married, he didn't drink as much. He couldn't, working two jobs, day and night to get the mortgage payments down, so he rarely interacted with her. Only once, Des had struck Janine, and Agnes said she would leave if he ever touched her again. There was a residual coolness when he spoke to Janine after that and he never offered any conversation unless Janine spoke first. It was almost like he had no time for her or avoided her. Janine was pleased when she got her first job at sixteen and moved out to share a house with girlfriends.

There was also an emotional distance between Lisa and Janine. It was not only the age gap—Lisa had just turned thirteen and Janine was now twenty-five—but also their physical appearance. Janine was consumed by jealousy over Lisa's growing beauty. Lisa was dark and exotic, which made her wild green eyes look like shamrocks. She was lithe in her physique. Janine was short and plump, and no matter how hard she tried with her diet, her waistline remained the same. She would look at Lisa and seethe. Janine's wiry hair was almost unmanageable, and when Lisa tossed her thick black mane, anger would flash across Janine's face.

Des would often comment to Agnes what Lenny, the young athletic boxer, saw in his stepdaughter. 'She's no beauty, but I guess opposites do attract,' he'd say.

'Well, Janine is the caretaker and dotes on him; she looks after his every need. He comes from a good, solid family, and they seem to be very comfortable financially. It's a good pairing if you ask me, Des.'

'It's bloody odd he thinks Janine looks like his mother! Was that the attraction? It's weird if you ask me. He's a talkative bugger, charming . . . could charm the birds out of the trees. Bit different to Janine.'

'What do you mean?' snarled Agnes. 'What's wrong with my daughter . . . err, our daughter?

Des didn't want to go any further. He wanted peace. But Janine was critical and judgemental and had the same acid tongue as Agnes. He heard a car pull up into the driveway and decided he would make himself scarce.

Agnes got up to greet her daughter. 'Come in, Janine. Where's Lenny?' she asked upon noticing he wasn't with her daughter.

'He's on a long cycle ride today, can't keep him off that push-bike. It helps with his boxing training. He says it's good for his legs.'

'You look lovely, dear,' Agnes commented as she led Janine to the kitchen and put the kettle on to boil. 'How are the wedding plans coming along?'

'Just great, Mum, no hiccups so far. The church and venue have been booked, and Lenny's parents will pay for the reception, photographer and the cars. Are you able to pay for the flowers in the church and bouquets?' Janine felt embarrassed to ask, but her mother nodded as she poured the tea.

'There is one other thing.' Her mother brought the two cups of tea over and looked at her daughter. Janine laughed. 'It's not serious, Mum, but people may ask why Lisa isn't a flower girl or part of the bridal party. We've had our differences as you well know, and I just don't want her involved. It's my wedding. What do you think?'

'Well, as you said, it's your wedding, so you can have who you want for bridesmaids. It doesn't have to be family. I have to agree with you, Janine. Lisa is not an easy girl in that I never seem to get through to her. She never speaks really, I mean to me as a mother. I feel like I picked up the wrong child from the hospital.' Agnes laughed and knew she would enjoy telling Lisa she was not wanted in the bridal party.

Janine nodded. 'I've never felt comfortable around her, Mum. I always feel as if she looks right through me. Maybe it's the age difference, but the silences when we sit together are very uncomfortable. I'm an adult and working, and she has just hit those teenage years, so who knows? *And really who cares? Certainly not me.* Janine kept her real thoughts to herself.

Janine knew in the back of her mind that Lisa was growing into a real beauty, and she did not want her to take the attention away from her big day. *It's my wedding and I'll have who I want. Not that half-sister, that's for sure.*

Agnes suddenly called out to Lisa across the backyard. Turning back to Janine, she said, 'We had best tell her in case she thinks she's going to be part of the bridal party. She hasn't mentioned anything but who knows with that silly girl what she thinks.'

◊

Lisa came into the house and looked at the two women. 'Shall I pour you a cup, Lisa,' Janine asked.

'No thanks, I'm fine.' She stood awkwardly, not knowing what they wanted. An uncomfortable silence filled the air.

Agnes cleared her throat. 'Janine wants to discuss a few things with you. This is just ladies business. Take a seat.' Lisa sat slowly, her mind already creating a mental tally of what could go wrong or what they wanted to discuss.

Lisa felt no warmth from them, and her first thought was to flee. If the discussion involved Janine's fiancé Lenny, she knew there was danger. Lisa felt very uneasy around him. He was tactile in his responses and seemed to leer at her when he was in her presence. Lisa was glad he wasn't here today. She couldn't put her finger on it but he stood too close, he watched her too intently and he was always trying to separate her from Mark so that she was alone. She forced herself to focus on what Janine was saying, her tone having an air of smugness while she patted her hair and smoothed it into place.

'Lisa, I just wanted to let you know that we've decided not to have you as a flower girl or bridesmaid.'

Lisa looked at her blankly. *Why are you telling me this?* she wondered.

Janine and Agnes were waiting for a reaction. They looked at each other surprised. Agnes glared at Lisa with peevish displeasure. Lisa knew she was expecting some sort of a reaction, but Agnes wasn't going to get one. She had learned over the years it was better to say nothing and not react.

'Is that all? asked Lisa, relieved.

Janine continued, 'Just in case you may have thought you were needed . . . you're not.' Her voice dripped with sarcasm.

Lisa smiled weakly. She didn't want to be in the bridal party. They had done her a favour. She shrugged her shoulders. 'Um, that's okay. It's your wedding. Whatever works for you, Janine.'

'Don't say it like that, Lisa,' snapped her mother. 'Janine is just trying to be polite.'

It didn't matter what she said or how she said it, her mother would always find fault. She really wanted to just go back outside with Mark and Cassius. She didn't care about the wedding, let alone to be in it. Just the thought of being that close to Lenny sent shivers down her spine. *Phew, I've dodged a bullet,* was all she could think.

'Oh, sorry, but really Janine, it doesn't worry me,' said Lisa. 'Whatever makes you happy.' Agnes just grunted.

As she walked away, Lisa felt her body sag. She wondered why her half-sister suddenly felt it was important to tell her this news. This was suspicious. They were always planning and scheming. Pigeon pair, her mother and half-sister. She let these thoughts go as she made her way into the backyard, looking for Mark and Cassius to take her mind off the disturbing conversation. There was an overwhelming sense of danger, a sense of impending doom.

As the wedding drew nearer, Lenny became a regular visitor. He engaged her mother easily and Agnes thought he was charming. Des thought he was over-generous with his compliments and narcissistic. Des often caught him looking in the hallway mirror. 'That bloke has a preoccupation with his appearance, always looking in the mirror, particularly his body. Probably takes more time in the bathroom than Janine.'

Lenny was older than Janine, turning thirty-two just before their wedding. He'd also been married before. When Agnes had asked why his first marriage dissolved, Lenny told her that his ex-wife was unable to fall pregnant, and he really wanted to start a family.

While everyone else was smitten with Lenny, except maybe her father, Lisa's instincts told her to keep her distance from him. If he walked into a room, Lisa walked out of it. She tried to hide her sour expression at the sight of him, and more than once, her mother looked disapprovingly, shaking her head but not saying anything. Lenny had a booming laugh and a grin that conveyed secret knowledge. He would always try to position himself near Lisa, stroking her arm if it was within reach, and he never stopped trying to make small talk. She didn't like him but would never repeat it. She only knew there was an unshakable sense of something being wrong with him. Staying away from him was going to be difficult as he would now be part of the family. *My brother-in-law. Ugh!* She shuddered at the prospect.

Sunday lunch was the obligatory baked dinner, and Janine had already arrived with Lenny. Every time Lisa looked up, she would catch him staring at her. He had cold, hard eyes that travelled over her body, and she hated his mouth, a cruel thin line, and he was always licking his lips. While Janine entered her mother's bedroom and began to show Agnes the wedding designs and patterns for gowns, Lenny chatted to Des about his boxing profession and the fights that were being planned for the near future.

'I don't understand why you'd want to get in a ring and get your head deliberately bashed about,' said Des. 'Although I can see your ears don't look like cauliflowers yet. Not a good look, mate.'

Lenny's laugh was hollow. 'I've been lucky so far, twelve wins.' Lisa groaned inwardly as she heard this for the umpteenth time. 'That's why I train so hard, so I move quicker. Sometimes if I'm out in the field surveying, I can knock off early from work and get to the gym and train more. It's all about the training.'

'But you get your brains battered when they do collect you with a good punch. Makes you stupid in the long run, mate. You'll get dementia. In twenty years' time you will be dribbling into your pillow in some nursing home,' said Des.

Janine appeared at the door. 'Lunch is an hour away, Lenny. Why don't you go back home and feed that collection of rabbits. I'm sorry I rushed you out of your mum and dad's house, but I thought lunch would be nearly ready.'

'Do you want to come, Lisa?' asked Lenny.

Lisa froze and shook her head. Fear clutched at her heart with its cold fingers.

Lenny continued. 'Come on, it'll be fun. Your mum said you have an affinity with animals.'

Janine turned to Lisa. 'He has quite a collection of rabbits, and they are so cute. You'll enjoy it.'

Lisa just stared at Janine, her pulse quickening and her muscles tensing up. Why was she being so nice? She'd never bothered before about animals or caring about anything Lisa liked. In her mind, Lisa was screaming for rescue.

'No, please, I don't want to go. I want to stay here . . . with my brother.'

She shifted uncomfortably, a feeling of panic spreading over her body. She didn't want to be alone with her sister's fiancé. Her gut instinct told her she would then be on a journey from which there would be no return.

'Don't be silly,' said her mother dismissively. 'It's a fifteen-minute drive. Just go with Lenny. You'll have fun. You know you love animals. Leave your brother here. His father has to trim his hair yet again. Bloody lice!'

'I . . . I said, I don't want to go,' Lisa whimpered. Images flashed through her mind of impending danger at being alone with Lenny.

'Lisa, please stop this nonsense,' her mother barked. She drew closer to her daughter and grabbed her arm.

'Do not embarrass me or our family,' Agnes hissed. 'You are going, and there will be no more of this rubbish.' There was deathly silence, and Lisa felt the terror coursing through her. She wasn't sure why she was so afraid, but an alarm was going off somewhere deep in her mind—an alarm she couldn't switch off.

Lenny looked pleased at the suggestion that Lisa accompany him, and a sly smile crept across his face. He was enjoying her fear. He quickly moved towards Agnes, trying to calm the situation.

'Come on then, Lisa. We'll be back in about forty-five minutes.'

Lisa felt helpless, withdrawing into herself. She knew there was no way out. Lenny motioned for her to come with him to his red sports car, taking her by the hand. Her legs felt like concrete on the slippery lino floor. The march to his car felt like a march to her hanging. Her eyes were downcast, her head hung low, but the rapid beat of her heart told her everything.

Lenny's grip was tight. She felt the clamminess of his hands before she tried to pull away. He opened the passenger door, and Lisa sat down. Lisa could feel the perspiration run down her neck. As they drove towards his parent's home, she began to feel physically ill. Lisa wished she had not been forced to go. She had no control. A sensation of helplessness swept over her. *What will happen to me?*

Lisa leaned towards the passenger door and shifted her body in that direction as they drove towards his parent's home. Unfortunately, Lisa also knew that his parents were away, so there'd be no-one else at the home to look out for her. Her limbs felt paralysed at this thought. Lenny was trying to make conversation, but she concentrated on looking out the window and was silent for the entire car ride.

Suddenly, Lisa felt his hand on her thigh. She pulled her leg away as they drove into a long driveway, not wanting to get out of the car. Thoughts were swirling in her mind about how to get out of this.

'I'll stay here and wait for you,' she said to Lenny as the car pulled to a stop. Lisa felt safer in the car. 'You can just feed the rabbits yourself.' Lisa looked around, her head darting back and forward, as if surveying the area, but not actually looking at anything. Her pulse was beating in her ears, blocking out all other sounds.

Lenny came around to the passenger's side and opened the door. 'No, you won't. You're coming with me. Now stop wasting time and come this way. We have to get back to your family for lunch.' And he started to pull Lisa out of the car.

As he dragged her towards the house, she noticed his breathing was heavier. Lisa wanted to run away. There was no need now for him to put on an act to impress others and it dawned on her just what kind of man he was. When they stepped into the house, it was still and empty. Lisa was shaking uncontrollably, terror sucked the very breath from her mouth.

'Just down this way,' Lenny murmured as he pushed her down the hallway. She moved slowly and had an uncontrollable urge to flee. He was directly behind her and kept bustling her through the rooms and then finally into his bedroom. 'This is my room,' he stated with a flourish. Lisa looked at him blankly.

Lenny closed the door. He had beads of sweat across his forehead and across his top lip. Lisa was repulsed, and shock coursed through her body, to the point that she felt she would lose control of her bladder. She shut her eyes tightly, her heart pounding. 'Just relax,' he whispered, his voice now lower, his breathing heavy.

Manoeuvering Lisa over to his bed, he pushed her backwards onto it, her legs dangling over the side. 'You don't need to tell anybody about this,' Lenny breathed. 'This is our secret, our secret little game, and if you tell anybody, no-one will believe you. They'll just think you're trying to cause trouble for me and your sister. You'll be sent to a Girls Home, just like Agnes is always threatening you.'

He stood above her, like an eagle looking at its prey, scrutinising her entire body. He unbuttoned his pants, and they fell to the floor. Lisa had never seen a man naked, and she grimaced at the sight of his erect penis. She began hyperventilating as Lenny kneeled to the ground, again squeezing her eyes tightly shut, not wanting to see, not wanting to feel. She felt his hands reach up and slide her shorts and underwear off. She tried to move away but he held her firmly in place.

Lisa was now naked from the waist down. She felt so exposed and was trying to focus her thoughts on anything but this to keep fear from taking over.

Lenny's hands begin to trace her slender young thighs. It were as if her body was not her own. Suddenly she felt something soft and wet between her legs, and realised it was his tongue. Lisa gasped in shock. It was a mysterious sensation. She tried again to pull away but his tongue kept tracing around the top of her thighs and between her legs. She wanted to scream and felt tears trickling down her face. She didn't know what he was doing or why he was doing it.

He kept circling his tongue between her legs then stopped to try and kiss her. She turned her face away in repulsion and attempted to push him off. His hand remained firmly on her chest, and his eyes glistened at the sight of her tender thighs and her young womanhood exposed as he looked back down at her body. She saw his right hand drop down between his legs and he began to massage his penis. Then he looked up at the ceiling and groaned. He shuddered and arched his back, moaning as his semen filled his hand. Lisa did not move. She felt a combination of both fascination and revulsion.

He finally stopped and handed her underwear. She watched him wipe the saliva from his mouth before he instructed, 'Remember what I said, Lisa. This is our secret, you do not tell anyone. Do you understand me?'

His voice was harsh and cold. 'If you say something, no-one will believe you, and they send girls away who lie. You will never see anyone you love ever again, not your brother or Cassius. And certainly not your Aunt Zena.'

Lisa could only nod, a sense of unreality settling over her. 'Okay,' he said. 'Let's go and see the rabbits, and then I'll take you home.'

Lisa followed him in a daze as she ambled through the caged rabbits. Nothing made sense, and she wondered what had just happened to her. It was a sensation of pleasure and a sensation of horribleness. Her mind was scrambling to understand.

On the drive home, Lenny touched her leg, sliding his hand up and down her thigh. Lisa pulled away. She didn't speak. When they arrived back at her home, she could hear her mother discussing marriage plans with Janine, but went straight to her room, feeling Lenny's eyes boring into the back of her head. She closed the door of her bedroom and climbed up onto her bunk, wanting to be alone. She felt worthless, and there was a clenching in her stomach.

Lisa clutched herself, touching between her legs. *What just happened?* her mind kept repeating over and over in a state of confusion. She felt pressure in her chest from forgetting to breathe, and her sobs were strangled with emotion and indignation. Her thoughts continued to tumble, *I want to tell every-one. I want to know what happened to me and why he was doing it.*

Mark had heard the sports car pull up and knew his sister had returned. He raced up to the house, ran inside and asked where his sister was.

Lenny said, 'I saw her going to her bedroom,' and watched as Mark made his way there. He knew he had reinforced upon Lisa that what happened was their secret and that she understood.

Mark bounded into the bedroom and stood on the lower bunk, his little hands just reaching to his sister who was lying with her back to him. He was excited to learn about the rabbits. 'How were the rabbits?' he asked. As she turned, he could see her puffy eyes. 'What's wrong, Lisa? Are you crying? Did the rabbits make you sad?'

'No,' she replied. 'I'm just tired, that's all. Your hair looks funny again. Dad seems to go shorter every time.' She smiled as her lovely brother pulled a face.

Lisa thought about telling Mark what had really happened, but what would a ten year old understand if she couldn't even make sense of what occurred? Then there was the reality of the threat. A Girls Home. She had read and heard of these places and how badly the girls were treated. She felt sheer terror at the thought of being sent away. Lisa lay in the blackness of the night. She drew her knees to her chest in a foetal position and thoughts of self-loathing and inadequacy began to fester like an open sore. She would soon have to face Lenny across the dinner table.

◊

'Lisa was extremely quiet over dinner, Des,' said Agnes in annoyance. 'Did you notice? She was picking at her food. I thought it was extremely nice of Lenny to offer to take her for outings. I have real concerns over her behaviour. She's up and down lately, so moody, even if she is thirteen years old. But if she keeps this up—'

'You're not on that again about homes and stuff! Leave it be. She's a teenager, and we have our own methods of discipline. Maybe more outings with Lenny and Janine will do her good,' said Des.

'Yes, Lenny is so thoughtful.' Agnes glanced across at Des with a look that radiated superiority.

FOUR

POINT OF NO RETURN

Des roused Lisa the next morning. 'Wake up! You have school. Mark is already up and dressed.'

Lisa turned her back to him, mumbling, 'I don't want to go. I don't feel well. I want to stay in bed.' He placed a hand on her forehead. 'You don't seem to have a temperature, so get yourself up, get moving, and we will have no more of this nonsense.' As her father was leaving the house for work, he reminded her that the Fairfield Show was on this coming weekend.

'You need to get the roosters and those silky hens ready for show entry. You know we enter every year. Can't let the team down.' Her father was always very proud of his entries. He always seemed to win. Little blue ribbons filled the garage. Lisa loved the show too, the carnival atmosphere, the big Ferris wheel and sideshow alley, where very strange people appeared. But this did not make her mood shift or her self-loathing fade. She stayed in bed.

Mark took off for school at the usual time, and Lisa could hear her mother clattering around in the kitchen. She knew her father would have told her that she was still in bed. It was only a matter of time before her mother's voice would be barking at her. Lisa heard her Agnes at the front door, waving Mark off to school. Start counting Lisa: One, two, three, four—

Agnes suddenly appeared at Lisa's bedroom door. 'Are you pulling a swifty? You may pull the wool over your father's eyes but not me young lady,' she spat and then stomped away. Not a spark of sympathy. Lisa buried herself under her doona. She lost track of time but finally heard the front door slam. Alone, her thoughts of self-loathing returned and then self-harm.

Lisa refused to leave her bedroom that day, apart from using the bathroom. She did not want to see or speak to anyone. The day turned to night and as she lay in bed, she pulled at her hair and muttered to herself. The next day, Mark tried to cheer her up.

'Come on, Lisa, you can't stay in bed, you have to help me with the chooks for the show. I can't do it on my own. If you stay in bed one more day, I heard them say they are calling in the doctors.'

What doctors?'

'I don't know. The ones who'll say if you're crazy or not. That's what Mum said. Come on, you have to come to school with me.'

Lisa bit her lip. *I must avoid questions.* She got up and splashed her face and came into the kitchen with Mark.

'Oh, I see. We're ready for school now, are we?' mocked Agnes, sipping on her tea. Lisa avoided her mother's glare. They made their lunches, and she followed Mark to the school bus. She felt like she was going through the motions in an almost catatonic state. Her mind was totally confused.

The weekend arrived, and it was time for the Fairfield Show. Lisa flatly refused to go. She wanted to stay in her room and shut the world out.

Des and Mark selected two beautiful silky hens and a big white rooster. Mark diligently groomed and brushed them in preparation for the show. They wanted to win again this year and place another blue ribbon in the garage. Bundling the hens and the big white rooster into their respective crates, off they went early Saturday morning. It was quite a big show, and people came from afar to enter all manner of stock. Lisa's father said it was like a mini Easter show.

After they left, Agnes made her way to Lisa's room, where she lay on her bunk with her back to the doorway. Agnes cleared her throat and as she spoke, her voice was harsh and abrasive.

'Now, Lisa, you need to snap out of this. Your father expected you to go to the show,' her mother snapped. As she reached over to touch her daughter, Lisa flinched and pulled away.

Agnes continued. 'Stop this right now. I will have to call a doctor. This behaviour is not right, and it's stressful to the household.' Sneering at her daughter she said, 'You'll get no sympathy from me.' Lisa just inched closer to the wall.

As she left the room, Agnes turned. 'They take troublesome girls away. You know that, don't you?'

Lisa's jaw tightened as she listened to her mother's footsteps fading away. *Why is everyone trying to get rid of me, send me to a home? I haven't done anything wrong!* she agonised, folding her arms around herself as a form of protectiveness while she rocked back and forward. She began to suck her thumb.

It was late afternoon when Mark reappeared, waving the blue ribbon. 'Hey, Lisa, here's your blue ribbon. I just groomed the ones you said to take.' Mark was jubilant, and a slight smile crossed her lips. He stood watching his sister intently.

He knew Lisa was in some sort of pain, and he'd heard his parents discussing sending her away. Mark stood on his bunk so that he could reach up to her. Lisa turned to face him and he took her hand softly. He put the ribbon down next to her.

'Lisa, you need to . . . sort of perk up, be happy or something. They will send you away. I heard them talking. You can tell me what's hurting you. I'm your best friend.'

Fear ripped through her body again. *Where would they send her and for how long?* She had difficulty swallowing with the lump in her throat and fought to hold back the tears. *My mother is just waiting for the right chance to get rid of me.*

'Thanks, Mark, but I just feel so frightened. Everything I do and say is wrong. Mum just jumps on me for no reason and I'm so tired of Dad belting me with the cord or them shoving soap in my mouth.'

'Come on, I'll help you get up. Don't let them send you away,' he repeated. 'I'll get a face cloth from the bathroom.' Mark returned and wiped his sister's face. Her hair was tangled and her appearance dishevelled. Dark circles were under her eyes. The energy he so loved about her was gone.

'You must try. Please try, for me,' he pleaded. Mark helped her down from her top bunk and placed her arm over his shoulder as they stood together. 'Let's go. You can fix yourself up on the way to the kitchen.' He watched his sister's shuffling steps and lethargy but at least she was up.

When Lisa entered the kitchen, her mother looked stunned. Lisa knew by the surprised look on her mother's face that she had already made plans to get rid of her.

'Sit down, Lisa. Let me get you a cup of tea. It's nice to see you out of the bedroom,' Des said. 'We've eaten but perhaps Agnes can make you a sandwich?'

'No, I'm not hungry.' Lisa sat quietly. 'Good you got some blue ribbons, Dad.'

'Yes. Mark couldn't wait to bring them home,' Des said proudly.

Lisa made a sad attempt at blindly watching the television. She stared vacantly and felt her world spinning. The doorbell rang, and Janine and Lenny appeared unexpectedly. Lisa inwardly groaned.

'Oh, Janine, Lenny, how wonderful to see you both,' said Agnes, her voice dripping with charm.

Des chatted about their entries at the show and held up the blue ribbons.

'You should come out to the show next year. It's a lot of fun,' enthused Des. 'They even have boxing out there, Lenny.'

Lisa ignored them and looked straight ahead at the television. She wanted to make herself invisible by retreating further into herself and made no effort to acknowledge Janine or Lenny. She felt his eyes roaming over her body, and the same feeling of terror coursed through her veins. Lisa wanted to run from this man but knew the consequences if she suddenly took off. Agnes scowled at Lisa, her eyes turning to slits. It was rude that she didn't acknowledge her sister or Lenny.

'Well, what brings you here at this time of the night?' asked Des.

'We were just passing. I'm dropping Janine off to the train station as she's staying with a girlfriend, who'll be the Matron of Honour,' Lenny explained.

'Oh, why don't you stay here tonight, Lenny,' offered Agnes. 'We have a blow-up mattress, saves you travelling back and forth.'

Lisa's head swivelled. *Mum, no! Please, no!*

Lenny looked at Lisa and smiled. She wanted the ground to swallow her up. Her feelings of dread returned, and she began shaking at the thought of him staying in their house.

Lenny casually looked at Lisa with a sick sense of power. 'No, that's okay, Agnes. I'm still painting the new house we just bought. Needs a few repairs and a major overhaul of bathrooms and the kitchen but we have plenty of time. We want to move in after the wedding. I have to keep moving. Mum and Dad have been great to put us both up. They don't want us to leave.'

'That sounds wonderful. I can't wait to see the house,' Agnes said, looking very pleased.

'Yeah, it looks great, Mum,' Janine said with an exaggerated happiness. 'We've done a lot of renovation work, and Haberfield seems to be a popular area for newlyweds. A lot of Italians, you know, the new arrivals, are moving there. It's kind of flash inner west not far from Sydney. When the house is finished, which is not that far off, I'll take you over to see it.'

Lenny leaned against the door. Lisa could feel his heavy gaze. 'As Janine isn't going to be here, I can collect Lisa tomorrow if you like, Agnes. I need a bit of a hand with some little things. Getting up and down ladders to change brushes, those type of jobs. But only if that's okay. It's obviously just for the day. I know Sunday is supposed to be a day of rest but a helper would be great.'

Lenny's thin lips were twitching as he offered the suggestion. Lisa looked at her mother and began to shake her head. The fear his words invoked must have shown on her face.

'No. Please, Mum, I'd rather stay here. I don't want to go,' she pleaded. She wished she could expose his ugliness to the others but she didn't know how. It felt like all the cards of life were against her.

'Yes, Lisa would love to help you, Lenny. I'll speak to her and let you know what time you can pick her up tomorrow.' Agnes smiled sweetly to Janine and Lenny. She showed them to the door and bade them goodnight.

◊

'Where's Mark?' Agnes asked her husband, after seeing her daughter and Lenny off. Lisa had already gone to bed.

'He toddled off to bed. Fat and full. But what's going on here with Lisa? Something isn't right,' said Des. 'She didn't greet her sister or Lenny, and there's a tension. I don't know. I can't explain. But you could cut the air with a knife. I know the girls have never been close but Lisa seems to really draw away?'

Agnes hissed. 'Well, you're right! It's not normal behaviour. Even you can see that. Just a whole lot of shit if you ask me. I don't think she's right in the head sometimes. Probably needs to see a shrink.' Des shook his head.

'Don't shake your head like that and ignore her behaviour, Des. Something has to be done,' spat Agnes.

'Let's speak to her in the morning. See what the problem is. The girl looks a sorry sight in case you hadn't noticed. She's too bloody thin.'

Agnes was taken aback and stood with her arms akimbo. Her tone was scathing. 'Don't feel sorry for the little bitch. She's manipulating the situation, being lazy and putting up more barriers to the relationship with her sister. Lisa is probably jealous her older sister has found a real catch.'

Des suddenly exploded. He could hear no more of Agnes' bitching. 'I'm going to the pub,' he yelled. There's too much fecking shit going on under this roof.' He stormed out of the house.

It was late when Des arrived home. From the bedroom, Agnes could hear him staggering around the kitchen. *Bloody useless Irishman.* She hoped he was too drunk to pick a fight.

Agnes swung her legs over the side of the bed early Sunday morning. It had been a restless night, even though Desmond had slept on the lounge. Agnes wanted the matter about Lisa sorted, so she marched into the lounge room. Her husband was snoring deeply.

'Des, wake up. Wake up now!' she bellowed and raised her leg to boot him in his ribs.

'What! Oh, feck, what are you on about now? If the girl doesn't want to go, let it be for God's sake, woman.'

'No, Des. We need to get this sorted. I don't want Lisa's behaviour to continue like this in our household. It's disruptive and inconsiderate.' Her husband just grunted in reply and turned over. 'Wake up, Des. You have to head to the markets and that auction this morning. You're taking Mark, so get going.'

Agnes then marched into Lisa's room like a general from the army on a mission. Lisa turned slowly and looked at her mother. Mark was awake and could see his mother was bordering on her usual volatility.

'Go to the kitchen, Mark, and get yourself some breakfast. Your father should be up by now.'

Agnes glared at Lisa and puffed out her chest like a broody hen.

'I'm going to make a few calls today, Lisa. I just wanted to let you know. Your behaviour last night was embarrassing. I think you need some psychiatric help. You ignore your sister, you won't help your future brother-in-law, who is only trying to be nice. Your behaviour is changing. You have become too much for me to handle and. . .and we don't want you here. My nerves are getting the better of me. I can't tolerate this anymore.'

'Tolerate what, Mum? I don't want to go there, that's all,' Lisa whispered.

'Don't answer back. You're going and that's the end of it.' She gave a crisp nod and left the room.

◊

Lisa was in turmoil. She had to comply or she knew Agnes would do everything in her power to send her away. Lisa pulled the sheets back and headed for the bathroom, telling herself to make an effort and keep going.

As Lisa entered the kitchen, Agnes put the phone down. 'Are you going to change your behaviour or shall I continue with this call?' her mother huffed. Lisa eased herself into a chair at the kitchen table. Her throat felt tight as the bitterness and confusion swept over. She peered at the woman who was her mother. *Wasn't a mother supposed to protect and nurture her children?* Hers only seemed to have it in for her.

'Yes Mum, I'm fine. I'll help Lenny and do what you want of me.' She ran her hands through her hair. Oppression swamped her, and her emotions were overwhelming, spiralling down into darkness.

'Do you want to tell me what's going on? Will this be your continual behaviour, ignoring people, refusing to help or are we just having a teenage episode. No wait. . .another bloody teenage episode. Too many for my liking.'

Lisa shrugged weakly and shook her head while looking at the floor. She knew that if she tried to tell her mother what had happened with Lenny, it would only add fuel to the fire burning in Agnes' eyes.

'What's that shrug supposed to mean, Lisa? Yes or no? I have just put the phone down to our local doctor and am expecting a return call. So, can you tell me what your decision will be before I take this further.'

Des suddenly appeared at the door. 'Come on Mark, we have a few things to do.' Lisa's eyes were pleading to him for help. *Please help me, Daddy.* But Des just shuffled Mark out of the kitchen and let the front door slam behind them.

Lisa was exhausted. 'Okay, Mum, yes, I'll go.' Tears began to burn her eyes. She desperately wanted to avoid any further conflict. Her voice cracked with emotion as she whispered, 'I will do better.' She could not look at her mother. Lisa knew she was blindly doing what she was being told to do, but there were no other options.

'Right, you had best eat something then. Let's make a start. You look like a scrawny bird. Even that is embarrassing,' Agnes barked as she placed some bread in the toaster and started to boil the kettle. Lisa could hear her mother speaking but she just sat there, staring at nothing. 'Are you listening to me, young lady.' Lisa turned quickly. 'Yes, I am,' she replied in a mono-tone voice.

After her mother left the kitchen to get ready for the day, Lisa sat alone feeling hollowed out and powerless about the present or her future, sensing that nothing would ever be the same. She buttered the toast and drank some warm sweet tea.

After showering, she went outside. The sun was strong on her face and she squinted her eyes. She called to Cassius. His big warm friendly face and wagging tail made her smile. Lisa had brought her uneaten toast outside and sat and fed him. *If only humans were more like dogs*, she thought sadly to herself, wondering when Mark and her father would get back. She hated being alone with her mother.

When she went inside, her mother was vacuuming and stopped the machine when Lisa came towards her. 'Well, that is an improvement. You can help me today if you have the energy. I need beds changed, so please strip the beds and carry the dirty sheets out to the laundry.' Agnes watched her daughter move slowly, but at least she was moving.

It actually felt good for Lisa to be doing something. She helped her mother throughout the day until they stopped for lunch.

'You can tell me if anything is bothering you,' Agnes said over sandwiches. Her voice was cold and insincere. At that very moment, Lisa could have easily blurted out what had happened. But she knew her mother and knew this would be a first-class ticket out of the house.

Lisa retreated inward. 'I just get a little down, that's all, Mum. It comes in waves and I want to hide in my room. To feel safe,' she said softly.

'Safe. Oh, for goodness sake! You are safe. You talk rot, Lisa!'

Agnes gave a quick, false smile as her lips curled back over her teeth. 'We will leave it for now but you do not fool me,' she retorted. Lisa knew she was waiting for the reason, any excuse, to send her packing. The situation at home was becoming extremely uncomfortable and made her feel physically ill. She was also nervously wondering when Lenny was going to show up and how she could get out of being forced to go with him to the new house to help out.

After finishing her chores, Lisa returned to her room. The fresh linen was welcoming, and she relaxed on her bunk. No matter how hard she tried, Lenny's face and what he had done to her, the strange feelings in her body and the repulsions in her mind, kept surfacing.

By early afternoon, Mark and her father had returned with boxes of fruit and vegetables. Lisa stayed close to her brother. They kicked a soccer ball about and played for hours with the dog. She was starting to think that Lenny wasn't going to turn up today, but then heard a car pull up in the driveway and his loud voice in the house. Bile rose in her throat. She stopped kicking the ball.

'Hey, Lisa, come on. Lenny is here,' Mark said excitedly.

Agnes appeared at the back door. 'Come on in, you two. We have a visitor.'

As they moved towards the back door, Lisa kept repeating to herself that everything would be okay. But she could feel the adrenaline shooting through her system. Mark shook Lenny's hand and then sat in front of the plate of cookies their mother had laid out. Lisa didn't acknowledge Lenny and avoided his gaze. She stayed close to her father, the stale smell of last night's alcohol filling the air.

'Right then, let's all sit and enjoy these new melting moments I made before Mark gobbles them all,' Agnes grinned. Lisa knew her mother was trying to keep things light, but again, with every movement Lisa made, Lenny's eyes followed her. She knew he was waiting for his next opportunity.

'Well,' Lenny said, quite breezily, 'I still need a hand with things back at the new home. Janine is away until tomorrow evening, being a long weekend and all. I would love it, Lisa, if you could find the time to help me. You'll like Haberfield. Lots of Italians, and they make great food. It's different to what we do here. I can take you down for a plate of pasta or even better, lasagne.'

'That sounds marvellous, Lenny,' said Agnes before Lisa could even utter a word 'Getting her out of the house might lighten up her mood. It's been a bit dark lately.'

Lisa's eyes dulled. She resigned herself to the fact that she had to go with Lenny. She had no fight left in her and could feel her spirit weakening.

'Come on, Lisa. It'll be great fun,' stated Agnes. 'As Lenny said, it's like visiting Italy, with lots of new shops and food, and we would love to hear your stories when you get back.' Agnes was trying to be jovial. The falsity made Lisa want to vomit over her shoes. Instead, she stood up, excused herself and left the kitchen.

Her mother looked horrified. She followed swiftly and grabbed her daughter's arm in a vice-like grip as she reached the bedroom.

'Please, Mum, I don't want to go,' Lisa beseeched, her stomach churning.

'That's enough of this bloody nonsense,' Agnes seethed. 'What's got into you? Rudeness is not a great virtue, and I'm not going to put up with it, do you hear me. My nerves are shattered. You'd better straighten out the shit in your head. Pack your bloody bag as it's a public holiday tomorrow so you can spend the night, and we will not hear another word from you. Come out when you are ready.'

Lisa resigned herself to her fate and knew pure evil waited outside. Who would believe her if she told them about the awful things Lenny had done and what he wanted to do to her. She would be accused of being a liar, just like he said, and sent away. Stuffing some clothes into a bag, her mind drifted off, thinking of the consequences. Her body trembled with fear at the stories about the girls homes she had heard in the school yard. Some girls being sent to those homes, they never saw their families again. She recalled some nights her mother would take great delight in reading articles out aloud from the newspaper about the Parramatta Girls Home. 'Just forty minutes away, Lisa' she would say with glee.

Agnes would look up from the paper and say, 'Good discipline there, Des.' A bitter smile would spread slowly across her face. Lisa knew it must be an awful place.

Mark wandered into the bedroom and watched his sister slowly pack. He could see Lisa was visibly upset and put his arm around her. 'Things will be okay,' he whispered.

'I just don't want to go with Lenny. I want to stay here with you.' But she knew Mark couldn't possibly understand.

Before she could say anything else, Agnes appeared at the door. 'Hurry up, Lisa,' her mother said impatiently. 'You have to get going. Don't keep Lenny waiting. I expect you to be on your best behaviour, and if I hear any bad reports, there will be repercussions. You're supposed to be helping your sister and Lenny to renovate their new home. Most girls would love to help. Lenny needs a hand.'

Lisa picked up the small bag containing her clothes and walked towards where Lenny waited. It felt like the walk of death.

Lisa had no words. All she felt was numbness and knew what was coming. She could see that Agnes wanted to strike out at her. Fury filled her mother's face.

'Great. Ready to go?' asked Lenny as Lisa appeared. She forced herself not to look at Lenny. She wanted to run away but where would she go? Who could she run to? And again, who would believe her?

Lenny opened the car door and murmured, 'Get in, I've lots to show you.' Lisa slumped into the passenger seat and began pulling on her hair. Small clumps of hair loss were beginning to show. She could not leave her hair alone. She began to bite her fingernails, and as they drove, she wondered if she could open the door and fling herself out of the car without injuring herself.

Lisa glanced sideways at Lenny's profile, and all she saw was ugliness and power. The gnawing tension in the pit of her stomach started to grow. As though feeling her stare, Lenny looked in her direction.

'Stop that,' he barked.

'Stop what?'

'Staring at me. You don't look at me unless I say you can. Do you understand?'

An unkind smile spread slowly across his face and she noted the change in colour to his face and neck. He pulled into the long driveway of the little cottage. High fences and hedges with large established trees provided privacy from neighbours.

'Here we are.' Lisa did not move; her posture was now rigid as she bit into her lip.

Lenny tried to pull her face towards him, but she pulled away. His eyes took on a wild-eyed look as he began to drag her out of the car. He seemed to enjoy her struggling and an evil pleasure showed in his smile.

'Stop struggling,' he ordered as he pulled Lisa to her feet. 'You're not very talkative. I hope this will change as I want us to have fun,' Lenny whispered as he slid his hand over her bottom.

He opened the front door to the house, and Lisa immediately felt trapped. He heart was beating wildly as he stood directly behind her, his arm suddenly coming around her waist. Lisa knew what was coming and squeezed her eyes tightly as if trying to shut out the image.

'I'll put your bag in your room. Be back in a minute.' Lenny looked at Lisa as he picked up her bag and she could clearly see his desire for her already. She wondered why he was so sexually drawn to her. Maybe he had a thing for virgins and the sexually pure. Or maybe he was just some sick paedophile! After all, she was only thirteen, a child really.

Lenny came towards her, and Lisa started to tremble. Her stomach clenched as she wondered what was going to happen to her next. She could tell that he wanted more from her this time and that he would do as much as he wanted this weekend. There was no-one to stop him and no time restriction.

He reached to touch her hair, and Lisa pulled his hand away. 'Stop touching me. I hate this,' she cried. Lenny stood back and watched her with an intense gaze.

'You are all mine this weekend, Princess. This is our secret, remember?' You will learn to like what I do. I know you like it. Think of it as a new adventure. Your sexual adventure.' He tried to cup her chin, but she pushed his hand away. She could feel his gaze travel over her body. Hungry eyes. He was toying with her, like a cat with a mouse. Lisa's face was stony and devoid of emotion. She just wanted to get this over with.

'I like that you have fire in your belly. It turns me on. In six months, you'll be asking me to do things to you.' He licked his thin, cruel lips, and she noticed the saliva building.

'There is something I need to ask you though, Lisa' continued Lenny. His voice had changed, so Lisa looked quizzically at him. 'Have you started your periods yet?'

Lisa blushed and wondered the relevance of this question in view of what he had done to her before. 'No, I haven't.' He seemed pleased with her response. Lenny stood up and grabbed her shirt, almost lifting her out of the chair. His enjoyment of dominance clearly showed on his face. 'You will do what I ask of you,' he growled, 'without question or I will have to punish you. Now, I want you to go and have a shower. There are clean towels in the bathroom.' Lisa didn't move, and his hand remained tightly gripping her shirt. He pulled her face close to his and raised his voice. 'Go on, clean up. I want you to clean yourself up and look pretty for me.' He pushed her towards the bathroom.

Having no fight left and resigning herself to her fate, Lisa went reluctantly to the bathroom. Locking the door behind her, she gazed at herself in the mirror while the shower was running. Her body was changing, and she now had breasts. Was this the attraction? Terror ripped through her like a violent storm as she thought of what was to come. Gripping the sink, she tried to steady herself from shaking, beginning to hyperventilate.

Her thoughts about the last assault kept coming back to her. Lisa sank to the floor. Bringing her knees up to her chest, she closed her eyes as the steam from the shower filled the bathroom. Lisa lay in the foetal position until there was a banging on the door.

'Lisa, open this door now or there will be trouble. I'll count to ten, and if there's no response, I'll call your mother. I'll just say you are uncontrollable and that I'm bringing you home.'

Lisa's eyes widened in alarm, and she began to whimper. 'Please . . . please don't, I'm okay.' Her voice sounded so childlike.

Lenny heard the click in the lock. Lisa stepped back as he opened the door and walked towards her. He curled his fingers through her hair, tugging her head backwards. His eyes fixated on her face and then moved over her body.

'I don't want you to give me any trouble; otherwise, as I said, I will punish you. Now get in the shower. I'll be back soon.' Although she felt powerless, anger and rage began to bubble under the surface. Lisa closed the door and got under the shower. The hot water trickled over her body and she began to shampoo her hair, closing her eyes to avoid the sting.

Her thoughts kept circling back to the worst possible outcome. She wanted to scream or find a way out to hide. But where would she go? Lisa let the water flow over her. She was in no hurry to exit the shower as she knew the predator outside the door was waiting.

Lisa flinched when she heard the bathroom door open and suddenly he came into view. Steam still filled the bathroom, but she saw he was naked and fully erect. He stepped into the shower. Lenny grabbed her from behind, pressing his hardness into her buttocks. Lisa tried to move away but he had both hands on her breasts, pulling her towards his body.

Lisa struggled, trying to push his arms away, but he was too strong. He pulled her out of the shower and turned the taps off. Lenny handed her a towel. 'Dry yourself,' he commanded, his eyes never leaving her body. He did the same, taking long slow wipes as if trying to tantalise Lisa.

He stopped and suddenly scooped Lisa up, carrying her to the bedroom.

'Please, please, Lenny, don't hurt me. I don't like this. I want to go home,' Lisa whimpered, tears in her eyes.

'It sometimes hurts a little, but after that, you'll want it all the time,' he said hoarsely.

Lenny pushed her back on the bed. Tears tracked down her cheeks. 'Stop whimpering,' he barked and suddenly slapped her face.

He pulled her legs to the edge of the bed and began to circle her clitoris with his tongue. 'I know you like this, I saw how you reacted before. Relax, Lisa, let your body take pleasure. I want to give you pleasure. I care for you.' Lisa squeezed her eyes shut. There was this sensation again, and she began to rock. What he was doing to her was wrong, but the pleasure it gave her body was locking her in. She felt ashamed. Lenny continued licking and biting her body. She moaned. It spurred him on, and he began to move over her thin body, licking and tasting every part of her. He moved back down and continued until Lisa shuddered to orgasm. She rolled over and began to sob.

'Don't cry. This is what you're supposed to feel. What I wanted you to feel.' His voice was raspy but soft. He went to kiss her mouth, but she pushed him away. She didn't like his smell and tried to get up.

Lenny pushed her back down and felt between her legs. 'Lisa, you're very moist. This is the part where it may sting. Try and relax.' He pushed her thighs apart with his knees.

Lisa had now disengaged and was drowning in her own thoughts. Staring blankly at the ceiling, her mind and body separated. As the tip of his penis pushed into her body, she gasped and tried to struggle, but he held her arms tightly above her head.

All the while he was pushing into her, he kept telling her to relax, that it was okay and that she would like it. Panic enveloped her, and she was breathing so hard she thought she would pass out. There was a searing pain and it felt like she was splitting in two.

He was moaning and sliding up and down telling her to move with him, but she could only try and block the act out. He plunged harder until he shuddered and moaned loudly, calling her name. It was his moment of release. Lenny lay on top of her, kissing her face, but she moved her face away, twisting her head side to side, trying to stop his attention.

He rolled off her, and she felt a trickling of warm sticky substance. Her pelvic area ached and there was a stinging sensation in her vagina. 'I hope I didn't hurt you too much. The first time is always the worst. It will get better,' he said coldly. Lisa didn't respond and stared blankly at him as he walked out of the bedroom.

Lisa heard the shower running and grabbed the towel from the floor to wipe herself, gasping in alarm as she saw her blood mingled with his semen. Reaching down, she touched herself between the legs and saw the blood was bright red. A sob escaped her throat. It was a moment of primal terror. Lenny finished in the shower and came back into the bedroom. He put his arm around her and tried to calm her.

'Lisa, Lisa, listen to me, this is all normal. Please listen to me. It's normal.' Lisa suddenly snapped. "Normal,' she cried. 'This isn't normal. You're not normal. You raped me. I want to get out of here.' She tried to slap him but he caught her hands.

Lisa leaped off the bed but Lenny stood in the doorway. 'You are not going anywhere until you calm down.' Lisa began to beat his chest with her fists until he grabbed both wrists. She bit down hard on his hands, and he slapped her hard across the head. She crumbled to her knees and lay on the floor, exhausted. Sobs racked her body.

'Stay on the floor until this passes. Why do you all react like this? You girls are so stupid. You should just shut up and enjoy it,' he ranted as he stormed out of the bedroom.

Lisa's breathing gradually returned to normal, and she lay very still on the floor. Her jaw ached from clenching her teeth. She felt pain where he had entered her and knew she had to find a way out of the house.

An hour passed, and then Lenny appeared in the bedroom. 'Get up, Lisa,' he snapped. 'You need to go and wash up.' His voice was all authoritarian.

Lisa looked at this man who had power over her and knew she had to play his game until she got home. Her world had changed. Where could she go? Where could she find a safe place? She decided to make a plan and escape when she got older, so they could never bring her back. Her innocence had been taken and destroyed. Now, she trusted no-one.

◊

While Lisa was bemoaning her fate in the bedroom, Lenny was in the kitchen, relishing his sexual power over the young girl and the way he had de-flowered her. God, how he loved innocent, young virgins. When it came to his soon-to-be niece, he rationalised his behaviour in that he thought he would teach this girl about sex and love, and maybe she would come to find his actions acceptable. He had been lusting after her young flesh since he first saw her, and now he had made his own sexual fantasy real. He couldn't believe she was in his house, completely at his mercy. That had been far easier for him to organise than he had anticipated. How blind her family were to his true intentions with her!

He felt his erection stir again. He was imagining her naked, just like moments before. Budding breasts, slender young thighs, the smell of her skin. He knew that sex was foreign to her, but at one stage, he was sure she had enjoyed it, reaching orgasm. How he wanted to devour her sexually, to feel every part of her young body and to teach her to do things to him. He knew he was being impatient, but the sexual pull towards Lisa was overriding any rationality. She was his to take, to conquer, to crush. He wanted to lay on top of her and penetrate her body. He wanted to hear her moan with pleasure or try to fight him. By now, Lenny was completely sexually aroused. He turned on his heel and strode back into the bedroom.

FIVE

THE CHANGE

Almost two years had passed since Lenny had infiltrated Lisa's world, and he had been sexually assaulting her at least monthly during that time. This was usually oral sex as she had started menstruating, but when he forced Lisa to have sex with him, he used a condom. It was now 1970. Lisa was fifteen and her behaviour had changed dramatically over that time, frequently answering back to her parents. Her mood was dark, defiant and aggressive, always on the attack. Although she was continually threatened to be sent away, Lisa knew when to back down and let things settle. If Agnes had her way, she would have already have been a resident at some institution but it was Des who kept persevering.

Lisa still hadn't figured out how to escape the hell her life had become but knew in her own mind it would be better to take off when she was closer to sixteen. In her turmoil, she frequently questioned the shitty life that swirled around her. She was lost without her aunt, who had taken an extended honeymoon with Alan in Europe while their homestead was being renovated. Alan's right-hand man was looking after the farm for them in the meantime.

Lisa had begun to self-harm and slash her abdomen finely with a razor. A trickle of blood would come from the wounds and the ooze seemed to quell her anger and sense of hopelessness. Whenever Janine was going to see her girlfriends, Lenny would suddenly arrive to take Lisa for a drive. He also seemed to always know when her parents were not around.

Recently, however, she had managed to avoid him with her belligerent behaviour or by feigning sickness. On one occasion when she was alone in the house, and he arrived, Lisa threatened to expose him until he raised the Girls Home and her being sent away. The fear of being sent there made her hold her tongue and let him have his way with her. Every time he invaded her body, she would take her mind away, picturing herself in a better place. Lisa counted down the days until she could release herself from this misery.

◊

It was early afternoon on a weekday when Agnes heard the phone ringing. 'Hello,' she said as she pushed her hair over her ear.

'Mrs O'Connor?' asked the caller.

'Yes, this is Mrs O'Connor.'

'It's the school, Mrs O'Connor. I'm Lisa's teacher, Miss Shaw. Is it a good time to talk?'

'Yes, it's a good time. How are you, Miss Shaw?'

'I'm fine, thank you, but I need to talk to you. Maybe you can come up to the school?'

'What's happened? I don't have time to come up to the school. What can I do for you, Miss Shaw?'

'Well, I wanted to let you know that Lisa's behaviour in the classroom has been extremely disruptive. She suddenly explodes over seemingly little things such as someone sitting in her seat. Her behaviour has been most unusual.'

Agnes was stunned into silence. 'Mrs O'Connor, I just need to know if everything is alright on the home front as Lisa's behaviour has changed so much over the course of the year.' Miss Shaw sounded hesitant asking the questions.

'Of course everything is alright. Why the devil are you asking me this?' harrumphed Agnes, her face flushed red from embarrassment.

Miss Shaw continued. 'Has Lisa told you about the accident she had at school nearly two weeks ago?'

Accident. What accident? 'No. There's been no mention of an accident. What type of accident are you referring to? Could you please explain what's going on.'

'This is difficult, Mrs O'Connor, and probably humiliating for Lisa. However, some two weeks ago, Lisa wet herself in the classroom. She seemed to be in a trance-like state and was certainly unaware that she had lost control of her bladder. We escorted her to Sick Bay, and she seemed to settle. She said she couldn't remember anything. Anyway, she was given a pair of shorts to put under her school uniform, and I asked her to bring the shorts back. She has yet to return the shorts so I thought I'd give you a call, mainly to see if everything was okay and obviously for her to return the shorts.'

Agnes put her hand to her mouth before apologising to Lisa's teacher. 'I am so sorry about this, Miss Shaw. Lisa has not advised me of any accident, let alone shorts that needed washing and returning. She should be on the school bus now to come home. I'll speak to her as soon as she arrives home. I will find the shorts, Miss Shaw, and get them back to you. I'm so sorry this has happened. Thank you very much for your call. I'll be in touch.'

'Don't be sorry, Mrs O'Connor. We're all concerned for your daughter, that's all.'

'Goodbye, Miss Shaw. I'll deal with the matter when my daughter arrives home.' Agnes again felt the flush of her cheeks. How embarrassing that her daughter had urinated in a public classroom and not told her. She felt the resentment building up inside her.

The front door opened, and Agnes waited for Lisa to enter the kitchen with Mark dawdling behind her.

'Mark, you can go to your room and do your homework,' Agnes instructed. 'I need to speak with your sister.' He scampered off, knowing there was to be some altercation. Whenever his mother stood with her arms folded, trouble was brewing.

'How was school today, Lisa? Is there anything you need to tell me?'

Lisa just glared at her. 'What do I need to tell you . . . it was just another day,' she replied as she opened the fridge door. Agnes pushed the door of the fridge shut. 'You don't need anything from the fridge, young lady! Pay attention to me! You are not running this household.'

Lisa didn't respond. 'Well,' Agnes shouted, eyes narrowing. 'Has anything occurred recently that I need to know?' Lisa stood with her eyes downcast, still not saying a word.

'You embarrassing little bitch. You have pissed in your pants, and the school has just called to ask for the shorts back that were provided to you. Where are they?'

Lisa didn't reply. 'I said, where are they?' Agnes moved towards her and grabbed her by the arm. 'Show me where those bloody shorts are or I'll get your father to take you aside. You either deal with me or him. Take your pick.'

Lisa finally spoke. 'They're under the house, Mum. I threw them under there. I just didn't know what to do. I couldn't remember wetting myself; it just happened.' Tears flooded her eyes, which only drew more anger from her mother.

'Well, you can crawl under there like the rat you are and give them to me so I can wash them. You can then return them to the school. You are disgusting for not telling me. I don't know what's wrong with you, but you're even more distant from this family. You are not one of mine with behaviour like this.'

Agnes grabbed Lisa by the arm and dragged her outside to collect the shorts. 'Now get under there and get them.' As Lisa crawled under the house, she was stung by the humiliation. As she handed the shorts to her mother ,the revulsion in her mother's eyes was evident 'You are a freak,' Agnes spat, her mouth twitching as the words spewed out.

'I'm sorry, Mum. I don't know why I did it. I didn't even feel it. I felt so humiliated myself doing that in the classroom.' The tears spilled onto her cheeks.

They both looked up when Mark spoke through the back screen door. 'Err, what's going on? Lisa, is everything okay?'

'Nothing, Mark' Agnes said curtly, asserting her authority. 'Get back to your room.' Mark turned away slowly. Agnes could tell that he felt sorry for his sister. He had never queried any argument or asked what was going on.

'Stop your blubbering; everyone can hear you. You've even upset your brother with your wailing like a banshee. The neighbours will think I'm murdering you . . . probably not a bad idea but I'd pay the penalty!' Agnes stormed inside.

◊

Lisa didn't let on to her mother that due to wetting her pants in class, she was being ridiculed constantly, to the point of de-fending herself in the playground or the toilet blocks from gangs of girls. The anger and shame consumed her. Most lunches were spent in detention now. Lisa made no apologies to any student or teacher.

When her father got home, her mother was waiting to tell him about the call this afternoon from the school. Lisa could only guess his reaction. She didn't need to wait long to find out. Her father suddenly appeared in the doorway of her bedroom.

'Get out here,' he ordered. Lisa walked slowly to the kitchen. Her eyes noticed the electric cord on the back of the chair.

'You are a dirty little cow and you are embarrassing to your mother and me. Your behaviour and your attitude these last twelve months especially has been very trying. We've had a gutful.' He grabbed Lisa by the arms, picked up the cord and belted her across the legs before she could move away. It was only one fierce lash, but the pain was intense. Her father let go of her arm, and she ran to the bathroom. Grabbing a small razor, she lifted up her shirt and slashed her stomach finely, the old scars still visible. She had a sense of release when she resorted to self-harm, watching the blood dribble down her abdomen.

Lisa stayed in her room until she heard her father's car start up in the driveway. He was headed for the pub to get his usual skinful. She wandered out a few hours later, and Agnes glanced over her glasses when she sat down next to her brother.

'There's no food if that's what you're looking for and besides, if there was, you're not getting anything.'

Lisa stared blankly at the TV then heard the car pull up outside. Des staggered back to the house around 10.00 p.m. He had obviously been drinking heavily, a good five hours. Agnes and the children would always be very wary of this type of situation due to his violent outbursts and physical assault when he had been drinking.

Upon entering the house, he saw Mark and Lisa in the lounge room and then looked at Agnes, who sat reading at the kitchen table.

'What sort of a daughter have you given me? His voice was slurred. 'The bitch wet herself in front of people. We are getting reports from school about her behaviour.' He began threatening violence. 'I'm going to smack your heads in . . . all of you.'

'Bloody idiot wife.' He advanced towards Agnes, who began to speak out, but Des slapped her hard across the face. 'Keep your fucking mouth shut.'

'Well, you set a good example don't you, Desmond!' she shrieked.

Lisa took Mark by the hand and they locked themselves in the bathroom, waiting for the storm to pass.

The following morning, Lisa sat opposite her father at the kitchen table. Agnes was still in bed. She felt edgy and was wary of his behaviour or what he would do. Sometimes the morning after was just as bad. But it was a Friday, and she always enjoyed this day of the week. It was sports day.

Des looked at his daughter sternly. 'I know you're in trouble at school. I've been told by the fathers of the children who work with me about your behaviour at school and being disruptive in the classroom. If this continues, I shall take you out of school.'

'You can't take me out of school, Dad,' Lisa beseeched. 'I haven't been fighting. I'm trying to defend myself. Since I wet myself, the girls have been taunting me. I try to stay away from them. Truly I do, Dad,' she said, raising her voice slightly. His eyes showed no compassion. Lisa bit her bottom lip and wanted to tell her father there and then what had been happening to her and the molestation that had been occurring. But it would fall on deaf ears.

'You are a minor and you have no control about what we say and do at this stage of your life. You're causing problems at home and at school and this needs to be corrected. Agnes is bereft at your behaviour. Her nerves are a mess, and I've had a gutful of all of you.'

She watched her father leave the table, collect his bag and head to work. Lisa remained at the kitchen table and looked up when Mark came in. He looked at his sister and quietly said, 'Lisa you have to behave, you have to be good or they will send you away. I heard them talking again. That's the plan.'

'When did you hear that, Mark?' Lisa asked nervously.

'Um, about two days ago, something about Parramatta.' Lisa's eyes widened and she took a sharp intake of breath. That Girls Home was about forty minutes away. The home was always in the papers. They called it an institution. Lisa recalled the reports regarding its administration were terrible. So many times she had listened to her mother read out different articles from the newspaper.

'Thanks Mark. You're very brave for telling me this.' Lisa grimaced, eyes sad and worried, her face troubled. 'I'm not the one at fault. I wish I could tell you what has happened. Maybe one day I will but I know I cannot stay here. It's madness.'

'Huh, where are you going?' Mark looked frightened.

'I don't know. I just want to find peace and warmth.' *And to stop being violated!* she said to herself.

Mark gently took Lisa's hand. He knew there was something that had occurred, and it must have been awful. 'Come on, Lisa, we need to get to school.' She followed him, her soul broken, her body battered. It would be hard to leave him.

SIX

RUNAWAY

Over the next week, all attention fortunately turned to Janine. Her wedding was in two weeks' time. It was to be a simple ceremony in Haberfield with fifty guests. The reception would be at a local venue. Agnes said it had to be simple to keep their costs down. She was grateful Lenny's parents paid for the majority of things. Agnes had always been frugal. Lisa hoped the celebration would take her parents' minds off relocating Lisa, or their plans to do so.

With the focus and attention now on Janine and Lenny, Lisa decided to make her move. She would leave home before the wedding. Today was the day. But she needed money and food until she found some sort of shelter. Where that shelter may be, she didn't know. She was running blind. Lisa changed into her school uniform, grabbed a few clothes, put them into her school case and walked with Mark to the bus stop.

When the bus pulled into their stop, she told Mark to get on, that she had a few things to do and would be home later. She instructed him not to tell anybody that she was not going to school. She hugged him and felt his warm heartbeat against her chest.

'I love you. Don't worry about me; things will be okay,' Lisa whispered. Mark looked pensive as he got on the bus. Lisa looked like a forlorn figure as he waved to her from the back seat until she was no longer in view. Lisa began to walk the two miles to the local shops.

When Lisa arrived at Franklin's, their local supermarket, she began to place a few items into the pockets of her school uniform and jacket. The store manager had been watching her closely from the moment she entered the store. It wasn't usual for a young girl to be in the store at this time of day, so Lisa stood out like a sore thumb.

Lisa reached the checkout, feeling very nervous. She began to tremble.

'How are you today, dear?' asked the cashier cheerily. Lisa looked into her face, thought that she was kind and hoped the cashier would not search her bag. She placed a small lollipop on the counter, a Rosie Apple, which was all she could afford. As she went to leave the supermarket, she felt a firm hand on her shoulder. 'Not so fast, young lady,' the store manager said.

Lisa turned to face the manager, her body shaking. 'Would you empty your pockets for me. I don't believe you have paid for everything,' he said calmly.

Lisa stuttered. 'I. . .I don't have anything in my. . .my pockets; all I bought was the Rosie Apple, this Rosie Apple, a lolly, um, .a lollipop. That's all.'

'I don't believe that's the truth, young lady. What is your name and where do you live? You need to empty out your pockets before I call your parents or the police. Make it easy on yourself and empty your pockets and open your school case, please. You do know stealing is an offence?'

Lisa remained silent, refusing to give her name. Instead, she reached into her pockets and began to place the stolen items on the counter. By this time, a small crowd had gathered, some of whom knew her. She was ashamed and felt her cheeks burning.

She saw Mrs Roberts, a neighbour who lived down the road, pointing at her and gossiping with the lady standing next to her. 'That's the O'Connor girl. She's been getting into a bit of trouble lately. A right little bugger,' Lisa heard her say.

Mrs Roberts peered over her glasses at Lisa with a look of disapproval. She approached the counter. 'Here, what's the young girl done?'

'Do you know her?' asked the store manager.

'Yes, she lives up the road from us. Her name is Lisa O'Connor. I've got her mother's phone number in my hand-bag.'

Mrs Roberts shuffled around in her handbag and pulled out a small diary. She read the number out loudly to the store manager with a look of triumph as he quickly wrote it down. He thanked her for her assistance and asked that they all move on. Although she had stolen, he felt sorry for the girl. Having daughters of his own, he noted the dark circles under her eyes and how painfully thin she was.

'You had best come with me, Lisa, as I need to call your parents. Shoplifting is a serious offence that is punishable by law. Do you understand the consequences of your actions?'

Lisa did not reply. They walked towards a small office at the back of the store where she sat down and listened as he dialled the number. Her breathing became rapid, and a facial tic developed over the left side of her face. She couldn't control the muscle. *This is not good; I have to get away*, her mind screamed.

'Is this Mrs O'Connor?' asked the store manager.

'Yes, it is. Who's calling?' Lisa could hear her mother's voice over the phone.

'My name is Trevor Martin, and I manage Franklins. I have your daughter Lisa here with me. Unfortunately, we have caught her shoplifting.' Lisa heard an audible gasp from her mother, and the line went silent for a long moment.

'Hello, hello . . . are you there, Mrs O'Connor? We do need to talk. Look, I'm sorry to bring you this bad news, but I thought I would call you first, rather than the police.'

Lisa sat quietly, listening to the conversation. No doubt Agnes was about to erupt.

'Right,' Agnes said sternly. 'Thank you for that Mr Martin. I'll get ready and be down there in about half an hour.'

Mr Martin had a kind face, Lisa thought. 'I'm sorry to call your parents, Lisa. But you have done the wrong thing.'

When Lisa lifted her head to meet his gaze, she could see he felt sorrow for her. His eyes were masked with sadness. Maybe he knew there was more to this than what met the eye.

A young girl escorted Agnes down to the store manager's office. Mr Martin and Lisa looked up as Agnes was introduced. Lisa could see the look of thunder on her mother's face and the hateful glare that was directed towards her. Her mother was an imposing figure standing in Mr Martin's office.

'I'm Lisa's mother. Thank you for calling.' Her voice was icy as it sliced through the air. Mr Martin, picked up on the tension between the two. The girl seemed to cower in fright. Lisa's mother was clearly the dominant force but there was nothing he could do to help. The situation was out of his hands.

'Right then, I'll leave you two alone for the moment. You may want to sort things out.' He quickly left the room and closed the door. Agnes looked at her daughter, and her eyes narrowed. A cold hard stare. Lisa could see her mother's chest heaving as she began to speak rapidly.

'There will be no sorting of any sorts. Come on, you little bitch, this is the last time, just wait till I get you home,' she snarled, dragging Lisa by the arm.

I don't want to go home. Please, Mum, don't take me home.' Lisa started to panic, pleading with her mother. 'I'm not safe there! Please!'

'Stop this,' Agnes yelled. 'Whatever has happened? Why has your behaviour changed? Can you give me a reason?' Her mother was red-faced and sweating as she grappled with her daughter, trying to drag her out of the store.

'It's Lenny!' Lisa screamed. 'He's been molesting me for a long time, and you have all just stood by and done nothing!'

Her mother's mouth flew open in shock, and she suddenly struck Lisa's face with the back of her hand. It was a stinging blow.

'You little liar. All the lies that spill from your grubby mouth. Don't be saying such awful things about your sister's husband. You are just jealous of her!' Her mother was fuming with so much anger that Lisa thought steam would come out of her ears. She had never seen her mother so enraged.

Agnes' voice was now shrill and carried through the store. 'You hateful, spiteful trollop. I'm sending you away. I never want to see your face again. I'll make the arrangements as soon as we get home. Your father and I will be glad to be rid of you.'

Lisa dug her heels in. She screamed at her mother. A high-pitched, guttural scream. 'I'm not lying. I'm not lying. Please believe me, Mum.' Her mother continued to drag her until Lisa struck out. She tried beating her mother's arm, and when Agnes failed to release her, Lisa bit down hard on her mother's arm.

'Sweet Jesus,' Agnes bellowed, clutching at the bite mark on her arm. 'You are no daughter of mine. Stop this nonsense; we are leaving. Just wait till your father hears about this. He will belt you until you can no longer sit down or stand!' Agnes tried again to drag her daughter out of the office.

'You will not be doing anything to me anymore!' Lisa just exploded. Her mind was like a hurricane. All the rage of the sexual abuse and humiliation were fuel to her mental fire that had slowly been burning the past two years. Mr Martin and some of his staff could hear the yelling, and he began to walk back towards his office to see if he could assist.

Breaking away from her mother, Lisa flung the office door open and began running through the aisles past Mr Martin, throwing cans into the air, pulling down food stands, anything that was in her way.

Her mother ran out after her, telling the store manager, 'Lock the door, call the police, call the police; she needs to be locked up. She's out of control.'

The staff at the checkouts locked the doors, and as Lisa got to the front entrance of the store, she was trapped. She banged heavily on the door with her fists.

'Open the door or I'll smash it down! Lisa wailed, desperate and frightened.

There were two bricks on the ground, which were obviously used to keep the door open. In her desperation, she picked up the bricks and hurled them with all her force against the pane of glass. It shattered and cracked, and Lisa grabbed a trolley and pushed it hard against the glass.

As the glass cracked and fell into pieces to the ground, she hopped over it and out into the street. Lisa was now running as hard as she could, her lungs gulping for air, running wildly to obliterate everything from her mind. She could hear sirens in the distance and knew they were for her. Her arms and legs were bleeding from the splintered glass, but she felt as if the storm that surrounded her had broken. She ran blindly until the police car swerved into the gutter, the doors flew open and the constables chased after her, restraining her against a wall.

She fought wildly, punching at the officers until restrained by handcuffs. They drove to the police station, and her mother arrived a short time later. Lisa was left alone while the police discussed the situation and what could be done.

'Mrs O'Connor, we have to formally charge Lisa now, and the damage to the store will need to be paid for,' said the young female, Constable White.

'Yes, I understand completely. My husband and I don't want any more of this. I'm going to have a nervous breakdown. We need to send Lisa away to rehabilitate or something. She's uncontrollable, pissing herself in public, disruptive at school, stealing. She's an abomination,' Agnes vented.

'The emotional side of things is out of our hands, Mrs O'Connor,' said Constable White. 'And while we understand how this can create unrest in a home, we have to look at the legal side of things only. She will be charged with public mischief and malicious damage. Just wait here and we'll make a few calls to a couple of institutions. Lisa is just in the next room. She's restrained with cuffs but you are welcome to speak to her. Just open that door there.' They left Agnes on her own and went to another room.

Agnes stared at the door and wrung her hands. A sly smile came over her face as she muttered to herself, *Boy you have really done it this time, little bitch, but you've done me a favour. You will never come back.* She cleared her throat and stood up, approaching the door. When she opened it, Lisa was sitting quietly. Agnes noted the handcuffs. *Good,* she thought, *she won't be able to strike out at me.* Agnes sat in the opposite chair to Lisa, still keeping some distance. Her daughter sat staring vacantly.

'Why did you do this?' her mother demanded. Lisa raised her head slowly. 'It's Lenny.'

'More lies. Stop lying! I wish I had drowned you in a bucket when you were born. You have been nothing but trouble. I never wanted you.' Her mother left the room, making a tsk tsk sound.

◊

Lisa gazed down at the floor, picking at her nails. She felt the tears spill down her cheeks. *I hate all of you. I hate myself. I'm damaged goods now. Nobody will want me. Worthless and dirty goods.* Lisa had a sinking feeling in her gut and an overwhelming sense of futility. All hope was gone now. She had never been wanted by her parents. Never loved. *I wish you had drowned me in a bucket, Mum. It would have been better than this shitty life.*

Constable White then entered the room, and Lisa kept her head down. The charges were read out to her and the sentencing fell heavily in the air. Lisa could only feel numb and despondent.

'Do you have anything to say, Lisa?' asked Constable White. 'These charges are serious. Your parents will have to compensate Mr Martin, the store manager, and I have had discussions with your mother regarding your behaviour. They think you need rehabilitation. We have also spoken to the school and they confirmed there have been issues there as well. Your mother also tells me you have been making accusations about a relative. Do you want to make any comments?'

Lisa gave a heavy sigh. Her response was mechanical. 'I don't want to go back home.'

◊

The young girl's eyes conveyed such sadness, and she seemed older than her years. There were so many times the young constable wanted to just hold them. The majority of them just needed love. Constable White shook her head as she left the room to discuss the arrangements with Mrs O'Connor, who sat waiting in an interview room.

'Mrs O'Connor, sorry to keep you waiting.' Constable White was surprised by the lack of emotion the woman displayed. She wondered what had driven the girl to do what she did today.

'Well,' said Mrs O'Connor. 'What do I sign?' She seemed overly pleased to be signing the papers. Another indication that there was trauma in the home. Why would anyone want to get rid of their daughter so readily?

'I have the papers here. The Parramatta Girls Home will accept her. It's a Reformatory and Training School for young girls. It's about forty-five minutes from your home in Fairfield. Due to the criminal charges and her behaviour at home and school, the Child Welfare Authorities have classified her as delinquent. They will assess Lisa there and, hopefully, they will be able to work through the issues that have caused her behaviour. There will be regular communication with you about her progress, and you can visit her any time you want in their set hours. Do you have any questions, Mrs O'Connor?'

Agnes shook her head. 'I just want her out of the house. I'm about to have a nervous breakdown. I'm so embarrassed by her behaviour. I mean, what will everyone think? She's a bloody delinquent. Just look at this bite mark. I shall leave her to the authorities. They can do what they want with her. What do I need to do now?' Constable White thought she was very matter of fact. Pragmatic? No. Her instincts told her there was a hardness to the woman.

'All you need to do is sign these documents, which is your release of Lisa to the Child Welfare Authorities and your acknowledgement of our discussions here at the station.'

Agnes perfunctorily signed the documents. 'May I go now?' she asked with a pinched expression.

'Yes, you can, Mrs O'Connor,' said Constable White. 'Do you want to say goodbye to your daughter or let her know when you may visit?'

'No, I have no desire to at this time. It's not a good idea. I don't want to see her at this stage. I'm glad to finally have some peace at home. Good day, Constable White, thank you for your assistance. I'll be in touch with the institution in due course.'

Constable White could only stare as Agnes swiftly left the room. *That poor young girl*, she thought to herself, recalling Lisa's downcast eyes and sagging posture in the interview room. What a sad and forlorn figure she was. The constable was sure that something significant had driven Lisa to behave the way she had, instead of delinquency like her mother had claimed.

SEVEN

IMPRISONED

Lisa sat in the middle of the two police officers as they drove to the Parramatta Girls Home. Light rain splattered the windscreen. It was a grey day. But Lisa was so emotionally spent that now she felt nothing.

When the police car pulled into the driveway of the home, everything looked desolate and ominous. A place of misery. The buildings were old and Gothic in appearance, and most had bars on the windows. There was no warmth to the buildings or the gardens, and the area was extensive with many dwellings. It looked like the pictures of those time-worn, bleak buildings in England in the poorest of areas, similar to pictures she has seen in history class. The overall appearance of the Girls Home was draconian, and it reeked of malevolence. A chill ran up Lisa's spine. This place had every mark of a prison, and Lisa feared the worst.

They were greeted at the front entrance by a woman called Eve, who was obviously well informed on Lisa's history and what had occurred. A short discussion ensued with the police officers while Lisa sat in the car.

Constable White came to the passenger's side door. 'Lisa, this is the Parramatta Girls Home. We need you to exit the vehicle, please.'

Lisa sat for a moment longer and then looked in to Constable White's eyes. The young police officer seemed to feel her pain. Constable White helped Lisa out of the car. 'Lisa, this is Eve, the superintendent's assistant.' The assistant offered a weak smile. She then turned to an older gentleman. 'This is Superintendent Ash, who will be monitoring your rehabilitation.' He was an older, portly man in an ill-fitting suit. He wore glasses, and his receding hairline accentuated his long thin nose, which was crooked. He chatted to the police officers, who left after a brief discussion.

'Come this way, Lisa,' commanded Eve. Her voice was military-like and there was a masculinity about her appearance. Her hair was cropped short, and her mouth was a hard cruel line.

When Lisa stepped into the building, the gloominess of the interior said it all. The walls were grey and filled with secrets. Lisa followed Eve into a small office and noted the name plaque on the desk: Superintendent Ash.

Eve stood in the corner of the room while Superintendent Ash closed the door. Lisa looked at him with suspicion. He opened her file and began to write, then peered at her over his glasses.

'Lisa, this is an institution', he began. 'You have been sent here due to your uncontrollable behaviour and your recent criminal offence. You will obey everything we tell you in this establishment and speak when you are spoken to. You will get to know the rules very quickly. If you misbehave, we will place you in an isolation cell, which is not the most pleasant of cells. In fact, the girls here who have experienced the isolation cell now call it the dungeon.' He smirked at the mention of the latter word.

At that moment, there was a knock at the door. 'Enter,' barked the superintendent. Two women appeared, dressed in the same uniform as Eve.

Superintendent Ash nodded at the ladies.

'Lisa, this is Glenda and Sharon, two of our wardens.'

He gestured towards the two women. 'Please take Lisa down to the showers and show her around the dorm and kitchen.' His smile was fake and his eyes watery. 'Lisa is a guest of ours, for how long, who knows.' He wiped a small dribble of spit at the corner of each mouth as his eyes raked over her body.

The women flanked Lisa and escorted her out of the office. When they were out of earshot, the taller lady, Glenda, nudged Lisa in the ribs. 'No funny business, bitch. We already know your file and why you're here.'

As they walked down a long corridor, Lisa felt an eerie sensation. It was as if the walls had voices, and she noticed odd scratchings on them. Some were the names of girls, and one spelled the word 'GRIEF'. Lisa felt her mouth go dry.

'We have to strip search you, Lisa. Do you think you might enjoy that?' laughed Glenda. They arrived at a row of showers that had no doors. Lisa noticed that the toilets opposite also had no doors, and the view from the toilets led out to a quadrangle. Glenda noticed Lisa staring. 'No doors here, dearie. Yep, that's right, the male officers can see right in when you have a pee.'

Lisa gasped. This was going to be a humiliating experience. Absolute degradation. Her mother was certainly getting her revenge. In the distance, Lisa could hear a girl screaming and screaming. It brought chills to her spine. She froze with fear and clenched her jaw.

'Get used to those sort of noises; they go on all day,' taunted Sharon. Lisa broke out in a cold sweat. She looked at the doorway she had just walked through, momentarily stopped and then turned to run. The two women knew exactly what she was going to do and both grabbed Lisa's arms.

'Let go of me. I don't belong here,' she wailed, trying desperately to kick out at them, her body bucking and struggling with restraint.

'Feisty bitch! Stop wriggling or you'll see another room you won't want to go back to,' barked Glenda.

The women were having trouble restraining her, so Glenda hit a buzzer on a wall close by. Lisa's now-erupting screams filled the air and she heard running down the corridor. A woman who looked like a nurse suddenly appeared.

'What's going on?' asked the nurse in an agitated voice. 'Can't you fucking see, Margaret,' bellowed Glenda. 'For God's sake, jab her in her arse to quieten her down.'

The two women pinned Lisa's arms, and Glenda swiftly kicked her legs out from under her so she hit the floor with a thud. Glenda then moved her body weight on top of Lisa.

Margaret quickly moved in and injected some sedative into her buttock. 'Breathe, Lisa, breathe,' ordered Margaret. To the others, she barked, 'Give her about five minutes and she'll be a lot quieter. I haven't given her a full dose in case she's allergic to the sedative, so you have about thirty minutes.'

'Thanks, Margaret,' said Sharon. 'I can see this one will be doing some time in the dungeon.'

'Get off her now, Glenda,' instructed Sharon. 'She seems to be slowing in her breathing.'

Lisa felt quite dizzy with the sedative oozing through her veins. The room seemed to float. It were if she was not in her own body.

'That's slowed her down,' remarked Glenda. 'Help me get her to her feet and onto that chair.'

Both women assisted Lisa onto a chair near the showers. She tried to speak but the words were scrambled, and she was dribbling.

'Come on, Sharon. Let's get on with it. The sedative will only last for about thirty minutes,' growled Glenda.

Pulling out a pair of scissors, Glenda smirked. 'No need for long, pretty hair in here.' She grabbed Lisa's ponytail and cut the hair clean off, holding it up like a trophy and twirling it in the air. 'Nice hair,' she commented as she let it drop to the floor. Both women laughed loudly.

Lisa's eyes scanned the floor and although she wanted to get up, her legs were too weak so she remained seated. 'Cute little thing you are. Scrawny, but you won't be putting on weight in here. Not with the shit that passes for food,' laughed Glenda.

Eve, the superintendent's assistant, appeared. She saw the ponytail lying on the floor and nodded her approval to the two women. Eve came to stand directly in front of Lisa.

'Can't have anyone looking different in here. We will teach you discipline, and you will learn to show respect and obey the rules. You will march with your eyes to the ground, speak when you are spoken to, and you are forbidden to use the toilet except during designated times. Our superintendent doesn't put up with any shit from you girls, and you will soon find out if you do give him or anyone else crap in this place.'

Lisa's head sagged. *This is my own living hell.*

'Remove her clothes and get her under the shower,' drilled Eve. They half dragged Lisa to the shower and Eve carried the plastic chair across for Lisa to sit on. 'Scrub her down and then search her cavities. Make sure you check under her breasts. Quite large for a fifteen-year-old scrawny girl.'

What Lisa didn't know was that Eve always enjoyed watching. She preferred girls, and it was well known at the institution.

The cold water made Lisa flinch, and she tried to steady herself by leaning against the wall but was pulled down into the chair. 'Let her sit like that for a while,' jeered Eve. 'Can't have her cracking her scone and dying on the first day.' The three women laughed.

It was about forty-five minutes later, and Lisa felt the fog in her head and body begin to lift. She had been sitting in the chair and was still wet from the shower. 'Where are my clothes?' she asked meekly, covering her breasts to hide her nakedness. Glenda and Sharon stood directly behind her. 'Oh, we are wide awake now,' said Glenda as she pushed Lisa's shoulder.

'Are you going to behave or shall we ask the nurse to pay another visit?' Sharon threw a towel over Lisa's legs.

The two women watched as she dried herself. Eve sat silently in the corner. The room was deathly quiet. No-one spoke, but Lisa felt their eyes tracing every part of her body. Although a little unsteady on her feet when she stood from the chair, she thankfully had no problem standing.

Drying herself with as much dignity as possible, she thought, *I must keep clarity of thought in here. God knows what they would do to me if I were unconscious.*

Eve finally stood up and spoke. 'Right then, we're going to do a little body search.' Lisa's lower lip quivered, and a muscle in her jaw twitched. Her first thought was to try and run or strike out at them but she knew the consequences would be dire.

'Stand still, this won't take long. And if you have a repeat performance, our nurse Margaret will pay us another visit,' avowed Glenda. 'Now, turn around and face the wall.' Placing a rubber glove on her right hand, she rumbled, 'No funny business, bitch. Sharon, get ready at the first sign of trouble.'

Tears filled Lisa's eyes as Glenda probed her vagina and anus.

'Turn and face me and keep your hands to your sides,' directed Glenda. She reached out and lifted up Lisa's breasts. As she did so, Lisa could see through her foggy eyes that the women were enjoying it.

'Clear,' said Glenda, ripping off the gloves. 'Nothing on this one.'

Lisa was mortified by the lack of human decency just shown to her. Her arms had fallen to her sides. She felt her life was futile, instantly recognising the dominance of others over her that she had felt so many times before.

Eve spoke. 'She has quite a shapely body for a young girl. On the thinner side, but long legs and full breasts.' The other wardens could see Eve was almost salivating. She did not like men. This was common knowledge amongst the screws.

Glenda handed Lisa a plain cotton dress, along with blue socks, a singlet, calico underpants, a nightdress and a pair of shoes. Lisa made no comment. This was a place of complete control, repression, discipline and power. She understood at that very moment, they would take every opportunity to punish her.

'Come on, then, hurry up, get dressed. We have to take you back up to the superintendent's office,' said Sharon.

The walk back to his office seemed to take forever. The drug had worn off, but Lisa still felt foggy. They knocked on the door, and Lisa heard him say enter.

He rose from his desk, turned to the ladies and said, 'That will be all, please. Close the door behind you.'

Superintendent Ash was a most unattractive man and his menacing aura filled the room. Lisa thought he would look good in sideshow alley at the Fairfield Show. He walked around Lisa and spoke quietly as he circled her, his fingers lightly touching her body as he spoke.

Lisa shivered, she knew this feeling and the consequences of that touch. Another paedophile, another monster. It was Lenny all over again, but worse. This man had more power. Her body stiffened, and she pressed her elbows into her sides, trying to make herself smaller or invisible.

'Shame about the hair, but you know, we like to have the girls all equal.' He bent to sniff her hair and curled a short strand around his fingers. Even his smell made her feel nauseous. 'It can be pleasant here or it can be very unpleasant. If you do what I ask you to do, then your stay here will be possibly enjoyable. Possibly.'

He turned around and stood against the edge of his desk, staring down at Lisa. She kept her eyes fixed on the opposite wall.

'I can see that you are growing into a real beauty. Your breasts are already developed despite your thin frame. I'm sure many men would love to see what is beneath the shirt. Now come then, Lisa. Do you have any questions about our institution or any matter about your stay here that may be floating around in that pretty little head?' Silence. 'You must have one question?'

Lisa made no response. But she wanted to yell at the top of her voice, 'Superintendent Ash is a paedophile creep.' The whole world should know but again, another person she should have been able to trust was pure evil. Just like Lenny. Her assumptions about the superintendent were right. She was now trapped in his world. Lisa sat very still but her insides felt like a cat ready to spring. The colour quickly drained from her face.

'I have tried to make conversation and engage you regarding any thoughts or questions you may have. You are expected to respond as a matter of courtesy.' The superintendent was becoming agitated at her silence, and the look he gave her was ferocious.

'I will ask you again. Do you have any questions?' Without warning, he suddenly struck Lisa's face with an open palm. Her eyes narrowed, and she sprang at him, catching him off guard.

She tried to scratch his face with her bitten-down nails. He grabbed her arms and swung her to the floor.

She looked up at him, her eyes blazing with hate and rage. 'I have known bastards like you,' she spat, masking her own fear with rage and false bravado.

Superintendent Ash left her on the floor, returned to his desk and pressed a bell. The same two women appeared. 'Please take Miss O'Connor to the isolation room where she will stay for two days until she learns the art of communication.'

Lisa had pissed the superintendent off. Badly. Glenda and Sharon roughly grabbed her off the floor and headed down a long hallway. Where she was going was obviously a good distance from the office and dormitory. 'This will quieten you down, Missy. I hope you are a fast learner,' goaded Sharon.

They unlocked a heavy door and when they entered the room, she knew why they called it the dungeon. There were no windows, and the walls were sandstone, as was the floor. A bare-walled dungeon used for torture. It was cold and no-one would hear her scream. They threw her into a corner, turned on their heels and locked the door behind them. Lisa sat on the floor and heard their footsteps fading up the corridor.

A small meal was served later in the evening. It tasted awful, and Lisa pushed the plate away after one mouthful. She had no idea what time it was until the lock was turned in her cell and the superintendent appeared. It must be late. There was no natural sunlight spilling through the small windows of the corridor, only the blackness of the night.

Lisa remained seated on the floor as he entered the room and pulled her knees up against her chest. The superintendent held a small black baton in his right hand.

'Do you like your new quarters? You can stay here for as long as you want, it's entirely up to you. The usual time frame for residents is two to nine days in the dungeon. But that decision is up to me as to how long you will stay. Getting to know you will be quite enjoyable. Right now, I want you to stand up.'

Lisa remained in a seated position, her knees drawn to her chest. 'I said get up, you little whore!' He grabbed her by the hair, slammed the baton into her knees and yanked her to her feet.

'That's better. Now turn around and face the wall. Put your hands on the wall where I can see them and then spread your legs.' Lisa bit down on her lip until she felt blood. She did not want to turn her back on this man.

Superintendent Ash pushed her to face the wall and banged the baton between her thighs making her stance wider. As Lisa placed her hands on the wall, he dropped the baton and grabbed her hips, pulling her towards him, lifting her dress as he did so. He licked the side of her face and then pulled off her underwear, kicking them down to the floor with his foot.

'If you don't cooperate, I will advise the authorities you are uncontrollable, and you will stay here for a very long time.' She heard him spit into his fingers and then rub her buttocks. *Please, God, no.* She felt the tears welling. His pants fell to the floor as his breath rasped in and out. She felt his erect penis pushing between her buttocks. 'Please, no. Stop. I'm sorry,' she wailed, tears spilling down onto her cheeks. Her pleading fell on deaf ears.

His penis entered her, and the tearing pain in her anus from penetration was searing. Lisa screamed and thought she would faint. She clenched her fists and tried to take her mind some-place else, far away from here. Superintendent Ash continued to pump away until he moaned and leaned against her. Lisa didn't know what was worse. The humiliation, the pain ripping through her body or him leaning against her. She wanted to vomit on him. She hated the smell of him. He was vile.

As he dressed, Lisa remained with her back to him. 'I'll see you tomorrow,' he promised as he left the room. The heavy door closed with a loud thud. The light switch on the outside was suddenly turned off and the room was plunged into darkness. Her anal area was so sore, and she felt a discharge, which she was sure was blood.

The room was so dark she could not see where any damage may have occurred. Lisa crawled on her hands and knees feeling for her underwear. Before pulling her pants on, Lisa wiped the discharge on her calico dress so she could see the colour of the discharge when she got into a lighted area.

Lisa now lay in the dark on the filthy floor. Her eyes were swollen and tired as she rocked herself back and forth, her arms crossed over her body. She was so frightened of the superintendent. How could she escape? How was she going to survive this place? Her heart and mind felt broken. Splintered. Exhaustion finally took over, but sleep was fitful until she heard footsteps heading towards her and the door opened. She had no idea what time it was—day or night.

'Morning, girly.' The door opened and light streamed in through the windows of the corridor. 'We have brought you your breakfast. Can't have you starving down here,' said Glenda. 'You haven't touched the meal from last night.' She laughed. 'I don't blame you, looks like shit, tastes like shit. Chef won't be happy.'

Lisa sat up and rubbed her eyes. Remembering she had wiped herself on her calico dress, she looked down at the area. It was dark with dried blood. She shuddered. It was painful to sit, so she got to her feet.

'Please, please help me. I have to get away from here,' she begged. Glenda just laughed.

'Stupid girl. No-one gets away from here unless the superintendent gives the nod. That's why you have to behave.' Lisa felt desperate as Glenda made her way to the door, making a dismissive grunt before closing and locking the door. But at least the lights had been turned back on. Lisa slid down against the wall, her knees buckling. Lying in a foetal position on the hard floor, she reached for the breakfast bowl. Breakfast was porridge, and it was full of weevils. She stared at the bowl, watching the weevils move in and out of the revolting food. The hours passed before she heard footsteps again. The door opened and she sat up, trying to focus, wincing at the pain in her bottom on the cold, hard floor.

The superintendent loomed in the light, and he closed the door behind him. The baton he used the previous night was in his right hand.

'Have you been a good girl? Are you cooperating?' he asked. 'They tell me you are not eating. Do I need to remind you that this could be your permanent residence for some time. We can't have you wasting away, can we. It will look bad if my inmates waste away.'

Lisa got to her feet and tried to back away, moving along the wall. She could feel the pain of the night before and knew she could not tolerate any more. Her eyes were wide with fear and she screamed for help. The superintendent scoffed.

'That will not do you any good. Go on scream, Lisa. It turns me on.' She watched his hand move to his crotch.

'Not a soul can hear you down here and not a soul can see what I do. That's why I enjoy it when you stupid little girls misbehave. I can do what I want to you. No-one sees but you and me. No witnesses.' He moved menacingly towards her, the black baton tapping on his thigh.

Lisa kept moving around the walls, trying to bargain with him and plead for leniency. 'Please, superintendent, I will behave. I promise, you won't have any trouble with me again.' Her voice cracked, and she felt her knees begin to buckle again. The sound of her heartbeat coursed through her ears.

'Be a good girl,' he commanded as he moved towards her, the baton still in his right hand. 'Come here, I haven't been able to stop thinking about you. Tasty little thing you are. I want you on your knees in front of me.' He raised the baton. 'I said come here.' Lisa crawled along the floor on all fours to kneel before him. He leered at her and licked his lips. 'That's better. I can see you are a fast learner.'

He unbuckled his pants, and they fell to the floor. She saw he was erect and her mind screamed, *Get to the door.* She tried to get to her feet but the superintendent pushed her down, striking her back with the baton.

'I won't ask you again. Get on your knees. If you don't, you can stay here for a few more days in this cosy room, and I will let the others have a turn. Men and women. You're quite the star with your pretty face.'

Lisa shuddered and slowly sank to her knees. He lifted up her chin. 'Look what I have for you.' He grabbed her hair and when she brought up her hand to stop him, he slapped her shoulder hard with his baton.

'Stop struggling and open your mouth.' He pushed his penis into her mouth. Lisa gagged and pulled back, but he struck the other shoulder with the baton. 'Do that again and you can stay here long-term. Lisa's eyes bulged and she squeezed her eyes shut. 'Suck it.' He moaned. 'Harder,' he roared and began to push himself in and out.

He grabbed the back of her head so she could not pull away. His thrusting became faster until she felt the warm flow of se-men spilling into her mouth. Lisa pulled away and vomited violently on the floor. She wiped her mouth and kept spitting to erase the vile taste he had left.

It was clear the superintendent enjoyed watching her humil-iation and denigration. He then abruptly left the room without comment and the door closed. The lights flicked off. Lisa screamed into the darkness of the room. *I will die or go crazy in here,* she was sure of it.

EIGHT

A NEW FRIEND

The following day the two women, Glenda and Sharon, appeared. 'You got your leave pass, Missy. You must have been a good girl,' said Sharon. They escorted her up to a common dormitory room. The light was so strong on Lisa's eyes that she squinted to focus. The room was devoid of furniture or fittings. There were thirty-six iron-frame beds set on opposite sides of the room and a single toilet in an adjoining annex. All the windows were barred. Lisa stood in shock. Her bunk that she had shared with Mark in their tiny room now seemed like luxury.

'How do you like your room, Lisa? Pretty fancy, huh,' sneered Glenda. 'Don't get any ideas about escaping. There are bars on all the windows, and the one door to the dormitory is locked at night.'

Lisa wondered what would happen if there were a fire. They would all be burned alive. Cooked chickens. The dorm was an atmosphere of fear with all traces of individuality removed. No privacy, no doors on toilets or showers and no lockers.

'By the way, we do body searches on a daily basis so you little shits can't hide anything, and your mail is censored too. And if your family has the inclination to visit you, and most don't, then it's only once a week.' Glenda seemed pleased with that announcement.

'Make yourself at home with our other residents,' said Sharon as they left the room. Lisa looked around. Some of the girls looked very young while others appeared hardened. They had all watched Glenda and Sharon bring Lisa into the room.

As she placed her only other piece of clothing on the bed, the nightdress, another resident tentatively approached her. She stared at Lisa before introducing herself.

'Hi, I'm Julie. I've been here for nearly six months. I'm hoping to be out very soon.' The girl looked nervous, and it was hard to guess her age. As she extended her hand, Lisa noticed the bruising on her arms. She looked at the short, slim girl with a bird-like frame who seemed curious but friendly. Although slight of build, there was a steely resilience and wisdom about her. She was the first real person here who had showed Lisa some warmth. Julie's face was kind, but like all the residents, her hair was shorn like a boy's.

Lisa spoke tentatively but felt calm before the girl who stood before her. 'I'm Lisa, and I'm hoping to be out very soon too. It's just so horrible here.'

Julie smiled forlornly. 'Yeah, we all hope we'll be out soon, but the superintendent doesn't let anyone out unless they have been here a minimum of six months. He enjoys us during that time, especially the new ones. Try and keep out of trouble and don't give him any excuse. He is rotten to the core and loves the power over us girls. He'll just keep molesting until he tires of us.'

Lisa's eyes filled with tears and she shivered. She was trapped in a living nightmare.

Julie continued. 'It's a real fixed routine. Breakfast is at 6:30 a.m. where we are mustered like sheep. You get given duties like cleaning the kitchen and laundry. We even scrub floors with toothbrushes.'

Lisa grimaced. *How long would it take to clean a floor using a toothbrush?*

'Um, we then do some schooling. Dinner is at 7 p.m. and lights are out at 9 p.m. sharp. It's very monotonous Lisa, but if you don't follow the rules, or you step out of line, the punishment is severe. They can withdraw your meals, you get sent to the dungeon and sometimes they give you drugs to quieten you down. If you keep on being difficult, they can send you to Long Bay Prison out at La Perouse or the Hay Institution for Girls for three months. You don't want to go there. I've heard it's far worse,' Julie exclaimed.

Lisa nodded and took a deep breath. 'I'm pretty scared.' Lisa's voice was barely a whisper. 'Thanks, Julie. It's good to have some sort of friend in here.'

'We heard some of the guards say you had been down in the dungeon,' said Julie, her expression guarded.

'Been there, and I'm not going back.' Lisa noticed the same fear in Julie's eyes as she felt herself.

'It was horrible, so horrible.' Lisa covered her face with her hands so Julie couldn't see her crying.

'So, the superintendent paid you a visit did he? Julie asked sympathetically. 'We all hate him. As I said, he loves to get new recruits. Takes a turn with them all. Likes to give it to you up the arse, so you don't get pregnant.'

Lisa winced at the memory of him sodomising her. She could still feel the pain. 'I'm still sore, and I feel so helpless,' whispered Lisa.

'The physical pain will fade, Lisa. Mine took about five days but I lie in bed and think about the things that go on in here. That's the mental pain. How do you fix that . . . I think it's unfixable. So try to keep out of trouble, then he'll have no reason to send you down there. The rules are rigid, and they try to break your spirit. One of the girls here was sent to the dungeon just for plucking her eyebrows!' said Julie, shaking her head.

'How old are you? What did you do wrong?' Lisa asked.

'I turned seventeen last week. Great place to spend a birthday, isn't it?' Julie had a sense of humour. 'My mother remarried, and my stepfather tried to have his way with me. My mother called me a liar so I smashed his car with a hammer. They said I was uncontrollable so here I am.'

Lisa offered a small smile, communicating acceptance. 'I'm fifteen, and I don't want to spend my next birthday in here.'

Julie knew it was tough, the first birthday in a place like this. 'When I get out of this place, I want to be a hairdresser. If I can do my hair, I can do anybody's. It's been cropped like yours but when I had my own hair before these mongrels butchered me, there were curls everywhere. Big tight curls that had a mind of their own.' Lisa smiled again; she was warming to the girl.

'But please, Lisa, be very careful of the superintendent and don't trust nobody in here, except me. The other male officers and the women are all the same. They love abusing you sexually and seem to enjoy beating you. I think it's called sadism. They are sick bastards, that's for sure. Oh yeah, and try not to be alone. Stick with me as some of the girls, the older ones, have formed predatory gangs and some of them will attack and rape you. Marilyn McPhee is the worst one. Stay away from her. I hate her, the big fat trollop. I call her Mutt Face. Mutt Face Marilyn. She singles out the weak ones. They say she has a tattoo just above her vagina which says "help yourself".'

Lisa spluttered, 'Help yourself?'

'Yep, that's what I heard. I've never seen it myself, but she likes the girls, that Marilyn, so never be alone if you see her and her cronies. I'll point her out in the dining room tonight.'

Lisa took a few deep breaths. Her brow furrowed as she took the information in.

'Oh, sorry. I didn't mean to frighten you, but that's what they do. Some of the girls here are real nasty. But you have to remember, some of them are hardened because they have been abused through childhood. Sexual, you know, incest and all that stuff. So they are hard, and then this place makes them harder. They've had riots here you know, the last one being in 1961.'

'Riots, what sort of riots?' Lisa asked.

'The girls all went on a rampage and destroyed every object and every piece of furniture they could find. It was pretty terrifying, apparently, girls running mad, other girls weeping hysterically.' Lisa was trying to visualise the riots.

'This place always feels like it's about to erupt. The screws will try to break you. They will bash and rape you and the abuse just continues.' Julie sighed her eyes full of despair. She had obviously been through the same sexual abuse in her own family and now had to suffer repeat performances in an institution that was supposed to care.

Lisa put a hand on her shoulder. She knew she had a friend. 'Has that happened to you while you've been here, Julie? Have the screws abused you?'

'Yes, but I learned very quickly to keep my mouth shut, do as I was told and stay out of trouble. It works. They think I'm the model inmate. I keep them amused. I even stand up to pee as I know they're all watching in the quadrangle.'

'That shower block and toilets are absolutely degrading,' agreed Lisa. 'I don't even want to shower or use the toilet.'

'As I said, they try to break your spirit, but to survive and get out of here, just play along. Pretend the toilets have doors and that the screws can't see you. Pretend they are not there,' advised Julie.

'Why are you telling me all this?' Lisa's curiosity was aroused.

Julie paused. 'You look so young and vulnerable, and your eyes are wide with fear. You looked like me when I first walked in. I just think we should all stick together and try to help each other, rather than tear each other apart.' Lisa hugged her and felt how thin she was, thinner than her even.

The women guards appeared and the thirty-six inmates were all marshalled into the dining room. A lot of attention was directed Lisa's way as she was new, but she kept her head down, said nothing and sat next to Julie. It was safer to form some sort of allegiance than be a loner.

'Over there,' said Julie, 'just to your right. Don't look yet as Marilyn is staring. She's the big girl with greasy ginger hair and the pug nose. A wranger. She's got rotten teeth too.'

Lisa didn't want to catch Marilyn's eye, so she waited five minutes before looking, even though she wasn't sure who she was yet. As she turned her head slightly, the description fitted aptly. *Marilyn Mutt Face. She deserved that name.*

'Boy, she does look tough,' whispered Lisa.

The meal was disgusting, and Lisa pushed it away. 'It's crumbed brains,' said Julie as she took a mouthful and then did the same. 'We get treated like we're dirt. All the screws call us sluts,' Julie said. 'We get told to keep quiet and that everything will be alright. But the women are the worst. If you ask me they are all a bunch of lesbian bitches.'

Julie abruptly changed the subject. 'Do you think you will have visitors?'

'I don't think so, my family, except my younger brother and my aunt, hate me. My aunt, who is my favourite, I think she must still be in Europe on her extended honeymoon. Why do you ask?'

'Girls who don't have visitors get kind of earmarked. It's almost a sign that no-one cares about them. More reason to stick with me, Lisa, and don't ever shower alone. Always have me there if you can, and try and hide those boobs,' cautioned Julie. She looked down at her own chest, smoothing her dress as she did so. 'I'm as flat as a tack. You could use me as an ironing board.' Lisa enjoyed her humour, despite the grim circumstances.

When dinner was over, the girls were marched back to the dormitory. 'March with your head down and don't talk until we get to the dorm,' instructed Julie. Lisa was grateful for a friend and one who was guiding her in this shit hole. The guards left and the door was locked. Lights were out at 9 p.m.

'I'm here if you need me, Lisa. Try not to get up through the night. Just stay put,' whispered Julie.

Out of the darkness, a voice growled. 'Shut up, you two. You are like fucking parrots.'

'Shut up yourself,' Julie fired back.

'Fucking bird-face dyke,' the voice spat.

'Night, Lisa,' Julie whispered.

'Ditto,' said Lisa as she pulled the sheets up over her head and closed her eyes. She tried to visualise Woori.

A month later, Lisa was doing laundry duties with Julie. When they entered the room with the washing machines, Julie pointed out Marilyn and two other girls to Lisa.

'That's unlucky,' whispered Julie, nudging Lisa in the ribs. 'We're stuck in here with them today. Keep your distance, Lisa.' It was Marilyn with her sodding cronies, Angie and Maureen. 'Come this way with me, and we'll iron today. All the clothes are there in the baskets. We get the shit work, that's why Marilyn is just feeding clothes through the wringers. A wranger on a wringer. Not much effort.'

Lisa noticed Marilyn watching them as they entered the laundry. Marilyn looked directly at Lisa, her eyes never leaving her.

'Who's your little friend, Julie? Cute, juicy little thing. You can't keep hogging her the way you do. We all got to get some of that.' Marilyn and her friends laughed. The tension in the laundry was building.

'Stay this side of me, Lisa. We're closer to the door.' Julie knew the door led to some stairs and down into a yard. They would be out in the open then if any trouble erupted.

'What's going on? Why do we need the door?' Lisa asked, her eyes wild, tension rippling down her spine. Her heart began to race even faster.

Marilyn stopped what she was doing and looked menacingly at the two girls. Her cronies stood behind her. She walked slowly towards Julie and Lisa, her index finger beckoning the girls to come to her.

'Don't come any closer. Get the fuck away from us,' Julie said as she picked up the iron. Her face was filled with a dreadful knowing of what was about to happen. She had seen it before.

They began to back towards the door. Lisa was behind Julie.

'Come on girls, let's play a little,' cajoled Marilyn. 'The screws are down having a meeting. We promised to be good, didn't we, girls. That's a lot of bullshit. Me, be good!' They all laughed.

'Come on bird-face, step aside. You know what I want.' Marilyn suddenly charged at the girls with Angie and Maureen. Julie knew she was no match for them and threw the iron at them. It missed Angie's head and bounced off the wall.

Angie, now inflamed, grappled Julie to the ground and began punching her face. Julie struggled violently until she felt the blow of the iron crush the side of her head. Angie got to her feet and laughed. 'Bird-face is going nowhere.'

Maureen was quick to move and flung herself at Lisa, knocking her to the ground. Lisa desperately tried to push her off and then Angie joined in, her body weight making it impossible to move.

'Come on, hold her down, I want to see what's under that uniform,' barked Marilyn. Lisa screamed wildly as she felt her underwear being ripped down by Marilyn.

'You are not going to screw me, you fat bitch,' yelled Lisa. She screamed and screamed until other inmates came rushing into the laundry quickly followed by Sharon and Glenda the prison screws.

'What's going on here?' barked Glenda. 'Back off, you bitches,' she cursed as she rammed the baton into Marilyn's back. Angie and Maureen had scattered to the back wall.

'Press the buzzer for God's sake, Sharon. Look at that kid over there; the blood is pouring from her skull.'

Lisa sat up, pulling her underwear back on, her heart breaking as she looked at Julie. The male screws burst through the door and quickly surveyed the mess, groaning when they saw Julie on the floor. Marilyn and her two cronies were dragged away by the men.

Sharon squatted over Julie's lifeless body and felt her pulse. 'She's dead, Glenda.'

'Fuck, fuck, fuck. What are we going to say to the superintendent. Stupid bitches,' moaned Glenda.

Lisa began to weep. 'Stop your fucking crying and get up on your feet,' barked Glenda.

'Cover her up, Sharon. Just grab a sheet from that pile. We have to say she fell down these back stairs. Maybe carrying the laundry to the clothes line and she tripped. Yeah, that sounds good. She fucking tripped.'

Lisa watched tearfully as the only friend she had was covered in a white sheet, the blood seeping through.

I have to get out of here, and in one piece. I'll not be alive in six months' time, she thought desperately.

NINE

AUNT ZENA RETURNS

Some months later after returning to Australia, Zena and Alan travelled down to Sydney for a rural conference on soil management. It was getting near Christmas, and the renovations to the homestead were nearly complete.

They had rung earlier and spoken to Des, who had sounded somewhat hesitant on the phone. Zena put it down to his lack of good communication skills on the phone. He never liked speaking on it. She looked forward to seeing him and chatting personally. She thought it odd that when she asked about Lisa, he was evasive, changing the subject quickly. Then he said he had to get off the phone to help Agnes.

As they pulled into the driveway of her brother's home in Fairfield, Zena spoke. 'I have a funny feeling, Alan. I never know what to expect when I come here. Suffice to say the visits are always unusual.'

'We shall see,' Alan replied as he opened the car door. Des came out to greet them when he heard their car in the driveway. 'Come in, come in. Agnes has just put the kettle on.' He opened the screen door, and they all headed towards the kitchen where Agnes sat slicing home-made fruitcake.

She looked up as Zena and Alan entered the room. Zena felt her iciness, but Agnes managed a lukewarm smile.

'How are you both going? Have you settled in to married life, Zena?' Agnes asked, smirking. 'I bet you just love the isolation, not to mention the blistering heat and the flies.' Zena removed her straw hat and pushed back her thick jet black hair that fell loosely around her shoulders. She was in good form. *This will be a game of words*, Zena thought. *Some things never change.*

'I adore it, Agnes. I adore everything, the lifestyle, the quietness and of course the big open spaces. The house is looking fabulous, and the renovations are nearly complete. Alan has been teaching me the best way to breed good foals from the broodmares and so far so good. We look forward to a new crop of foals towards the end of the year.'

Agnes cocked her head to one side. 'What type of foals are you breeding?'

'Australian stock horses. They've been especially bred for Australian conditions. They're very hardy and noted for their endurance, agility and good temperament. Des could tell you all about them as well, but their ancestry dates back to the arrival of the first horses in Australia, brought from Europe, Africa and Asia. So they have a long history and are valued as a working horse by stockmen and stockwomen throughout Australia.'

'Well, I can see you're quite excited,' Agnes replied as she poured their tea. The house was unusually quiet. 'Where are the children?' asked Zena. She looked directly at Agnes and then her eyes swept across to Des. She knew immediately something was wrong. Her gut instincts had never let her down.

Des cleared his throat, and Zena watched his hand circle the cup. He was clearly nervous and fidgety. 'The boy is playing with his mates down the road, and . . . well, Lisa has been sent to Parramatta Girls Home.' Zena's eyes widened as she sat opposite the couple who appeared to have no emotion at the mere statement and remained expressionless.

'What the devil has gone on! Why is she there?' Zena's voice grew louder, and Alan placed his hand over hers. 'It's okay, Zena. I'm sure there's a good reason,' Alan ventured as he looked at Des searchingly.

It was Agnes who spoke. 'Lisa was caught stealing, and we deemed her behaviour as uncontrollable. She was too much of a handful, causing all sorts of problems at home and at school, and I was nearly having a nervous breakdown. The police were called to the shop where she was caught stealing, and she became violent and aggressive. She has been formally charged.'

'I don't believe this,' Zena exclaimed. 'She was a kind girl, and always honest in her presentation. Lisa has never been aggressive, let alone violent. Something must have happened for her to behave in this manner. How can I see her? Tell me what I have to do. I would very much like to talk to her because as you know, we wanted her to come and stay at Woori this Christmas. We'd hoped she could have stayed last year, but with our extended honeymoon, this wasn't possible. But she was so excited about the prospect of spending a Christmas with us.'

Des looked at Agnes, but no words were exchanged. Agnes rose from her chair and spoke. 'I don't think that's a good idea, Zena.' Her expression soured.

'Why not?' Zena demanded. 'I think it would be a very good idea. Lisa and I have always had a sound relationship, and I would really like to speak to her. If you don't give me your permission, and I'm hoping that you sincerely do, I will go to the Home myself.'

'Zena,' Alan said, 'We need to calm down. I know you care very much for Lisa, but she is not your daughter. Maybe it's best we leave this to the authorities.' Zena stood up abruptly, ignoring her husband's comments.

'Do I have your permission to go to the Home, Des?' She deliberately ignored Agnes and looked directly at her brother. Her presence filled the room, and Des knew she was a force to be reckoned with.

Her brother spoke haltingly. He knew that Zena would go to the Girls Home and ask to see Lisa whether they gave their permission or not. He was in a no-win situation with his wilful sister. 'Look, I don't see that there would be any real harm, so I'll give you the address details.' Zena tapped her foot as he walked over to a kitchen cupboard and pulled out some paper to write on.

Des handed Zena and Alan the address. 'We will ring the superintendent at the Girls Home and let him know that you are on your way. They have strict visitation days but as you have travelled a long way, I'm sure he'll be flexible. I gather that is what you want to do right now?'

'Yes, I do,' Zena replied as she picked up her hat and beckoned Alan to the door.

Zena looked at Des as he followed her out. 'I will let you know how I get on and what transpires. Thank you, Agnes, for the cup of tea, but I need to speak to your daughter. My gut feeling is that something is wrong but as I said, I'll let you know if I find out anything that may assist in going forward. Sometimes children and young adults feel more comfortable talking to a relative or a stranger if something has happened that they don't feel they can tell their parents about.'

Alan linked arms with Zena as he escorted her to their car. Agnes and Des followed them outside but made no further comment. They both appeared to be somewhat stunned by Zena's forthrightness. As she swung her legs over the seat, she looked at them disdainfully. 'I will get to the bottom of this,' she said firmly and closed the door of the car.

As they drove silently to the Parramatta Girls Home, a million questions swirled in Zena's head. 'I can almost hear you thinking, Zena,' Alan said quietly.

'You know me well,' she replied. As they pulled into the driveway, a portly man came out to greet them.

'Good afternoon, Mr and Mrs Smith? I am Superintendent Ash. Mr O'Connor called regarding your visit today. He said you had travelled a long way, so we are making an exception. Please come this way. The staff are bringing Lisa down to the guest arrival room.' Zena watched him walk away. She did not like to judge people on a first meeting, however, the man with the long, thin, crooked nose had watery eyes and she felt no trust in him.

They sat down in the stuffy guest arrival room, which had an awful musky smell. Zena knew the institution was poorly run from previous media coverage, particularly after the riots, which had received strong media coverage a few years back. Her niece would feel extremely uncomfortable in this jail-like establishment.

'This isn't right, Alan. Lisa has always been a good and kind girl. The relationship she has with Agnes has always been troubled but this is not the behaviour I would expect from her. Something has gone horribly wrong.'

'It's not your business, Zena. She is not your daughter,' Alan said.

'I accept that she is not my daughter. But it is my business. I so strongly disagree with her being institutionalised like this. It doesn't seem like a place for first offenders as they have classified her. And she is definitely not a delinquent. It's a poor description. This place is more like a jail. She is my niece and I aim to get to the bottom of this situation and get her out of here.'

As she finished her sentence, the door to the left of where they sat opened slowly. Lisa was ushered in by a large woman whose name badge said Eve. Zena almost gasped at Lisa's appearance. She was painfully thin and the dark circles under her eyes were visibly noticeable. There were scratch marks on her neck as if fingernails had tracked around the circumference of her throat, which was red raw. Zena and Alan rose slowly and walked towards Lisa, who stood with her head bowed. Zena looked at the woman and stated firmly, 'I'd like to speak to my niece in private.'

'Yes, of course, Mrs Smith,' Eve replied. 'I shall be just outside if you need me.' Her voice was filled with sarcasm. 'I won't be needing you,' Zena retorted. Eve left the room swiftly.

'Come here, darling girl. Alan and I are here for you.' As Zena hugged Lisa, she could feel how frail her body had become. Zena stepped back, but her arms remained on Lisa's shoulders. She looked into Lisa's eyes. Lisa spoke before she could. 'She called you Mrs Smith. Are you married now?'

'Yes, Alan and I married overseas in London. I'll tell you more about it when we have the time. Right now, I need to know what has happened.'

Lisa's eyes were downcast and tears spilled down her cheeks. Zena's heart began to ache. 'I know what you've done, the stealing, but I also know for you to do this thing, there must have been a very good reason. Do you want to tell me?' Lisa's eyes searched her aunt's lovely face, then looked across to Alan.

'You can speak and tell me what has happened. I'll make sure no harm comes to you. Don't be frightened,' Zena said softly. Lisa began to sob, and Zena took her into her arms once more. She stroked her head softly.

Lisa could smell her perfume and felt her aunt's strength. She wanted to stay there forever. 'We will both try to get you out of here; you can come to Woori and stay with us like we planned. Would you like that?' Zena asked earnestly, hoping the girl had not changed her mind.

'Oh, yes, yes, please, Aunty,' Lisa said as she wiped her eyes. 'But I don't know how that will be possible. They said I have to stay here for six or nine months. I don't want to stay here any longer; it's horrible.'

'How long have you been here now?' There was pain in Zena's voice.

'About four months. I hate it, just hate it. I cannot last in here. I want to get out and go to Woori, like we planned.' Lisa began to shake.

'Listen to me now, Lisa. You have to try and stay out of trouble while Alan and I seek permission for your removal from this God-awful place. Promise me you'll be good and that you will stay out of trouble no matter what happens. You must be strong. If you don't play by their rules, I just know they'll keep you in here and use any excuse, particularly if you misbehave.'

'I promise,' Lisa whispered, tears welling up in her eyes again. Her aunt hugged her fiercely.

'We are going to leave you now as we'll head across to see the superintendent.' Zena left Lisa sitting in the guest arrival room as they walked down to the office of Superintendent Ash.

'United front. The kid looks like shit, absolute shit. Skinny as a branch,' Alan whispered.

The superintendent's door was open, and he sat writing as they approached. He put his pen down when he heard their footsteps and stood to greet the couple.

'So, how's it all going? As you can see, she is being well looked after. Have to teach some of these young girls respect for authority.'

Zena saw right through him. Being looked after. What bloody rubbish! Thin, dark circles under Lisa's eyes and bruises on her arms and legs, the markings around her neck. Sure. But she knew she'd have to turn on the charm to get her niece out. She had to find his weak spot.

'Oh, yes, I can see you are a wonderful, compassionate human being, and the girls must thrive under your care. You have done a splendid job here, but I really think it's time for Lisa to leave. I know she has only been here for four months and that you usually have the girls here for a little longer, but when I explain to you our plan, which I add, was discussed many months ago with Lisa's parents, you will understand my reasoning. May I have a quiet word with you, Superintendent Ash?'

'Yes, of course,' he said as he removed his thick glasses. Zena turned to Alan. 'Would you allow me the time to discuss Lisa's best interests.'

'No problem. I'll head back to sit with Lisa. I can tell her about the farm and the new foals that will be arriving.' Alan stood up. 'I'm not far away if you need me.' Zena knew what Alan meant and watched him as he closed the door behind them.

'Now then,' Superintendent Ash said as he sat opposite Zena in his worn leather chair. 'She is a bright girl, young Lisa, head strong, but we have got her into shape.' He gazed down at Zena's breasts.

Zena could read his thoughts. There was his Achilles heel. He dribbled slightly at the corners of his mouth as he continued to stare at her breasts. Zena found him repulsive, and she hoped that Lisa's time in the place would be very short. It would be if she had anything to do with it.

'As you know, Superintendent Ash, I have spoken to Lisa's parents this morning and am quite shocked at what my niece has done. I think, you, as a very well-educated man would agree, it would be in her best interests to remove her from the city and its environs and anyone who has been a bad influence on her. Alan and I would take full responsibility.' Zena paused. 'As you can appreciate, in a remote and isolated place, there is nowhere to go to. She can't drive, and the walk to the nearest town would kill a healthy adult. So you see, we would have her in our full custody. It would be one less resident to look after. One less expense for the authorities.'

Superintendent Ash shuffled papers as she spoke. He knew she was right. One less resident. One less headache. Her exit would free up a bed for a new recruit. He smiled at the thought.

Idiot, Zena thought. *Trying to look important shuffling his papers.* He pressed the intercom button and cleared his throat. Eve promptly answered.

'Yes, superintendent,' said the military-sounding voice.

'Eve, the young girl, Lisa, is still in the guest arrival room with her uncle. Could you bring them down to my office.'

A few moments later, Alan and Lisa entered the room. Lisa sat next to her aunt. Alan stood at the back of the room. Zena glanced at him and knew he felt the same as her. Alan wanted to pull the bastard over his desk and give him a good belting.

'Now, Lisa, your lovely aunt has queried whether she could take full responsibility for you and that you would reside with her and her husband Alan on their property. Would you find this suitable or would you prefer to stay in the home?'

Zena noticed Lisa picking at her nails with a general nervousness that had never existed before. *Was it the home or this man? What has happened here?* she thought desperately.

Lisa looked at him and said quietly, 'I think that I would very much like to live with my aunt and uncle, Superintendent Ash.'

'Very good, I shall clear this with your parents first and then the authorities, and I shall let you all know in due course.'

'How long will that take, Superintendent Ash,' Zena asked, smiling sweetly.

'Well, today being Thursday, we may have clearance by Monday. I'm not quite sure.'

'Oh, my dear superintendent, are you able to pull any strings? A man of your power and stature would surely be able to move mountains. I'm sure with your reputation that the authorities would listen to you, particularly given the fact that we live in a very remote area, so there will be no room for temptation or escape. Just hard work.' Zena almost purred, and Lisa could see she was working the stupid fool.

Zena continued, 'We have to go back to the property. As you know, it's a very long distance from the city to the bush, so it would work so much better for us to take Lisa with us as soon as possible rather than on another return trip. I would be so grateful if you could possibly manage this.' Again, she fluttered her eyes and pressed her body across the desk, the outline of her breasts clearly visible.

'We're staying at The Boulevard in Sydney. If we leave now, you have the whole afternoon and a few days to organise her release. Would that be possible? Is that enough time, Superintendent Ash?'

Alan suddenly interjected. 'We could stay until Monday or Tuesday into the following week? I can get the boys next door to go over and feed the animals.'

Zena looked at the superintendent. Alan was like the second troops rallying to the cause. More time. No excuse. She rose slowly and extended her white-gloved hand.

'So, you see, we'll make ourselves available while you advise the authorities. Please ask them to call me at The Boulevard if they have any concerns.'

The superintendent kissed her hand, and Zena wanted to quickly pull it away but she was using her feminine charms so let him linger. Zena then turned to her niece, her back facing the superintendent.

She winked at Lisa but said sternly, 'I know this has been tough, Lisa, but you can't do the wrong things and expect to get away with it. So now we must amend our ways and start a new beginning. Do you understand, Lisa? You will come to the country with Alan and me, and you will work hard at doing the right thing. Should you cause any problems, you'll be straight back here. I will have no hesitation calling the superintendent.'

Lisa gave a faint smile. 'Yes, Aunty, I promise to do the right thing.' Zena kissed her niece on the forehead then turned back to the superintendent.

'Thank you once again, Superintendent Ash. I look forward to hearing from you either this afternoon or tomorrow. I am sure the authorities will understand. My husband Alan has a few heavy-weight friends in the political arena who may also be able to assist the process.' They left the building and walked towards the car. Out of the corner of her eye, Zena saw the superintendent standing at his window, watching them drive away.

'I'm hoping that my charm can work miracles, Alan. He is an awful man, and I need to extricate my niece as soon as possible.'

Alan nodded in agreement. 'Yes, I got that feeling too. I wonder what goes on in that place. By the look of Lisa, lots. As I said, she looks like shit. I didn't like him either, Zena, and that doesn't happen too often with me. And by the way, who are my heavy-weight political friends?' Zena laughed. 'I don't know, but that line always helps.'

◊

Lisa remained seated in Superintendent Ash's office. He turned from the window and remarked, 'Your aunt is a splendid woman. Lucky man, that Alan.'

'Yes,' replied Lisa. Superintendent Ash walked over from the window and placed his hands on the arms of the chair and leaned towards her. Lisa cringed at the smell of stale tobacco on his breath and turned her face away. He licked the side of her face. She wanted to kick him but could hear her aunt's words running through her head: *Remain in control. Stay out of trouble.*

'Maybe just one more time. I can pretend it's your delicious aunt I'm fucking,' he whispered into her ear.

Lisa felt the bile rise in her throat and a cold dread spread across her body. She knew what was coming but had hoped her aunt would come to get her before he invaded her body again. It was not to be.

The superintendent picked up a set of keys on the wall and told her to follow him down to the isolation room. He closed the door behind them. Lisa stood looking at the superintendent from across the room.

'Take off all your clothes,' he said hoarsely.

Lisa didn't move, so he began to unclip the baton on his hip. She quickly fumbled at her calico dress and lifted it over her head. 'Now your panties, shoes and socks. I want you completely naked.'

He licked his lips as she stood naked before him and rubbed his erection through his trousers. He commanded, 'Come towards me and stand with your legs apart.' Lisa's legs felt like lead, and her heart began to race. What plans did he have this time? He had not asked her to turn around, and he had not asked her to get on her knees.

'I want you to masturbate in front of me, play with your clitoris.' Lisa's eyes widened with humiliation and shock. She did not want to do this but could hear her aunt's words.

'Hurry up,' he barked as he unbuttoned his trousers and they fell to the floor. He stepped out of them and stood directly in front of her. 'Pull my underwear down, bitch.' Lisa grimaced as she pushed his jocks to the floor. He stepped out of them and stood back to look at the trembling girl.

'Touch yourself.' Lisa froze and then felt the baton slam into her shoulder. She began to touch herself. The superintendent's eyes blazed. 'More, enjoy it, bitch. Do it more.'

He began to masturbate, his eyes leering at the sight of the young girl rubbing her clitoris. His strokes grew faster until he moaned with pleasure and then ejaculated over Lisa.

He brought his hands around her buttocks and pressed her body to his lips. Lisa squeezed her eyes shut and began to shake involuntarily. 'I'll miss you,' he said standing to his feet. When he closed the door behind him, Lisa let out a bloodcurdling scream.

TEN

RESCUED

Lisa lay sobbing on the floor of the dungeon. She raked her nails across the floor and screamed silently, *Please, please, Aunty. Get me out of here.* She passed in and out of sleep until she heard footsteps. The door opened and Glenda appeared. *What day was it? How long had she been here?*

'Get your clothes on, girly. No time for lazing around. Have to get you back up to the dormitory.' Lisa threw the dress over her head and followed Glenda, her legs heavy, her body aching. The girls were all in their beds so it must have been after 9.00 p.m. Standing in the darkness, Lisa shivered, making her way to the small bed. She still felt so alone without Julie. A voice whispered in the dark, 'They got rid of Mutt Face and her cronies.' At least that was something of a relief.

Three days later, Eve appeared in the laundry where Lisa was working.

'You've got an early release, you little bitch. Not quite sure how you managed that but you have to go to your dorm, pack your things and be down at the guest arrival room in one hour. If you're not down there, you can stay with us,' Eve snorted.

Lisa scurried out of the laundry, her heart pounding. There was nothing to pack, so she was in the guest arrival room in far less than an hour. As she waited, she looked down at her nails. They were bitten to the quick, and there were bruises on her arms and legs. At that moment, she heard a car in the driveway. She crossed her fingers it was her aunt and uncle, and then she heard Zena's familiar voice. It was music to her ears.

'Superintendent Ash, how good of you to personally greet us on Lisa's last day. May I thank you for the clearance of red tape and for the discussions with Lisa's parents.'

Lisa heard the superintendent reply, 'Here are Lisa's discharge papers. I will be sorry to see her go. She was really being rehabilitated to our expectations. Just sign here, Mrs Smith.' Zena quickly signed the two copies. 'There will be follow up calls from child welfare officer. These should occur within a week, and you can discuss any problems or issues you are having with Lisa's behaviour.'

'Thank you, superintendent. You really exceeded my expectations. Done and dusted on a sunny Monday. Where is my niece?' Zena asked sweetly.

Lisa heard them all walking to the guest arrival room where she sat anxiously waiting. Her heart raced as their footsteps approached the door. It was an instant relief when the door opened and she saw her aunt's face and Alan standing next to her. She wasn't dreaming. It was happening. It was real.

'Do you have any bags, Lisa?' asked Alan. The superintendent interjected. 'No, she doesn't. She arrived in her school uniform, which we have since disposed of. I have a paper bag in my office that contains her shoes and socks.'

Zena interrupted, 'We have no need for them, superintendent. Perhaps someone here can make use of the shoes. Come dear, we have to get on our way. Thank you once again for all your assistance, superintendent.' Lisa saw her aunt was clutching the discharge papers closely to her chest as if expecting someone to snatch them away.

Zena extended her hand to Lisa as they walked to the blue Zephyr parked outside. Alan opened the rear door for Lisa, and she quickly slid in. She made no acknowledgement of Superintendent Ash nor did she look in his direction.

Superintendent Ash stood at the front door, his gaze never leaving the car. As Alan drove slowly past, Zena asked him to stop the car but to keep the motor running.

'I want to see his face, Alan.' Zena was almost purring at the thought. 'By the way, superintendent, I will be sending a letter to the Ombudsman asking for a full investigation into this place. It seems a few of the girls have complaints.' He went pale and a look of astonishment spread across his face. Zena could almost see his mind ticking over, *A full investigation! What had Lisa said? What girls had fucking complained?*

◊

The car pulled slowly away and moved through the two black gates. Lisa felt her wounded body go blissfully limp into the soft leather seats of the pale blue Zephyr. Her mind was full yet blank. She had only known pain and terror and abuse in the family home and then more of the same in an institution that was supposed to rehabilitate her. She began to cry and laugh at the same time. Elation and relief. If she had not experienced the pain, the sorrow, the anger and the horror, she would not be sitting in the back seat. Lisa suddenly shouted, 'I'm free, I'm free,' and punched the air. Tears ran freely down her face as she shook her head from side to side in disbelief.

◊

Alan looked across to Zena. She met his gaze and he read her thoughts. They both knew it was a long road ahead. They both knew there was more to this than met the eye. They needed to know the initial source of Lisa's anger and why she had rebelled. Zena knew there would be a good reason.

Alan watched the girl in the rear vision mirror. She looked exhausted and seemed to be bruised physically and mentally. She was a young girl that had known terror, he sensed this, but he hoped now that her heart would also come to know love.

His wife could give that in abundance.

PART TWO

SPIRIT COUNTRY

ELEVEN

RED DUST

As they left the city and travelled up over the Blue Mountains, heading west, Lisa slept. Alan had decided to stay overnight in the country town of Bathurst and after dinner, get an early night. They pulled into the Best Western Motel, and Zena leaned over to look at her sleeping niece.

'Still asleep. I hate to wake her, Alan.' Zena gently shook Lisa. 'Wake up, my darling girl. We're staying overnight. It's too long a drive, and we can get an early start in the morning after breakfast.'

Zena checked in to a family suite that had two separate bedrooms. She didn't want Lisa to be alone or let her out of her sight. She expected the worst to come. Would Lisa open up? Would she have nightmares? How would she react?

She could see that Lisa was very tired to the point of exhaustion. As they reached their suite, Zena put her arms around her. 'Safe now. We are both here if you need us,' said Zena tenderly. 'Why don't you have a shower and then we'll head down to dinner. Alan has put a small bag in your room, which has a few things I bought for you.'

Lisa nodded as she felt the warmth of her aunt. Zena's hazel eyes softened. 'I am no psychologist, Lisa, but when bad thoughts or bad people come into your head, try and think of good things. I've done that in the past, and sometimes it works to concentrate only on the positive. I have no doubt you have suffered terrible things. You don't need to tell me now but I am hoping you can trust me to support you when you do.'

'I'll try and think of good things, Aunty, and things did happen . . .' Lisa's voice trailed off and then she headed for the bathroom, not wanting to break down.

Stepping under the hot water, Lisa suddenly had an image of Lenny in the steamy shower. Closing her eyes tightly shut, she tried to remove the image that flashed before her. She began to take deep breaths and visualised Woori, silently telling herself, 'Think of good things. Think of good things. Please go away. You're not in my life anymore.'

The warm water felt good and Lisa felt clean, with the dirt of the institution washing away. Wrapped in a bathrobe that hung behind the door, Lisa wandered into the bedroom from the ensuite and saw the small treasures on the bed. Tears welled. *You are so kind to me, Aunty.* A new blue gingham dress, bra and panties were laid out on the bed for her, with some new sneakers on the floor.

Lisa peered inside the bag and there were new Volleys, a pair of sandals, shorts, T-shirts and jeans. Lisa could not remember the freshness of new clothes and held the blue dress delicately in front of her.

Zena knocked softly on the adjoining door. 'How are you in there Lisa?'

'I'm good, Aunty. I'm just looking at this lovely new dress. I don't know what to say. How did you know my size?'

'A good guess. I hope they fit, darling girl. I know you've lost weight. Is it okay to come in? Are you decent?'

'Yes, just in a bath robe that was provided, please come in.' Zena sat on the side of the bed and took Lisa's hand. 'I know we have a lot to get through and work out and it's all before us, but we will and we can do it.' Lisa's eyes portrayed gratitude. She held up the uniform from the Girls Home.

'Here, give it to me, Lisa, I am putting this into a paper bag, and we will burn the dress when we get home to Woori.'

Lisa smiled. Her first real smile in what felt like forever. 'Yes, and I would like to light the match, thank you,' she said, holding her new dress to her chest.

Zena replied, 'I'll leave you to it. Come out when you're ready. Alan is wanting to eat.' Lisa closed the door and changed into the new clothes. They were a bit loose, but the new clothes felt good against her skin. Lisa whipped the towel off her head and then walked to the mirror. Her hair was still short, and the tufts stood out like wild grass in a paddock. It will grow, she thought as she ran her fingers through her hair.

As she stepped into her aunt's adjoining room, Zena commented, 'Well, that looks a lot better!'

'Yeah, a bit loose, but I feel clean and fresh. I don't know how to thank you both.' Lisa put her head in hands. There was momentary silence, and Zena came to her side, putting a reassuring arm around her. 'Things will get better, I promise.'

They walked across a small courtyard, and the evening colours filled the sky. 'What beautiful colours, pinks and purples,' Lisa said as she felt an enveloping feeling of safety flanked by her aunt and Alan.

The dining room was empty when they arrived. It was a typical country restaurant. Big windows and pictures of cattle and landscapes.

'What about steak, chips and salad, Lisa?' asked Zena.

Lisa nodded, 'Sounds good,' although she knew she did not have much of an appetite. It still felt like she was dreaming. Her body still ached from the assaults, but she had just used a shower and toilet that had doors with no-one watching. She felt a sense of peace at last.

'Make that three,' Alan told the waitress.

As the plate was placed in front of her, Lisa looked at it carefully and turned the plate around a few times.

'What's wrong, kid?' asked Alan.

'Um . . . nothing.'

'But you looked at it like . . . I don't know, as if it wasn't real.'

'I know it's real, Alan. I was actually looking for weevils.'

'Weevils!' exclaimed Zena.

'Yes, our food, particularly the porridge, seemed to be always accompanied by weevils.'

Alan and Zena stared at her in shock.

After dinner, they settled in for the night. The feeling of no-one watching and no-one entering her room to violate her was like a balm to her soul. How could she ever repay her aunt's kindness? Right now though, she was ready for bed. Fatigue came easily, but when Zena knocked on the door of her room, Lisa startled. The memories of doors opening or people wanting to enter her room always represented danger. She sat straight up in bed, tightly clutching the bedcovers to herself.

'How are you, Lisa?' Are you feeling any better?' Zena asked as she sat by Lisa's bedside.

'Yes, Aunty. For the first time I feel as if I belong, like I'm actually wanted.' Zena hugged her niece and then sat back.

'Do you want to tell me about the marks on your neck or the bruises on your arms and legs.' Lisa hesitated and then shook her head. 'Not now, Aunty, but I will. I just can't right now.' She felt her bottom lip quiver just at the mention.

'Okay, try to get some sleep. We'll see you in the morning.'

Lisa lay back down. The bed was soft and warm, and the sheets were crisp and clean. The sensation of being loved was overwhelming. She had always known her aunt was deeply fond of her, but now she was astounded by how much and how she was able to get her out of the Girls Home so quickly. Her living nightmare had stopped. She thought how lucky she was that she had been discharged early, before drifting into a deep sleep.

◊

The sun rose early, and Alan stirred. He looked at his beautiful wife sleeping next to him. He never got tired of that sight. The job had been done by getting Lisa out of that dreadful institution, but his instinct told him there was a lot more to be revealed.

He put the kettle on in their suite and began to get ready for the drive ahead. He hoped Lisa would love the outback as much as his wife. They were childless and probably would remain that way. Zena had had terrible cysts on her ovaries as a teenager, and they were so large that surgery had been required. One ovary and fallopian tube were removed and the other ovary was damaged in the process. The cysts were multiple and scar tissue had developed. They were both disappointed that they couldn't have children of their own. He looked forward to having his niece around.

'How did you sleep?' Alan asked as Lisa opened the door to their room.

'A few bad dreams, but I did get some sleep.'

Alan knew she would have a continuation of these memories. Nightmares, guilt and a lack of trust. They needed to know what trauma she had experienced. They would take everything in their stride and reach out for professional help if needed.

◊

The chatter over breakfast in the dining room was unusual for Lisa. She was used to silence. Laughter and discussions regarding the day ahead and forward planning were all new to her. When they spoke about Woori, it sounded so exciting. Lisa could not wait to get there.

After breakfast, they began the journey to Dubbo. The road was long and straight, and wildlife frequently crossed their path. There were no houses, and Lisa watched the beautiful bare landscape changing in foliage and colours. This was the outback. No fibro shacks side by side, like in suburbia. As they travelled the dusty roads, even the dead trees that reached to the sky looked like weathered arms reaching out. Just like her.

'Where are we now? I'm totally lost,' Lisa remarked.

'On our way to Dubbo, Walgett and then Carinda. Once we get over the Blue Mountains and head west, we belong to the bush,' Alan said with a grin.

Alan turned to Zena. 'We have to stop in Dubbo to collect the Land Rover, so how about we stop for lunch there as well. Can't have the girl starving. I think she has found her appetite.'

Zena laughed. 'Yes, I think she has. I need to get some more poultry and ducks at Walgett as well as a few other supplies for home, now there is an extra mouth to feed.'

Alan chimed in. 'I need to get some more fencing material as well. There are a few holes in some areas. Have to keep those dingoes out.'

'Dingoes!' exclaimed Lisa.

'Yeah, kid. They do a lot of damage, especially at lambing time. You can ride the boundary fences with me. Then you will know why we're always fencing. The dingo fence we call it.'

Lisa watched out the window as the landscape continually changed shape. The red dust began to swirl as they drove, covering the blue Zephyr. The trees became sparse. The open plains were enormous and vast. So much land.

'What is Dubbo like, Aunty,' Lisa asked excitedly.

'It's an interesting country town. A lot of history. Alan is the history buff, so he can tell you more. But for me, there are a lot more stores than in Walgett and Carinda, so I try to do as much shopping as I can there.'

When they arrived in Dubbo, it was a small country town. People stood around chatting and were very friendly. No-one appeared to be in a rush. The men wore big hats like the one Alan wore, and the utes that were parked all had kelpies or cattle dogs in them. 'Good working dogs, Lisa,' Alan explained. 'They go all day. I've got plenty of them.' Sadness crossed Lisa's heart when she saw the cattle dogs.

Her thoughts turned to Cassius, the old blue heeler at home. Lisa wondered how Mark and Cassius were faring. Lisa missed her brother terribly but knew he would be okay. He was always her mother's favourite. She smiled when she thought of him waddling, playfully teasing her and always looking out for her. *I so wish I had him here with me.*

Her attention returning to her surroundings, Lisa noticed there were no big stores in Dubbo apart from Woolworths. Alan said the first European settler in the area was Robert Dulhunty. He arrived around 1830 and chose some grazing land, calling it Dubbo.

Alan went on to explain. 'It's an Aboriginal name, Lisa, maybe from the Wiradjuri tribe. It means red earth. Wheat and wool is what they do here. Some of the old buildings are really beautiful architecturally. We'll just take a quick drive around, and I'll point a few things out. You can both have a history lesson.'

Lisa saw her aunt smile. Alan loved to talk history and he was trying to engage Lisa in her new surroundings.

'There is the Court House, built in 1885, and just over there is the Anglican Church, built around 1875. A famous architect from England designed it. I really like Saint Zena's Catholic Church just over there. It has stained glass windows but the rose window was donated by Duncan MacKillop, the uncle of Saint Mary MacKillop.'

'That's a really beautiful church, Alan,' Lisa said wistfully. Alan winked and said, 'Just time for two more. There's the Old Dubbo Gaol, built in 1848. It closed in 1966, so is now just a tourist venue slash museum. Kind of spooky as it tells the life stories of the inmates and has the gallows pole with the hangman's equipment. Eight men were hung there.'

Lisa went quiet. 'I don't want to visit there.' Something about the jail had spooked her.

Alan quickly changed the subject 'Okay, last one, the Milestone Hotel. Built in 1881. It was also run as a casino and a brothel.'

Zena laughed. 'Just think, Alan, you could have a cold beer, lose a fortune and visit the local ladies all at the same time.'

Alan chuckled. 'We're done now,' he said. 'This tourist guide is getting hungry!'

Zena filled up with petrol after lunch while Alan said his goodbyes and headed off to get his Land Rover. 'See you lovely ladies both at home.' He waved as he headed off down the street.

'How much further, Aunty, until I see Woori?' Lisa asked her aunt eagerly, which seemed to please Zena.

'Oh, we have about five hours to go. We have to stop in Walgett to get some poultry and the fencing gear. But then it's Carinda and home. It's a long way, and I will need you to help me open the gates as we pass through the property. Lots of gates, Lisa, so when we're closer to home, get your sandshoes on so that you're comfy as well as protected from the cat's heads.'

'Cat's heads? What are they?' Lisa wondered out loud.

'Think of a bindi, the size of a small marble, with horns. When you get one in your foot you just can't walk,' explained Zena.

Lisa rummaged through the bag her aunt had provided with the items of clothing and toiletries and then removed her sneakers. When she pulled out the Volleys, another memory flooded in. Her favourite shoes. It was sports day, where her athleticism was apparent. She wondered what she would do about school now that she would be living in the bush, but she kept these thoughts to herself. Somehow, her aunt would have worked this out.

'Perfect,' her aunt said. 'We have about four hours in front of us.' They headed to Walgett, the blue Zephyr covered by the red clouds of dust.

'There's not a lot in Carinda, Lisa, which is why we get as much as we can in Walgett. Carinda just has the general post office, petrol station and of course a pub. Every country town has a pub.' Zena laughed.

Lisa slept part of the way but each time she woke, the warmth of the scenery flooded her being. Enormous stretches of land under a big blue sky on the open highway flew by. Freedom. They finally arrived at the Walgett Co-Op store, which was full of everything and anything you could want for a farm.

'This is amazing,' Lisa said as she stepped through the door. She was taking in all the smells. 'Is that leather?'

'Yes. And hay and everything else you find on a farm. I love it too, Lisa. The smell of leather and hay, the smell of rain in the outback, and of bacon sizzling in the mornings, all washed down with good cup of tea. A good sense of smell is something you need in the bush.' Lisa walked alongside her aunt, who chatted easily to the staff, and watched her as she selected the mallard ducks and chickens. Zena also ordered more fencing wire for Alan due to the dingoes breaking through.

'Chicken is considered a luxury food, as are eggs. Don't really know why . . . but we have always eaten them. Wait till you taste my bacon and eggs or my Sunday chicken roast. Alan said he has never tasted better.' Lisa couldn't wait to taste Zena's cooking either, the way she described it. She thought of Agnes' cooking. Cardboard.

The Co-Op staff followed Zena to the Zephyr and lined the rear of the car with old hessian bags. They loaded the crate of poultry and ducks into the back of the Zephyr Station Wagon.

'Where will the fencing wire fit, Aunty?'

'It won't. Alan will have to pick that up in the ute next time he is in Walgett. But they have to order it in. It comes up from Sydney. Everybody uses it. The dingoes can be a problem, but with the extra help over the shearing season, we get a lot of fencing done.'

Lisa moved to the front of the vehicle and loved being able to sit closer to her aunt.

As they drove through the town, Zena pointed out the Walgett RSL. 'That's where Alan and I provide entertainment nearly every month on a Saturday. Usually in summer, but sometimes we do a winter special. You must come; it's a lot of fun and we both love music. Alan plays the saxophone, and I sing and play the piano. My mother always sang at home and played the piano. I learned from her and then I did further training when I went to London.'

'Really?' Lisa had no idea of her aunt's musical talents. 'I would love to come to the RSL, Aunty. I'm amazed at what you know!'

'Well, your granny had a piano in her home, and she taught us the basics, and of course, she loved to sing. But after completing my Primary School Teacher's Certificate, and then saving for a few years, I decided to take off overseas. Travel broadens your whole outlook. I loved London and Europe. As I said, when I got to London, I had private lessons in piano and singing. We'll go there one day, I promise you. Maybe for your birthday next year. You'll be sweet sixteen then.' Lisa couldn't believe what she was hearing. London for her sixteenth! How her life had changed in such a short space of time.

The day grew hotter, and her aunt had the windows closed as they headed to Carinda. The dust seemed to sneak into the car despite the windows being up, and the car began to smell of chickens and ducks.

'Cripes,' Zena exclaimed. 'Those ducks and chooks are really starting to get on the nose, but there's not much I can do about it, Lisa. They are doing what comes naturally. It's not a problem when they're outside but certainly when you're travelling, ducks and chooks are not pleasant in a confined space. The smell of chook or duck poo is awful in the heat, let alone in this car.' They would be very grateful to reach their final destination.

By the time they got to Carinda, both women exited the vehicle rapidly. Zena dusted herself off, as did Lisa.

'Come on,' Zena said. 'I feel the need for a strawberry milkshake. 'Me too,' replied Lisa. She could already feel the cold milk filling her dusty throat. 'We can't be too long, Lisa,' Zena added, 'or the poultry will roast in their own juices in the back of the Zephyr.'

Zena had parked her car just near a milk bar with some shady bloodwood trees, so they sat in the shade as they sipped their milk shakes.

Lisa hugged her arms to her body. 'I'm pinching myself, Aunty. It's like I've gone from one life to another. If it . . . if it had not been for you, I'm sure I would have died in that place.'

Zena sighed and took Lisa's hands as if trying to reassure her. 'I have no doubt that if we did not live out here in isolation, I think your extrication would have been much more difficult. Going forward, let's try to think positive thoughts. You have a lot to tell me, and the child authorities will keep in touch. You also have to complete your education. It's so important, Lisa, and yours has been badly interrupted.'

'Are you going to send me away, Aunty, for education?' Lisa asked, her lower lip trembling. She couldn't bear the thought.

'Good grief, no. We can do this via School of Air Australia. This is basically a two-way radio for country kids. So, you can do some chores in the morning, and then I'll show you how to hook up to the radio for a three-hour lesson. But right now my priority is just getting you settled. I know you've been through a great deal. You'll let me know about it when you're ready, and only when you're ready.' A feeling of being cocooned in warmth and safety spread through Lisa's body. Her aunt had always been her greatest supporter.

Zena changed the subject. 'Anyway, back to the RSL. I don't think the board will mind my niece assisting. We'll ask if you're allowed inside the RSL. If not, you may have to play outside with all the kids. They roam the streets playing, and it's quite safe. Some of the parents are inside the RSL, so it's a mixture of white and Aboriginal children. We can periodically check on you between our breaks. If the cinema has a picture playing, you can also go to that if you want.'

'What sort of music do you play?' Lisa wanted to know.

'Well, anything really. Jive music, so there's a bit of twirling about, slow dance music for the older group, and of course, people in love. We'll give you a private recital at home.'

'That would be great; I can't wait to hear you play.' Lisa smiled. It must be a nice feeling to be in love. She wondered if she could ever be intimate with someone or have a normal relationship after what she'd been through. These thoughts started to upset her. The words 'damaged goods' flooded her mind, so she immediately tried to think about something else.

'Some of the shearers come into town just for a bit of entertainment and to see the local ladies. A few romances come and go and also a few marriages, so we must be doing something right,' laughed Zena.

They finished their milkshakes, and Zena returned the silver containers.

'Let's get going; it's not long now until we reach Woori. It's about one and a half hours before we get to the farm and drive through all the gates to reach the homestead. I just hope we don't pass out with the smell of those ducks and chooks in the car! Let's go, kiddo. Homeward bound.'

As they swung out onto the highway, Zena increased her speed. They could see a red dust cloud up ahead. 'What is that, Aunty?' Lisa was fascinated.

'It looks like a big dust storm, doesn't it? But it will probably be a stock truck, and the red dust cloud you see is what he's creating as he travels. I'll have to overtake him; otherwise, we'll sit in this dust cloud. And between him and the dust, as well as the smells in the back, we'll both choke.'

Her aunt increased her speed as she began to overtake. The dust billowed around them making vision difficult. Lisa had never seen a woman drive so fast, and her aunt showed no fear. As she began to overtake, she waved to the driver, beeped the horn and kept her foot planted on the accelerator. She was right, the dust was choking.

'I don't know which is worse Lisa, the red dust or the smell of those chooks and ducks. Thank God Woori is not far off! I will pull over at the next rest stop,' said Zena. 'Be good to stretch our legs and get some fresh air.'

Further down the highway, a rest bay appeared and Zena pulled the Zephyr into the shade. When they exited the vehicle, Zena pulled out a water bag and poured two glasses of water into tin mugs as they both breathed in the smell of the bush. 'That's better,' remarked Lisa and they both laughed.

The same truck Zena had overtaken previously suddenly appeared and the driver slowed, making his way down into the rest bay. As he exited his cabin, he saw the blue Zephyr and waved, walking towards them at the small table they were sitting at. He took off his big hat and Lisa could see his weathered face and strong tanned hands. They were as big as gold-mining pans. He was missing a few teeth when he smiled.

'You were flying, missus. Must have been in a bit of a hurry.'

'Indeed I was,' replied Zena. 'If you had a crate-load of ducks and chooks in your car that were pooing everywhere, you'd have your foot on the accelerator too.' She chuckled.

With that, he laughed. 'You're darn right with that one, not to mention my dust storm.' He tipped his hat, put it back on his head and disappeared into the bushes. 'Let's move Lisa,' Zena urged as not much bush was covering what he was about to do. 'When you've got to go, you've got to go.' Lisa followed Zena back to the car and they took off.

'He's a typical truck driver, Lisa, a real bushy. They're the salt of the earth, and I'm sure he works like most, seven days a week, sunup to sundown. These men are the backbone of the west. They thrive out here. It's in their blood.'

As they drove, the landscape became even more sparse, but Lisa loved it. They passed many mobs of kangaroos and emus that chased the car. Lisa laughed at the inquisitive emus, her aunt slowing down at one stage so they could keep up.

The first gate for the road leading into Woori came into view, and Zena stopped the car while leaving the motor running. 'I'll show you how to lock and unlock the gates. It's easy, but you must make sure the gate is shut tight and the loops secure. It's very important as we come through the gates that you shut them properly. You don't know where the stock are or even if they're in the paddock, but every gate must be closed behind you. And another thing, whenever you exit the car, look down on the ground before stepping out just to make sure you're not stepping on anything.'

'Like what?' Lisa seemed puzzled at that statement. 'Like a snake or a frilled-neck lizard', her aunt replied. You'll see a few of those in your travels. So rule number one: Look where your feet are going, survey the area quickly and only scream when you're in extreme danger. You'll always come across kangaroos, emus and wild pigs. As you have seen, the emus are quite funny, curious creatures that will chase the car. Another thing. If any animals have babies, the mother or father is always very aggressive. So keep your distance. They're just protecting their babies but they can be hostile to humans.

'The afternoons and the evening have a peacefulness to them, and there is always something to see. It's great to watch a storm when we do get them. The lightning strikes light up the sky,' Zena told Lisa as she opened the car door and tentatively looked down for snakes.

As they drove further, Lisa stopped counting the gates and watched the paddocks go by. They seemed to go on forever. They came to one more gate and Zena said, 'This is the last gate, Lisa. Once we get through this one, we're home. You can begin to take control of your own destiny now. That is, you can question things and learn things. I hope this new chapter in your life is a wonderful journey.'

TWELVE

WOORI

For the first time in her life, a feeling of elation enveloped Lisa. Contentment was moving under her skin and the sense of freedom was overwhelming. As buildings came into view, her aunt slowed. 'Welcome to Woori, Lisa,' her aunt said as they headed towards a white homestead. They passed the first large corrugated building with lots of paddocks and equipment.

'That's the shearing shed and men's quarters directly opposite. The smaller building is the shower complex,' Zena explained. 'When Alan built those, everyone said he had rocks in his head, but it has paid off. The shearers get their own rooms and an open shower block, so that's why we get the best of the best workers. Treat them well and they always return. Shearing starts around July and August, and we have a lot of jackaroos, roustabouts and wool classers around at that time. Some of the shearers bring their gins or lubras, and the blacks set up their own camps. Just remember, they live by their own laws but there's always much laughter in the black's camp. And of course, there are even more dogs and picaninnies running around. As I said, the place comes alive.'

'What's a gin or a lubra?' Lisa asked. 'I thought gin was something you drank. My mother did.' Zena was amused, and a smile spread across her face. 'The names are used by us white folks. I don't like it myself, but it's for the Aboriginal women. You'll see the girls here, and the men use the women. It gets lonely at night, they say. I turn a blind eye to it, and sometimes the women even fight for the men's affection. Some of the women even bring their picaninnies. Thank God Jack keeps them all in line.'

'Who is Jack and what's picaninnies?' Lisa queried.

'Jack Pettigrew is the overseer of the men and the season. He's basically Alan's right-hand man, and he kept the farm going while we were overseas these past couple of years. He's a big gregarious bloke who doesn't put up with any nonsense. Very well respected,' smiled Zena. 'The dictionary describes children of black descent as picaninnies. In Portuguese, it's actually an affectionate term for little, but I don't think some white men mean for it to be affectionate. So, in this case, picaninnies are the babies or small children.'

'But don't the Aboriginal women have names?' asked Lisa, full of questions about this new world.

'Of course they do, and you'll meet a few as they set up their own camps around the property. I let them come and go as they please and even offer food, but they're very resourceful and gather their own foods and bush tucker, while the men kill kangaroos or goannas for meat. I have a great respect for all of them.'

'Do they speak to us?'

Zena laughed. 'For sure. Some may be a little suspicious of us and vice versa, but you'll meet two women who stay around Woori permanently. They came one year and never left. Binna is a very elderly lady who is almost blind, and her daughter is Ningali. Their camp is not far from the river, and we often take food out there when we ride. Binna is a great storyteller and very spiritual. You'll enjoy her Dreamtime stories about their culture. I'm sure you'll love to sit with her as I have done many times.'

'Why do they live here?' pressed Lisa, her curiosity peaked.

'That's a fair question. I don't know, and I have never asked. Binna and Ningali just set up one day after a shearing season and they never moved,' answered Zena. 'The jackaroos are also great stockmen and trackers, and the Dreamtime stories by a fire are always amazing when told by them. There are some who are more spiritual than others. They are the healers. The women can likewise teach you about food gathering. It's a different world to ours.'

Zena and Lisa passed another two large yards. 'That's my chook shed and the pig yard. We keep them away from the house so there's no smell,' said Zena. 'The larger shed stores the hay, feed and other grains. Further down is a small open dwelling with a tin roof, and that is for Alan. He uses it for a bit of shade and to hang the wedge-tailed eagle heads. The eagles take the lambs, which is not good, and Alan gets a bounty for a head.' Lisa pulled a face. She thought of her father and how he removed the heads of the chooks on the chopping block. They always got up despite having no head and ran around before collapsing.

Zena noticed her grimace and explained, 'They are huge birds, Lisa, and have a great wing span—about six feet. The eagles are our largest birds of prey and are very good hunters; they can work singly, in pairs or even groups. They can kill animals as large as a kangaroo. There is talk of stopping the bounty on dead eagles, but they are either shot or poisoned because they take the lambs. Alan takes the head as the scalp is proof that he's killed one.' Lisa shuddered at hearing this. She had a lot to learn about the country. It was so very different to suburbia. Her thirst and the seed for knowledge about the bush had been planted.

Finally, they pulled up outside the white homestead. 'It's beautiful,' Lisa breathed. It looked like a big white palace to her. Large and rambling with a bullnose verandah that wrapped around the house. Opposite the homestead there was another small house. Surrounding both houses was a large cyclone wire fence, ten feet high. It was like a compound.

'Is that another smaller house?' Lisa queried.

'No, Lisa, it's what we call a Tack Room. We keep all the saddles and bridles and a few other items in there, which you will see. I think it's much too close to the main house but Alan wanted it close in case he needed to saddle up quickly. I love the smell though, all the rich leather. On the other side of the Tack Room there are a few paddocks. You cannot see from here but when we saddle up, Alan keeps the horses we are riding there or if a mare is in foal, he'll use the yards to do night watch.'

'What's that . . . night watch?

'We just keep the mare close by and sit with her until the foal comes. They usually come in the early hours of the morning. So if they're in that yard, Alan can come up to the house and get a cuppa or whatever if he's hungry or needs something. They foal in the early hours so the mother can get the foal up and drinking. If the foal is born in daylight hours and lays on the ground, the blasted crows may come and pick the foal's eyes out.'

'Oh, God, that's awful.' Lisa tried to imagine the crows and the helpless foal.

'Why do you have such high fences, Aunty?'

'Protection really. Have to keep those wild animals out, and I also have a little garden and veggie patch. I use the bore water for my garden, and the only thing green is the grass inside the compound.'

Lisa noticed the bore, previously mentioned by her aunt, and across from the bore were about twenty dog kennels. Dogs of various sizes and colour were chained to each kennel and all were barking. Zena explained, 'They're all working dogs, and Alan uses them for the sheep. When we ride down to the river, we invariably take a few dogs in case of pigs. He'll also take a few when he goes spotlighting overnight.

'What is spotlighting?' Lisa giggled. 'I'm asking so many questions, Aunty. Sorry!'

'That's how you learn, darling girl, so keep asking. Spotlighting is when you take the utes out with strong lights on the roof and the bull bar, while you look for kangaroos or pigs. These are to feed the dogs. We are both good shots and very humane when we kill any animal. It's part of country life, and having no supermarkets we have to provide food for our animals. You'll see just how many kangaroos there are.'

As they got out of the car and walked up to the homestead, Alan sauntered out. He wore khaki shorts and a long-sleeved shirt rolled up to his elbows. His legs were long and tanned, and he looked very relaxed. When he smiled, all you could see were his white teeth.

'Hi ladies, good to have you back.' He stubbed out the cigarette that had been dangling in his mouth. His smile was broad. Yes, he was a handsome man who was comfortable in his surrounds. He walked towards Zena and kissed her on the lips. Their affection for each other was very clear. He came around to Lisa and kissed her on the cheek.

'Welcome to Woori, Lisa! We both hope you'll be very happy here. There's a lot to learn, but I'm sure you'll be a great pupil. Come, your bedroom awaits. I'm sure you'll appreciate the shower and getting the red dust off you, not to mention the smell of those ducks. I could smell you ladies on the wind before I even saw you.'

'I bet you could! You can get them out of the back of the Zephyr, Alan. I ordered your fencing material. They'll have it there in a week's time. We'll go clean up.'

'Well, this is home. Home sweet home as they say,' Alan said as he carried their luggage up into the house. Lisa didn't know where to look first. The kitchen was a long galley style with warm wood, which extended into a large dining area. There were Aboriginal paintings and landscapes of the outback all over the walls.

The lounges were brown leather and rich rugs filled the rooms, covering the Kauri floor boards. The ceiling-to-floor windows so were huge that every vision of the outback surrounding them was captured. There was a big fireplace in the sitting room, which contained a huge library. Zena's piano was in a corner with Alan's saxophone nearby.

'It seems odd to have a fireplace, but it does get cold in the winter, and it's lovely to sit by the fire,' said Zena. Lisa followed Zena down the hallway where she stopped and said, 'This is your bedroom.'

Lisa gasped as she looked in the room. It was huge, and there was only one large white four-poster bed. She had always shared with her brother in the bunks so having this much space was very luxurious. The sheer and flowing curtains were white, and a beautiful patchwork quilt of various blues covered the white quilted bed. French doors opened out onto the verandah. Lisa felt like a princess. She flopped onto the bed and crossed her fingers. *Please make this last. I never want to leave.*

Her aunt smiled. 'Just make yourself comfortable. There's also the wardrobe and chest of drawers. You can hang what clothes you have in your bag, but don't worry about clothing at this stage as we'll head back into Walgett at some stage and purchase some new clothes at the haberdashery. Come out into the kitchen when you're ready, no hurry,' Zena said as she gently closed the door.

The pain from the Girls Home was still ever-present in her memory, but with every passing moment, Lisa concentrated on a new beginning, safe surrounds and the love from her aunt. 'I will get stronger. I will feel better,' she told herself.

◊

Alan was seated in the kitchen with two cold beers when Zena walked in. 'Has she said anything or mentioned something that we need to know? I thought the long drive may have loosened her tongue,' Alan said as he handed a beer to Zena, which she sipped appreciatively. It had been a long, dusty drive.

'No, not as yet. She was a little quiet initially but chatted about where we were heading and the things that we were encountering along the way. She loved the red dust billowing behind the Zephyr. I think what we have here is a broken and wounded soul. Splintered into many directions. This will be a long healing process, Alan.'

'All things in good time, my darling,' he comforted, and they clinked their beers.

'I think it's important to get her into a routine. A busy one, so it keeps her mind off things. Chores, school and, of course, fun. But as soon as she provides any information, I'll write a letter to the police for further investigations into that institution. I know things occurred there of a very bad nature, and I want that place investigated, not only for Lisa, but for the girls still in there and also the ones that will be sent there. I will not rest easy until that task has been completed. But my gut feeling is when she does tell me, it will be vile.'

Alan kissed her forehead. 'You are a wonderful woman, my dear wife,' he said. Lisa appeared sheepishly in the doorway. 'Am I interrupting?' she asked.

'Heck, no,' Alan laughed. 'I would get you a beer, kid, but you're still a little young. There's a nice cool lemonade on the table for you.' Alan continued, 'Dinner will be about one hour, but for now let's go and sit on the verandah. It's my favourite place at the end of the day, and you'll see why, Lisa. The animals will start to arrive, and we can see the beautiful colours of the outback sky as we kiss the day goodbye.'

◊

There were big comfortable lounges and cushions all along the bullnose verandah. Lisa tucked her legs up underneath her and relaxed into a lounge. She suddenly felt very sleepy from the weariness of the travel but more from the mental fatigue and anguish that filled her thoughts. The end of the day crept over her body, but the horror of the abuse was there when she closed her eyes. A whirl of emotions flooded her being. She felt the beatings, the sexual abuse, and all the pain and humiliation bubbling under the surface. *When will the turmoil leave? When will these memories leave me*, she agonised.

Opening her eyes, Lisa tried to block out her thoughts and feelings by watching a number of different animals as they came to the bore. The kangaroos hopped slowly to drink at the side of the waterhole. 'It's amazing that those roos start life as the size of a pea, and some of them end up being about seven foot tall,' mused Alan.

The wild pigs grunted and shuffled a bit further down by the bore, but Lisa loved the long-legged emus the most. They moved gracefully past the house to take up their position. 'They are so big, Alan.' Lisa was amazed. 'I so love their feathers.'

'Yep, big and powerful birds, but the damn things can't fly. The Aborigines say when they lay their eggs, it is a totem of fertility.'

It was wonderful to watch the animals from the safety of the compound. It was all so natural, and Lisa felt that she had always belonged. No-one spoke. No-one needed to. Everybody was breathing in the visual beauty. *I wish you were here, Mark*, she thought.

As the sun began to slowly set, Zena rose from her chair and said, 'Okay, you two, we had best make a move and get some dinner before you both fall asleep. Lisa, you can help me set the table, please. This can be your chore of an evening.' Lisa jumped up despite her tiredness. She was more than happy to help her aunt.

Over dinner, they chatted about the wildlife they'd seen that afternoon as well as the approaching season. They decided to head into Walgett in a week's time to pick up the wire fencing and to shop for Lisa's clothes.

Alan commented, 'The wire is arriving at a good time as the boys can give me a hand along the fence line. Bloody dingoes. Heard they made a mess up at John McGregor's property. Found twenty dead lambs, and a few others had to be put down as they were mauled so badly. Only littlies, about three months old. They'd been bitten on the tail end of the loin area. The dingoes attack the kidneys there,' he explained to Lisa.

'Oh, that's so horrible,' said Lisa, aghast. 'Those poor baby lambs.'

'It's like having a murderer hanging about, Lisa. When you see the dead lambs, it really hits you personally, and of course there is the financial loss that accompanies it. That's why we're always fencing. Bloody dingoes cost me a fortune; the fence has to be nearly six feet in height.'

'Why can't you just shoot them?' asked Lisa.

'Because they're bloody sneaky and usually come out at night when we're in bed. You often see the males in packs and you can hear them howling at night. The first boundary fence was built in the 1880s to keep the rabbits out. Around 1948, it was converted to a dog barrier, now known as the dingo fence, to help the sheep. The jackaroos shoot the dingoes if they're about, and we also bait them, but I'm always worried with the baits in case our dogs get them. It's a terrible, agonising death.'

'You'll have to show me how to fence, so I can help you then,' Lisa replied.

'Deal, kid,' smiled Alan. 'There were a few young jackaroos a couple of seasons back who worked like Trojans. Did a great job helping me with the fencing. So the wire coming in around this time is good.'

With dinner finished and dishes finally done, Lisa made her way to her room. The covers had been turned down, and she slid leisurely between the sheets. A warm breeze blew in from the open windows, and the ceiling fans made the white curtains shimmer. She whispered in the dark, 'This is my home, where I belong.' Lisa fell asleep to the melody of the night.

There was no screaming in dark corridors, and she slept until the first nightmare intruded into her consciousness. Lisa felt herself shaking as Lenny's face moved towards her. Her breathing was laboured, and she was in a lather of sweat. She began to grind her teeth and screamed out, 'Stop, stop, please stop,' as she felt herself being pulled down. Lisa sat up crying, sweat soaking her body and bedclothes.

Zena had heard the yelling and quickly entered the room. She sat next to her niece, placing an arm around her shoulders.

'Bad dream?' Zena enquired gently. Lisa nodded, feeling the tears stream down her face. Her head was on Zena's shoulder.

'You'll probably have more of these, Lisa. But at some stage, I need to know what has happened as I've thought about seeking help from a professional.'

'No,' Lisa cried. 'I'm so ashamed. I don't want to see anyone.' Her body was rigid, and the anxiety came in waves.

'Breathe deeply, Lisa, and try to relax. You are in a different place now. Reassure yourself that you're safe now. Alan and I are here to help and protect you. If you need to talk to me at any time about what has happened, then just say, 'Aunty, we need to talk.' I will not force you to tell me. You'll know when the time is right. Just remember that when you have a bad dream, I'm right here across the hallway.'

Zena went to get some water and a warm face cloth. 'Here, drink this.' Lisa gulped the water and then wiped her face.

'Do you want me to stay?' Zena asked softly.

'No, I'll try to sleep, thank you, Aunty.' Lisa wriggled back under the sheets.

'Okay,' Zena replied, smoothing her niece's damp hair back from her forehead. 'I'll leave this small bed lamp on. You don't have to sleep in the dark. Does the darkness frighten you?'

'Yes, a little.' Lisa's voice was barely audible.

'I'm right here,' Zena comforted as she bent to kiss her niece. 'I'll leave the door half ajar. Is that alright with you?' Lisa nodded.

Zena stayed until Lisa slept peacefully, but her vulnerability shimmered around her.

◊

Alan was sitting up in bed, waiting for Zena. 'Nightmare?'

'Yes,' Zena admitted, a worried expression on her face. 'And I would say a bewdy. She's not offering any insight as yet, but it's not far off, I feel. She may need professional help, but she says she's too ashamed to speak to anyone. They have psychologists in Dubbo, but for the moment, I may ride out and speak to Binna. She's a spiritual healer and does the Aboriginal cleansing ceremonies. This may give Lisa the strength she needs to reveal what's actually happened to her.'

◊

The following morning when Lisa opened her eyes, all she could hear were the magpies and kookaburras. Despite the nightmare, it was the best sleep she'd had in a long time. The nightmare came to her mind, but she tried to push the intrusive thought away, concentrating on the sounds of the birdlife instead.

The house was quiet, and she could hear no movement. *I wonder where they are? Why is there no sound?* Lisa stretched, quickly changed into her jeans and t-shirt, then went out into the kitchen. There was a note against a glass of water: Help yourself to breakfast. We are up and about early but not far away from the house. Love Z & A.

Lisa could hear horses whinnying and looked towards the Tack Room. Just to the left of it, there was a post. Alan came into view and had a beautiful black horse tethered while he placed a saddle it, before coming into the kitchen with Zena.

'Morning, sunshine,' Alan said as he came into the kitchen, ruffling Lisa's tufts of hair. 'How did you sleep? I thought I could hear you snoring.' Lisa blushed.

'He's only joking, Lisa,' Zena laughed. 'You'll get used to him. But right now it's time for bacon and eggs.'

They made no mention of the nightmare, keeping it light. 'Yum,' Alan said. 'Make it a double helping for Lisa. She needs a bit of meat on her bones and then we can all go for a ride around the property. Not too much on your first day as the bum will get a bit sore, but it will give you the basics of riding.'

Lisa tucked in to her bacon and eggs with gusto. 'Good appetite,' Alan remarked with a smile. 'You'll need that extra helping to get you through the day. Did you notice the black mare outside the Tack Room?'

'Yes, I did,' said Lisa as she quickly swallowed the last bit of bacon. 'She's so very beautiful, but why do you have her legs hobbled?'

'The mare is young and green, so I'm breaking her in slowly without breaking her spirit. Animals, like us humans, respond to kindness. Her name is Noir, which is French for black, and she was my wedding gift to your aunt. She'll produce beautiful foals.' Lisa thought to herself, *Yes, we do respond to kindness* as waves of gratitude swept over her. *My wonderful aunt and her husband.*

'Let's go,' Alan said after they'd cleared away the breakfast table and dishes. 'Zena has saddled up two extra horses around the back of the Tack Room. Tidgy and Neddy are two older bay geldings. Neddy is the smaller of the two and very quiet. He'll look after you. All you need to do is sit tight, take control of the reins and follow Zena.'

Lisa followed her aunt and uncle outside and tried to appear confident. Zena put a reassuring arm around her and whispered, 'Baby steps. You'll be fine.'

Alan gave Lisa a short discussion on a horse's anatomy, running his hands gently over Neddy's body as he did so, always speaking softly, always stroking as he moved around the horse. Lisa liked the smell of the horses and their beautifully muscled bodies. She wanted to be a good horsewoman like her aunt. Alan explained, 'They are creatures of flight, Lisa. That is, they'll run before thinking.'

'We'll sit you on Neddy and lunge you around at first,' said Alan. He helped Lisa mount the horse, giving her instructions as he did so, and then he hooked a long lead to Neddy.

'Okay, Lisa, firm reins without pulling at the mouth. Gently press your ankles into his girth and Neddy will step forward. I'll move him around for you until you get the hang of it.' Lisa pressed her heels and Neddy took off in a circular motion. It felt wonderful. Alan spoke to her constantly, moving the horse from a walk to a trot. 'Rise up as he breaks into a trot,' instructed Alan. 'Then when you're ready, just squeeze his flanks and he'll move into a steady canter.'

Lisa couldn't wipe the smile off her face. When she returned to where Alan was standing, he was full of praise. 'Very good,' he grinned. 'I think we have a star pupil.' Her aunt agreed.

Alan slipped the lunge lead off Neddy, and Zena mounted Tidgy.

'This is the beginning of another journey for you, Lisa. Remember what I said though, "Horses are creatures of flight". You are the master, so keep a firm hand and learn from your aunt, We'll ride over to the shearing sheds and around the perimeters of the property so you can get your seat and legs,' said Alan.

'Give Neddy another gentle squeeze, Lisa. A shift in your weight and the movement of your thighs and ankles, or even your backside, will tell your horse what to do. These are known as aids,' instructed Zena.

Alan rode up beside Lisa. 'You're a natural, kid. You sit well. If your genes are as good as your aunt's, you'll be an excellent horsewoman.' He cantered past Lisa and then dismounted when they reached the shearing shed. He tied up Noir to a post, and Zena and Lisa followed.

'Have a wander around and stretch your legs, Lisa.' She swung her legs over the saddle and slid off. 'That felt great, Aunty. I so want to learn more.' Zena smiled. Lisa was glowing and coming more out of her shell. Her confidence was evident.

'I'm so glad, Lisa. The ride down to the river is really lovely and there's lots to see along the way. It's a good ride, and I know your backside will be sore, but it'll be well worth it as you get used to a saddle. The horses that we break in all do well with this ride.' They all walked towards the shearing shed and male quarters where the shearers would stay during the season.

Lisa poked her head in. There were rows of beds in a single room and a large communal kitchen. The shower and toilet block were situated opposite. Alan said there were no flushing toilets for the shearers, just long drops.

'The shearers and roustabouts usually sleep in here, but it's not uncommon to see them sleeping under the stars, particularly the Aboriginal jackaroos. The blacks have their own camps,'

Zena clarified. As they rounded the back of the shearing shed, there was a large separate paddock along the fence line. A beautiful bay stallion was rearing onto his back legs. Lisa couldn't take her eyes off the stallion. 'He's truly lovely,' she breathed. 'Why is he up here, sort of isolated?'

Zena spoke. 'That is Alan's stallion, Khartoum. He gets the mares in foal. When all the girls are locked up, we let him out for a run. You'll see this afternoon. We let the dogs off for a run as well as this big boy.'

The stallion snorted as he ran up and down the fence line. His nostrils were flaring, and he kicked up the dust. Lisa thought he was a truly magnificent beast. She looked forward to the afternoon to see him in full flight.

The cockatoos squawked above their heads as they watched Khartoum. 'There are so many of them,' Lisa exclaimed.

Alan overheard and chimed in, 'Bloody nuisance they are. There are way too many. White cockatoos and bloody galahs. Zena loves them with their pink breasts and grey wings. They're a festoon of colour when they take off in large groups. But they're still a bloody nuisance.'

Lisa noticed an open tin shed about eight-hundred metres from where they stood. There were things dangling from the roof line. 'Are they beer cans or something?' she asked.

'No,' said Alan. 'They're eagle heads. I shoot them so they don't take the lambs.' Lisa looked uncomfortable and remembered Zena had pointed this out to her on the drive in.

'Dingoes and eagles, Lisa. I have my bloody hands full,' Alan said, laughing.

'Let's head back now, Alan,' Zena interrupted gently. 'I want to show Lisa what she needs to do in the Tack Room. I also want to show her the yabbies and how to catch them in the bore.'

'What are yabbies? Lisa asked.

'I'll give you a long piece of thick string. You tie a piece of meat to the end and throw it in the bore. You'll feel the yabbies latch on. That's when you give it a good yank and pull it out of the water. These will be our entrée tonight. I'll go down to the bore with you and then leave you to it. I cook them in butter and garlic. Alan loves them. They're like a prawn, and it's also a lot of fun catching them,' said Zena.

After finishing in the Tack Room, they got ready to head to the bore for some yabby catching. Zena handed Lisa the string and took some small pieces of meat from a freezer. She picked up a bucket, and they opened the gate closest to the bore.

When they arrived at the bore, Zena instructed, 'Tie the piece of meat to the end of the string like so. Make sure it's tight so it doesn't slip away. Those yabbies have big nippers.' Lisa copied her aunt. She was ready to have a go.

'Remember, yank hard and quick. Stay away from the nippers or you'll lose your nipper, and it's a long trip to the hospital. You can throw your catch in the bucket. I'm thinking positively as I know you'll bring back a bucketful.' They both laughed as they made sure the meat was secured tightly.

Lisa squealed when she felt the first strike and pulled quickly. She slung the string so hard that the yabby landed well away from the bore. 'Well done, Lisa,' her aunt exclaimed as she pulled another in. 'We'll need about thirty yabbies, and I'll leave you to it. If there's any danger from anything out here, just move quickly back to the compound, forget about the yabbies and don't squeal unless you're in mortal danger!' Zena stepped back into the compound and disappeared from view.

Yabby catching was such fun, and the bucket was filling quickly. Lisa only changed her meat once. The dogs on the other side of the bore watched her closely, often barking when she got a yabby out of the water.

'Sorry, guys,' Lisa apologised, looking down at the clawing yabbies. As she came up the back steps, her aunt was at the dining table with music sheets. Zena looked up over her glasses and whistled.

'That didn't take you long,' she said as she looked into the bucket. 'Look at the size of them! Well done, my dear. I'm sure you'll love the way I cook them.'

It was late afternoon when they heard the sounds of a dirt bike. 'It's Alan. He's heading up to Khartoum and will then come back for the dogs. Come,' said Zena. 'Let's go out on to the verandah. Khartoum usually races up past the house and does a full circle.' Alan came into view, letting all the dogs off their chains. Lisa then saw a cloud of dust and the magnificent stallion galloping, tail up and spread behind him as he raced up the road, pig rooting and clearly happy to be free. The horse's muscle depth was apparent, and Lisa stood in awe.

It was a good hour before Alan had settled the dogs and locked Khartoum away. Over dinner, they made plans for the river ride the following day. Lisa couldn't believe how wonderful the yabbies tasted. Her appetite was returning in full force.

As Lisa was getting ready for bed, Zena knocked on her door. 'Come in,' Lisa called out.

'How was your day?' asked Zena, sitting on the chair next to Lisa's bed.

'I loved it, Aunty. It was so much fun, and I so look forward to the day's ride tomorrow and obviously learning more and more from you and Alan.'

'Splendid. Are you missing home?' Zena asked.

'No, not at all, apart from my brother,' Lisa sighed.

'Well, don't fret. When things settle, we'll get Mark up here for a visit. I don't want to rock the boat at this stage. Having taken you, Agnes would freak if I asked for him too,' explained Zena.

'That would be wonderful,' Lisa enthused. 'I would love to have Mark here. I just hope my mother doesn't try to stop that visit.'

'I don't see any reason for her doing that, Lisa. You know Agnes is pretty difficult, particularly with me, but I think when things settle, she would let Mark come up here for a visit. Anyway, I'm glad you had a good day. Always remember, I'm here for you. If you need to tell me something, then don't hesitate. I won't judge you, I'm just here to listen. We'll do as we did last night, leave the small lamp on and the door half open. The bad dreams may come again, from time to time. We'll have to work through these. But I'm right here,' Zena said reassuringly.

'Thank you, Aunty. That means a lot to me.' Lisa was relieved. Someone she loved was finally there to listen to and support her. 'Sometimes I feel lonely at night,' revealed Lisa.

'Lonely?' Zena queried.

'Yes, I was so used to having Mark there and knowing he was just below me. I know that sounds so weird, but when you share a room with someone, it feels odd to suddenly be in a big room on your own. Sometimes I think I'm dreaming all of this. I expect someone to burst into the room anytime, like a warden or just someone to take me away.'

'It will be an adjustment, darling girl, but this is reality . . . your reality, so keep thinking positive. This is your home. You'll enjoy the ride down to the river tomorrow,' Zena reassured. 'We'll have to get up very early before the heat kicks in, and we'll travel slowly as Noir will be hobbled part of the way to settle her down on the ride out. We should pass Binna and Ningali; I always take them a few food supplies. I'll introduce you, and perhaps if you feel comfortable, you can sit and chat with them. Full of stories those two, especially Binna.'

◊

After Zena said good night, she realised that she must talk to Binna about her niece. Alone. There was significant mental scarring with Lisa. Zena could tell. She hadn't revealed anything yet, but with time she would. The Aboriginal spiritual healers were revered and did amazing work in their communities. Binna was a legend. She had also become a good friend.

As she lay down next to Alan, Zena told him of her plans. 'I'll head out when I get a chance, the sooner the better. You know the Aboriginals connect the spirit to the mind and body. If one is broken, they think you are out of sorts, or something like that. Binna has always been respected as a healer, and although her sight is going, she feels and hears everything. I want Lisa to sit with her.'

'Yes, I can see your reasoning,' Alan agreed. 'It's good we're teaching her and showing her lots of different things. Yabby catching was just a bit of fun, but it's all new and nurturing the girl. If I had to speculate, I'd say Lisa is a wounded bird. More than that, I think she's a very damaged spirit who has faced unspeakable adversity.'

Zena was now more determined than ever to speak with Binna alone. 'Goodnight, husband. I'll find a way to heal my girl, to open up her heart and mind. As you said, something significant has occurred to damage her spirit. I have so much respect for the Aboriginal healers and hope Binna can reach out to her.'

THIRTEEN

BINNA AND NINGALI

Lisa was looking forward to the ride and to meeting the Aboriginal women her aunt had described. They sounded fascinating. Healers. *What could they do?* she wondered.

The three horses were ready to go. 'Come over this way, Lisa,' said Alan. He ran his hands over Noir's rump and down her legs. He lifted her feet and all the time, he kept talking softly to the mare.

'I want you to do the same, Lisa. Feel the horse, let it smell you and hear the sound of your voice. Let her know your touch. Move over here to her side and begin slowly. It's all about trust.' Lisa ran her hands gently over the mare and felt the softness and the muscle. *Such power*, she thought. *Yet look how they trust.* She was loving getting to know the horses.

After petting Noir, Zena mounted Tidgy with ease and Lisa followed suit with Neddy. Her aunt rode next to her. She reminded Lisa, 'Don't forget to keep your back straight and keep your reins firm but not pulling at their mouth. Stay in control. Use your feet as an aid. Lots to remember, but suddenly it will just click. Your thigh muscles will become stronger as well as a lot of other muscles you didn't know you had.'

Lisa couldn't stop smiling. It felt so natural, and she was very comfortable on Neddy. 'How much longer to the river, Aunty.'

'About two hours, Lisa. But we'll stop when we get to Binna's hut, which is not too far from the river.' Lisa watched both her aunt and Alan; they never seemed to shift in their seats. Noir had settled nicely for Alan, but he said he would keep her hobbled until they stopped at the women's camp. The mare needed to be tired out a bit before removing them.

By the time the little hut came into view under a large bloodwood tree, the horses were sweating. Lisa could feel the stiffness entering her body, particularly her legs. She'd be happy to get off and stretch. The two Aboriginal women were squatting by a small fire, the thin grey smoke curling into the air.

'Don't be frightened, Lisa', said Zena. 'The ladies are from the Wailwan Weil tribe group. Most of them dwelt on land stretching from Brewarrina to the Warrumbungles, but by about the late 1800s, a few of the Aboriginals moved towards the Carinda area, which is Macquarie Valley country. Some of the Aborigines are also around the river banks at Cuddie Springs. Nothing to be frightened of; they're people, just like you and me. They have their own culture, live by their own laws and tell wonderful stories.' Zena motioned Lisa towards the women.

'Good morning, ladies,' Zena greeted. 'I have some tucker for you.' She handed the parcel of food to the younger woman, Ningali.

'Thank you, missus. You wanna sit down?' Ningali asked as she gestured to a space next to her.

'Yes, we will, Ningali. Thank you. I want to introduce my niece Lisa to you both. She may be riding out here regularly, sometimes with us and sometimes on her own when she has the confidence.' The two ladies smiled. Lisa noticed the absence of many teeth.

Ningali was thinner, younger and taller. Her hair was wild and untamed with streaks of grey. She was very dark like Binna, with a broad nose and full lips. Her smile was cheeky, and she laughed easily. She had beautiful brown eyes that were like pools of comfort and peace.

Binna's eyes were milky in appearance, and Lisa remembered her aunt had said that her sight was very poor, almost blind. She was thicker in the waist than Ningali and moved very slowly. Her skin was a shrivelled leathery brown, and her white hair looked ethereal. There was an aura of confidence and intelligence about her that filled the air. Wisdom.

'She very pretty, good looker, your niece,' commented Ningali. Zena and Lisa sat cross-legged opposite the women and swatted away the army of bush flies. No-one was particularly bothered by the black swarm, which always made its appearance at dawn.

'We're on our way to the river, so we can't stay too long, and Alan looks impatient already. He doesn't want it to get too hot,' explained Zena. Ningali waved to Alan as he took the hobbles off Noir.

'Boss fella ready to get on his way. You come visit, Lisa. We teach you how to find bush tucker, track people and animals, and birds too, dem good eating, and maybe you speak our language, learn some bush songs,' offered Ningali.

Lisa smiled. The two women were so different in looks, presence and language but she was very drawn to them. She wanted to learn more from them.

'Okay, we must be on our way. If you need anything, just let Lisa know. I have a feeling she'll be a regular visitor,' Zena said with a twinkle in her eye.

The elderly lady Binna said something to Ningali in their own language.

'Binna wanna feel you, Lisa,' said Ningali. 'Feel your spirit. Come, come here, sit closer.'

Lisa moved across the dirt floor and sat cross-legged opposite Binna. Her craggy hand lifted slowly, feeling Lisa's face. She spoke softly, almost like a chant and in her own native tongue. Lisa didn't move, and her gaze never left Binna's face. She was mesmerised. The old lady picked up a mixture of red dirt with sand. She let it filter through her hands four times.

'You do same now,' Binna instructed. Lisa picked up a handful of the red sand mixture and let it run through her fingers four times.

'Dis is in honour of da four elements. Water, fire, air and da earth,' Binna explained. She had her eyes closed and continued chanting. When she finally stopped, Lisa looked at Ningali. 'What did she say?' Lisa asked kindly.

Ningali was still squatting, and her fingers traced signs in the dirt.

'Binna smart. She say Lisa is da good earth and good spirit. But Binna feels big sadness. Maybe spirit bin broke.'

Lisa looked down to the dirt and lifted her gaze as Ningali continued. 'Binna say, Lisa, your baby, she never leave dis place, dis country. She belong.'

The old lady continued to trace Lisa's face. She finally stopped and opened her milky eyes. Binna spoke in her own language and then placed her hands together. She sat so peacefully. Lisa was curious and fearful at the same time. *How can the old lady feel my spirt, that I feel broken?* she thought to herself.

'How does she feel things in me, Ningali?' Lisa asked.

'Binna, she great healer. Healers are able to catch sickness and heal da people. Healing gives us back to ourselves. Not to hide or fight anymore, but to sit still, calm our minds. We listen to da universe, allow our spirits to dance on da wind. Drift into Dreamtime. Healing give us back our country, ourselves. Healing help 'em to stand in our rightful place. Healing not just about recovering, missus. Healing not about what lost or what bin broken. Binna's healing about life. Enjoy your Dreamtime, your life. Keep us new, keep us here . . . grounded.'

'That's so profound, Ningali,' said Zena. 'But I think it's time to go now, Lisa. Thank you, Binna, Ningali. Lisa will no doubt see you again.' Zena rose and she could see that Lisa had been touched by what the old lady had said. They joined Alan, mounted up and began to ride towards the river, the women and their fire disappearing from view.

'I loved them, Aunty,' Lisa gushed. 'I could feel their spirit, feel their energy. They made me feel different. But I couldn't take my eyes off their legs, they were so skinny. How do they walk for such long distances?'

Zena laughed. 'They are quite stoic, Lisa. Strong women. Yes, I love them too, but a lot of people don't, so just be aware of that.'

Lisa frowned. 'Why not?'

'I guess they just don't understand them or their culture, and they don't like their colour. They are racist,' informed Zena. 'One day things will change. They are changing slowly, but we still have a long way to go.'

'Well, I like them. It was like Binna could see into me, Aunty. It was scary but fascinating at the same time. I felt so drawn to her.'

'Binna is a healer, Lisa. You have to remember theirs is a 60,000-year-old culture, encompassing the mysteries of the universe. I've heard stories about Binna. There are many parallels between traditional healing and methods employed in counselling such as developing trust, being held in mind and spirt as well as developing shared understanding. I have no doubt trust will play a big part in you going forward.' Lisa silently agreed with her.

The river came into sight, and it was very welcome to the eyes. After dismounting, their saddles were removed and the horses waded in near the banks to drink and cool off. Alan had roped them all together to avoid them running off and tied the last length of rope to a tree.

'It's a long walk back, Lisa, so when you're out here on your own, always remember to tether your horse tightly,' Alan advised. Lisa nodded. *It would be awful to walk home,* she thought.

Zena laid a small blanket on the banks of the river. The trees were filled with birds, and their voices and songs filled their ears. As they had lunch, Alan asked, 'What did you think of those black women, Lisa?'

'I really liked them, Alan. I cannot wait to sit with them, get to know them and hear their stories.'

'Yes, they're all great storytellers of the Dreamtime, and they are the original owners of the land. There's a lot of turmoil over this, which will probably get worse with time. Things always get worse before they get better. Their men are great horsemen, which you'll see when shearing time comes around.'

'I love it here,' Lisa said as she lay back and looked at the canopy of trees. 'It's so quiet and tranquil.'

'You're a real bushy true and true, Lisa. This is a special place. I even proposed to your aunt right here. Think we were skinny dipping at the time,' laughed Alan.

'Oh,' murmured Lisa. She shuddered at the thought of nakedness. Zena quickly noted her reaction.

'Shhh, Alan.' Zena admonished.

'I think we should all go for a swim. Cool off,' remarked Alan.

'No, I'll sit with Lisa on the bank here,' Zena stated. 'We're cool enough. Off you go. We're happy to watch.' Alan appeared a few moments later in a pair of long shorts. He dived into the river and quickly surfaced. 'Bloody beautiful in,' he said as he swam around.

'Are you confident to sit with Binna and Ningali again?' asked Zena.

'Oh, yes. I would love to hear their stories.' A smile crept over Zena's face. She was pleased. Lisa was drawn to them and hopefully open up to these women.

◇

On the journey home, Zena gave more riding instructions to Lisa. They waved to Binna and Ningali as they passed by but kept moving. Lisa could feel the stiffness in her thighs and was getting hungry as the homestead came into view. When they got to the Tack Room, the dogs were barking to be let off.

'Can I leave you two with the saddles and feeding?' Alan asked. 'I want to head up and let Khartoum off. Can you hose the horses down and put them in their yards, Lisa, and then start letting the dogs off, please.' Alan kissed Zena on the cheek, headed to the dirt bike parked nearby and took off.

'Are you sore, Lisa?' Zena probed.

'Yes, Aunty. A little, but more so stiff,' Lisa revealed as she removed the saddles.

'Nothing a good hot bath and an early night won't fix. I'll get some hay if you want to lead the horses down to their yards for a quick hose.' Khartoum raced by and Noir began to pace along the fence.

Zena said, 'Noir certainly likes that Khartoum. Be interesting when they finally do get together. Mating season is around September, and we're hoping she'll be ready by then.'

Khartoum made his way to the fence line, and Lisa noticed his erection. He was stirred by the mare. The dust was flying as he repeatedly turned, and both horses whinnied loudly.

'He's teasing her,' Zena explained. Lisa was shocked and didn't know which way to look. Dark thoughts swirled in her head when she saw the horse's erection. She winced. It did not go unnoticed by her aunt.

'This is nature, Lisa,' Zena started to explain. 'What's wrong, darling girl? Please tell me if something is bothering you. We've had such a wonderful day. You know you can tell me anything or ask me anything for that matter. Never be hesitant.' Lisa sat on the steps leading to the Tack Room and her aunt sat next to her. 'I know its nature, Aunty, but—'

'But what? If you speak, it's sometimes better to get it all out. Keeping things bottled up never works.'

There was a guarded silence from Lisa, and the moments that passed felt like hours. 'I know, Aunty. It's just so hard.' Lisa began to weep uncontrollably and tremble as she tried to speak through choking sobs. Zena put her arm around Lisa. Her grip was encompassing and reassuring.

'Here, let's just take a moment. Breathe, Lisa,' she said as she wiped the tears from her niece's face. 'You can tell me now or later, it's up to you, but I'm ready to help you as I do know something has gone on. I have to call your parents later today to let them know how you are and how things are progressing. Not the most pleasant of tasks discussing things with your mother but if I keep you here, that's what I have to do.'

Lisa shuddered at the mere mention of possibly going home. 'Aunty, I never want to go back home. Please....p...lease . . . tell my mother I'm doing very well. I'm doing very well.' Her voice got louder as she started to panic.

Zena remained calm and spoke quietly. 'Yes, that's no problem, Lisa, but what happened at home to make you feel this way? Perhaps let's start there.'

Lisa's sobs gave way to a deep sigh. She picked at a thread in her jeans, not knowing what to do with her hands. She began to hyperventilate as all the awful memories flooded her being, and finally she gushed, 'I . . . I just don't know, I don't know where to start.' The words caught in her throat, and the anguish in her voice was evident. She put her hands to her face and sobbed into them.

Zena held her niece tightly and stroked her head. 'Let's go back to where it started. Can you start with what hurt you initially? What caused you to steal from the supermarket?'

Lisa suddenly jumped to her feet and began pacing in the dirt. 'I hate him, I hate him, he said it was our secret. My mother wouldn't believe me. It was horrible. I felt so frightened. I wanted to run and hide. I was made to do horrible things.' Lisa was crying, her voice strangled with emotion. 'It was my step-sister, Janine . . . her husband. I hate him. I hate him so much. He molested me.' Lisa was shaking and purging away all that was buried inside her, her speech almost garrulous. She fell onto her knees, wailing, her hands clawing the dirt.

Zena was horrified. She got to her knees next to Lisa, holding her tightly.

'It's not your fault, Lisa. It will never be your fault.' Zena's voice grew stronger. Lisa could sense that her aunt was outraged that her own brother had done nothing to protect his daughter. How could Agnes not see something was wrong?

'My darling girl, it's out now, we can build on this, and I'll get the monster who did this. I will not rest until I see justice. Why didn't you say something, Lisa?'

Lisa wiped her nose with the back of her hand. 'Sorry, Aunty. But I did. I told my mother. She didn't believe me. And he said if I told anyone, I would be sent to the Girls Home, but I was sent there anyway. I shouldn't have done what I did, stealing stuff, but I was just trying to escape, get away.'

'Shhh now. You have nothing to be sorry about,' Zena reassured as she pulled a hanky out of her jeans.

'I so wanted to tell someone, Aunty. You have to believe me.' Lisa began to tremble. 'I didn't know where I was going when I tried to run away, but I just wanted to feel safe.' Lisa clung to her aunt, sobbing.

'It's okay, take your time, darling girl,' Zena said as she stroked the back of Lisa's head.

'I lost control in the supermarket. I just panicked. I didn't want to go home and I was so angry inside. I wanted to break things, destroy. I didn't mean to do it but it was the anger.' Lisa's voice trailed off.

'It's not your fault,' Zena repeated.

Lisa cleared her throat. 'I didn't understand at first what Lenny was doing. Mum had always said she wanted to send me away. Lenny said I would be sent there if I spoke up. I told Mum about Lenny, but she didn't believe me. She just said I was jealous of Janine and that I had made it all up.' Lisa rocked back and forward until her tears finally stopped.

'I am going to get that vile creature for what he's done to you,' Zena asserted, hugging her tighter. 'Do you have enough strength to tell me what happened at the Girls Home? I know something has gone on there too. I didn't like that superintendent one bit.'

Lisa paused. Visions of the superintendent and her friend Julie flashed before her.

Zena sensed her hesitation. 'Maybe another time, Lisa? Perhaps this is enough for now,' her aunt soothed.

Lisa felt the tightness in her chest. Scenes flashed through her mind of home and the institution and she continued to rock back and forth, holding her arms across her chest. Tears came to Zena's eyes as she saw the pain in her niece's young face.

They sat crying in the dirt together. Lisa clenched her fists as she spoke. 'That was awful too, even worse. Superintendent Ash had an isolation room; the girls called it the dungeon. He sodomised me there as well as other stuff. And I saw . . . I saw my friend Julie killed in the laundry.'

Zena gasped. 'Bastards, those evil bastards.' She stood up, her anger rising, hand on her stomach. To Lisa, it looked like her aunt wanted to be sick. She knew that telling her this had really shocked Zena.

'Excuse my language, Lisa, but I am just so angry, so bloody angry. I feel murderous. I could squeeze all those people's heads to a pulp. The authorities will know all about this, and I will inform your parents. How could they have subjected you to this!' Zena was livid.

'No, no, please don't,' begged Lisa. 'I'm afraid my mother will take me away from here or the authorities will put me back in that home.' Lisa tugged at her aunt's hand and more tears spilled from her eyes. Zena was now fierce and protective. She pulled Lisa harder to her.

'It will be okay, Lisa. I promise you. Nothing will harm you while you are here. No-one will take you away.' They sat in the dirt until Lisa's breathing calmed and they had both stopped crying. Their tears mingled with the red dust.

'Lisa, I'm glad you told me. No-one should have to keep all this bottled up inside. We can perhaps seek professional help for you. There are lots of things we can do to help with the healing process. Now, let's head up inside. A shower and cup of tea with some quiet space may be a good idea at this stage.'

Lisa felt so drained, and her eyes were red and puffy. 'You don't hate me for saying these things, Aunty?'

Zena looked shocked. 'Hate you? Goodness no! I love you for saying these things and trusting me enough to confide in me. It clarifies the whole picture now and why you reacted in such a way. I'm just so sorry no-one was there for you. Right now, I could give your mother a rocket and blast her to the moon. And as for those two men, I only wish for them to die a horrible death. But we shall have to travel the legal way in terms of justice.'

As they returned to the homestead, Zena walked to Lisa's bedroom with her, never taking her arm from her niece's shoulder. 'Wash up, darling girl. I hope you feel a sense of relief now. I know exactly what has happened and I can help you deal with it. I'm also going to get justice for you. You just take your time, and I'll bring a cup of tea in for you. Try to relax and again, please keep thinking about what I said: It's not your fault. It never has been. It never will be.'

◊

Zena heard the shower running and went to her own bedroom where she broke down. *Now I have to be strong for her,* she thought. She wiped her eyes, combed back her hair and headed to the kitchen.

Taking a cup of tea into Lisa's room, her niece sat staring solemnly out the big bedroom window, a white fluffy towel wrapped around her body. Zena said softly, 'I just want you to rest. Telling me all this information today must have been emotionally exhausting, and I wonder how you even coped at all at either place. Well, the short answer is: you didn't. You survived. Drink this, and I'll pop back in after I get dinner ready.'

She kissed Lisa on the forehead. 'I love you, and Alan and I will stand by you.' Zena's eyes filled with tears. 'Hold it in Zena,' she told herself sternly and quickly left the room to start dinner.

Alan wandered through the back door. It had been a good day. He took one look at Zena and knew something must have happened to make his wife look so drained. Her eyes were red and glistening with tears. He walked towards her and took her in his arms. 'So, my gut feeling is that someone has spilled the beans. I wondered where you were, and why the dogs were still on their chains. I've let them off myself.'

'Our gut feelings were all correct but it is so much worse than you can possibly imagine. I have to call Agnes tonight and also contact the police.' Zena was so distressed.

'The police!' Alan tossed his hat onto the table. 'I'll put the kettle on; it's going to be a long conversation.'

FOURTEEN

HEALING

Zena's throat felt tight. Rage pounded in her chest. She knew she was about to get hear ear chewed off. This was not going to be an easy conversation. The phone rang out five times before finally being picked up.

'Hello, Agnes, it's Zena. Have I got you at a good time?' The tension crackled down the phone.

'It's a bit late, but we've been waiting for your call. How is Lisa? Are you managing to keep her out of trouble? Is she pulling her weight or being lazy?' Agnes asked sarcastically. Zena gritted her teeth. *You are never any bloody different Agnes.*

'No, she's been a real gem . . . no problems whatsoever. Lisa seems to love the land and everything we do. She is delightful and learning a great deal.'

Agnes harrumphed, and there was a long silent pause. 'Well, I always said, she is just like you.'

'I am not sure that is a compliment or—'

'Take it how you want,' Agnes retorted. 'I don't care as long as she is not embarrassing us, or you, for that matter. See how you feel when she does.'

'On the contrary. In fact, I would go as far as to say, I would be proud to call her my daughter,' replied Zena. 'I am calling for two reasons. The first is to let you know, as I have already mentioned, that Lisa is doing very well and wants to stay. She does not want to come back home. The second reason is that she has advised me today that Janine's husband, Lenny I believe that's his name, interfered with her sexually.'

Zena heard the sharp intake of breath and could picture Agnes clearly. 'That's a bloody disgusting lie,' Agnes spat venomously, the hostility rippling down the line. 'That little bitch, I could wring her neck,' threatened Agnes. 'She is just making things up. She always does. Tries to manipulate everything. Little bugger she is!'

'That's exactly why she didn't inform anyone. Fear of the repercussions. Lenny also threatened her and said no-one would believe her and that she would be sent away to a Girls Home.' There was no response, so Zena continued. It felt as if she were sailing a boat into a huge storm. 'As a mother, you must have noticed the dark circles under her eyes, the loss of weight and the absolute change in behaviour?'

The serpent rose its ugly head. 'You have no right to criticise me. You don't even have children. You're barren. It's a wonder Alan married you. Useless cow! How would you know what to do in any situation regarding kids. You don't even know what you're saying.' Agnes was fuming.

Zena interrupted. 'You disgust me, Agnes, but before I go, I want you to know exactly what has happened to your daughter. While in the Girls Home, she was sexually assaulted and sodomised by the superintendent. Lisa has given me fairly graphic details of what has occurred, both in the family home and the institution. I will be contacting the police as well as writing an official letter to the Child Welfare Authorities. No doubt there will be a formal investigation and hopefully charges will be laid.

Lisa will provide me with written details and understands she will have to be interviewed.'

'I don't believe a bloody word of this,' Agnes shouted, trying to talk over Zena. 'You both deserve each other!'

'I am asking you for custody of Lisa. I think it would be very detrimental to her if she came home,' Zena asserted.

'You can take the stinking little liar! I don't want her back here, neither does her father. She's a bloody delinquent. An embarrassment to this family!'

Zena clenched her teeth. 'Am I able to speak to my brother please, Agnes?' She heard the phone being thrown down. Des would be nearby and would have heard part of the conversation.

There was rustling and muffled voices and then she heard things being smashed. Zena could picture the scene in her mind. The hurricane had started. Hurricane Agnes.

'Zena,' her brother's voice came on the line in an almost hesitant manner. 'It's me, Des.' His voice sounded agitated.

'You have no doubt got an idea of my conversation or shouting match with Agnes,' Zena stated. There was silence on the other end of the line. 'Des, Lisa has been sexually abused in her own family home as well as at the Girls Home. No wonder her behaviour changed so dramatically, which obviously led to the final scenario at Franklins!'

'Well, I'm not convinced this has happened until I have proof,' Des argued.

'What! Why wouldn't you believe your own daughter, Des. For God's sake! How could a thirteen-year-old virgin make up these stories! What has happened to her is inhumane, horrendous. Shocking beyond belief. Both these men need to be exposed and sent to jail. Lisa is your own flesh and blood. Don't just sweep it under the carpet and forget about it!' Zena yelled down the phone.

'I don't want to talk anymore, Zena,' Des responded almost robotically.

'Alright, then I will get the proof and in the interim, I am asking for custody of Lisa. She does not want to come back home. Who could bloody well blame her! She wants to stay with us.'

'Fair enough' replied Des.

'Is that all you can say, Des? Fair enough! She is so fragile and damaged, but who wouldn't be after going through all that.' Zena sounded exasperated.

She was again greeted with silence, but he was still on the line. She could hear his laboured breathing even though his hand was over the phone to cover the voice in the background. No doubt he was getting instructions from Agnes.

'Right then' he suddenly spoke. 'We don't want her back, either. She has caused Agnes a lot of distress, and I really feel this angst and unrest would only continue. I know it's been a troubled household from time to time but we don't want to cope with her behaviour.'

Zena was taken aback at his apathy. *Bloody fools. They have erased Lisa from their lives. At least I got what I wanted. I get to keep her. Spineless bastard. I can't believe you are my brother*, she raged internally.

'Your behaviour is nauseating, Des. I will make all the necessary enquiries into seeing that justice is done for Lisa. You will no doubt have the police call you in relation to the allegations, which by the way, I don't believe allegation is the correct word. It's fact. I am yet to prove this, but just give me some time. Lisa wasn't the only girl abused in that place you put her in to. Others will come forward. Des, please . . . it doesn't have to be like this—'

She heard the line click and go dead. Zena sighed. Her brother was lost to her. She only prayed that Mark would live out his childhood unscathed by the pair of them.

'Well,' Alan said as Zena entered the lounge room, patting the seat next to him. Zena sat down and put her head on his shoulder. 'I had a feeling Agnes would react like this but I expected more from my brother. It's like they don't and won't ever believe Lisa. They see her as an embarrassment to the family and would rather just sweep it all under the carpet. But Agnes has never liked me. For all the years I've known her, she's been critical. Maybe because I've done so many things that she never did. Maybe she would have liked to have had a career and travelled. Falling pregnant at sixteen stopped all of that. She's jealous, I suspect, or like so many, just disappointed with her life.'

Zena sat up straight and continued. 'Anyway, it's a done thing. I need to start the ball rolling and contact the police and the child authorities. Agnes and Des don't want Lisa back, which is a relief. I couldn't stand a fight with that woman, but I don't know how she can desert her own flesh and blood. Even a cat takes its kittens.'

Dinner was a sombre affair. Lisa had fallen asleep earlier, no doubt from emotional exhaustion, so Zena just let her sleep until morning.

◊

Lisa woke and felt sore from riding, but smiled. It was a good soreness. A weight had also been lifted from her shoulders after all that emotional release yesterday. She had recounted the worst experiences of her life to someone who not only believed her but also loved her. She didn't get punished. Lisa's heart felt the pain but it was like the demons who had invaded her mind had finally left. She wanted revenge and she wanted justice. She knew if she could have survived the abuse, she could steel herself to provide the necessary information to help put those awful people away. Lisa felt jittery at the thought but she kept hearing her aunt's words: 'It's not your fault.' Her aunt was right—it did feel good to get it all out.

Her bedroom and the rest of the house were very quiet, and all she could hear was the chortling magpies and cockatoos. She made her way to the kitchen and looked at the ticking clock. It was just after 10.00 a.m. Lisa couldn't believe how long she had slept. There was a note on the table: 'We're up at the shearing shed, didn't want to disturb you. All good. A & Z.' Lisa pondered the last two words. All good. Did that mean she could stay?

Lisa could hear a motorbike in the distance. The sound got closer until it finally pulled up at the house. Her aunt appeared at the back door and spoke as she removed her boots. 'Morning, darling girl. How did you sleep? We're just back for a cuppa. Alan is not far behind in the ute.'

'I was a bit restless at first, wondering what is going to happen now, and the nightmares came again.' Lisa looked hesitant and there was a flightiness about her as if waiting for the unknown to strike.

''Your note said all good. Um . . . what does that mean?'

'Well, I spoke to your parents last night, Lisa, and to cut a long story short, I asked for custody,' Zena informed her.

Lisa's mouth flew open. 'Gosh, what did they say?' Her breathing quickened.

Zena continued, 'I expected the usual animosity and anger, which I got in bucket loads, but I also told your mother about Lenny and the home, and that no doubt there would be an investigation after I advise them what you have told me. Agnes said what I expected: that you were lying. Anyway, the final result was good for us. She said she didn't want you back. So kiddo, for now you're ours. I just have to go through the appropriate channels to apply for custody of you. I'll also contact the police as well as Miss Fothergill at the child authorities. We are on our road to justice, Lisa.'

Lisa sat down, so many emotions flooding through her. She looked up at her aunt and said in quiet voice, 'Knowing they don't want me back, that hurts . . . it hurts a lot. They must have never wanted me.' Her face was full of sadness. 'But, now I'm with you and Alan, that does make me feel great. I've always loved you.'

Zena put her arm her. 'You have a new start, Lisa,' she said. 'You are with us now and no-one will ever take you away. But first comes the hard part.'

'What?' Lisa looked puzzled.

'When you've had breakfast, I wonder if later today, we can put pen to paper and recall some of the things that have happened to you. Maybe start with the family home first. What do you think?'

Lisa grimaced. Her mind was racing. *Where to start? There were so many things.*

'I know it will be painful and difficult, but it's the information that will be needed for the police. Can you do that, Lisa?'

'Yes, Aunty. I can try and remember when everything started at home and then I'll write down the awful things Superintendent Ash did.'

'Good girl, try and remember as much as you can of every awful detail. I know it will be hard on you, but it will only help things when there is an investigation. I can sit with you when you begin if that helps to support you. It will be emotionally draining and will bring the horribleness back but there is no other way.'

Lisa felt her face tingling with heat as humiliation flooded her being. She baulked at the thought of having strangers read about what she had been through. Her aunt believed her, but would they? She hardened her resolve and knew her aunt was right. 'I want justice too, Aunty. When did you want me to start this?'

Zena advised, 'Well, the sooner the better, but I want you to take your time. This will be an emotionally raw experience for you. The memories and trauma may cause you to break down, which is why I've suggested I sit with you. But then again, you may like your own space. Only you can tell me what you want to do. It will no doubt stir up things in your head, Lisa, and the nightmares will keep coming, possibly worse than ever. But the unfortunate thing is that if you do not do this, they get off scot free. We need justice to be served, for you and for all the other girls. The evidence needs to be concrete.'

Lisa nodded. She thought of Julie and the rest of the girls at the home.

'I'll try and start this afternoon. Please sit with me, Aunty.'

'Of course, my darling girl.' Zena hugged her. 'If you can talk, I can write. We can stop and start as much as you want. No going back. We go forward, but we can take our time with your notes about the sexual assaults. You can stop if you feel overwhelmed. We are not in a rush; what we want is all the detail. I guess what I am trying to say is that you don't have to sit in here all day, day after day to complete it. We can go slowly.'

'Thanks, Aunty. I understand. But just telling you yesterday, it was like sudden freedom. As if the sorrow and pressure that has disabled my mind and body for so long was released from this vice-like grip . . . from all this fear I've carried for so long.'

Zena looked surprised. 'You expressed that very eloquently, Lisa.' Standing up she said, 'Okay, let's start in a few hours then. Alan wanted to take you around today and show you a few things. Your farm education continues. Alan says you are his star pupil.' Lisa smiled. No-one had ever called her a star.

'I'm heading out to see Binna and Ningali.' She kissed Lisa quickly. 'See you later, darling.'

As Zena left to get organised, Lisa wandered down the stairs and over to the Tack Room. 'How did you go, kid? Sleep well? I heard you had a big day yesterday,' Alan said. Lisa let out a gush of breath.

'Come sit down,' he gestured as he pulled a small stool out. 'I'm hoping you feel relieved after telling Zena everything. A lot has gone on, kid. Terrible things that should never have happened. But not all men are like that,' Alan said softly.

Lisa gave a tentative smile. 'It's good not to feel frightened all the time. I've been carrying it around for so long. There were some days I thought I'd go mad. All this stuff in my head.'

'I cannot imagine the things you've suffered and how you endured these assaults, Lisa. But know that we will do everything we can to get justice for you. Always believe we are here for you,' said Alan solemnly.

Her bottom lip trembled. Alan put a protective arm around her shoulder. 'Come on, I have a few things to show you.'

'Am I really a star pupil?'

'Yep, kid, like a big sponge. A true bushy.' He took her hand as they walked to the ute.

Alan drove a mile up the road, and they stopped at a large tin annex and about four pens. Two big peppercorn trees provided shade. There were pigs of different sizes. The floor was straw and mud, and the pigs clearly loved lying around in the mud.

Lisa laughed. 'It smells awful, Alan. Dung and urine . . . and those pigs, look at them, they are so filthy but look so happy.'

'Yes, I know, Lisa. It's that saying . . . you know . . . happy like a pig in mud. I try and get up here early as the smell is not as bad. The sun seems to make it real ripe. We get the pigs when we go pig shooting; they're meat for the dogs. Sometimes the old sows have babies, so we take the babies and hand feed them until they're weaned. We eventually kill them for consumption. No corner shop here. Have to be self-sufficient. We feed them a mixture of corn and soybean and leftover scraps. If the chooks have been laying a lot of eggs, I'll add a few eggs for protein. So over there in that shed is all their food we buy from the Walgett Co-Op when we go into town.'

'What's that shed way over there?' Lisa asked.

'It's a long-drop dunny. There are a few scattered around the place. But hold your nose in those places, too. If you have to use one, you'll be real quick, let me tell you, not only for the smell but the flies. They're like a black swarm, could carry a bloke away,' he chuckled.

Alan continued pointing things out to her. 'That's the Chook Hilton over there. It's very well fenced, even has a wire floor to keep the foxes and dingoes out. So the forty-four gallon drum has their pellets, but Zena will give you a scrap bucket that you can throw in for them. They scratch around doing what chooks do. That smaller bin is the grit. It's like sand or a coarse dirt. Helps their gizzards to grind up wild foods.' Lisa tried to take it all in.

'So, Lisa, two extra chores . . . pigs and chooks. Make sure they always have water and that they are fed once daily. Come on, we'll do everything together and then head back so you can hook up to the School of Air and then perhaps start making a few notes as Zena suggested.'

'That was fun,' announced Lisa as she hopped into the ute.

Alan asked, 'By the way, how is the derriere today? Do I need to give you a pillow for tomorrow's ride?'

Lisa smiled. 'No, I think I'll be okay. I do like to ride.'

Alan nodded. 'Yep, kid, know the feeling. Man and beast. It's a powerful thing. I'm now tidying up down at the shearing shed. The shearing will start in a couple of months. The place comes alive then, you'll see.'

'Who will be here?' Lisa asked.

'Stockmen, shearers, wool classers, a cook and a few jacke-roos. We go from three people to about twenty-five or thirty. If the shearers bring their women, then there are a few more mouths to feed, but the blacks set up their own camps and usually get their own meat.' Lisa pulled a face. She rather liked her world of three.

'Does it worry you, Lisa, that a few new and different people will be around?'

'Um no, not really, I just don't want things to change.'

'Everything in life changes, you just go with the ebb and flow, kid. Anyway, the crew are a lively bunch and a lot of fun. You'll get a good laugh out of them. I sure as hell do, especially the blacks. They have a good sense of humour and tell things as they are. Real characters. I'll drop you off at the house and head down to the shearing sheds.'

When they pulled up at the house, the Land Rover was gone. 'Zena must have taken it,' Alan commented.

'Yes, she was going to see Binna and Ningali,' Lisa informed him. Alan nodded. His wife didn't waste time.

'See you in a bit,' said Alan. 'Go easy on yourself, kid.'

Lisa headed to the office. School of Air first and then she released a huge exhalation of pent-up breath.

FIFTEEN

HORRIBLE RECOLLECTIONS

The Land Rover kicked up dust as Zena sped along the country road, having decided to drive out rather than ride. It was quicker, which would give her more time with Binna.

'Hi ladies, I've brought you some more tucker,' Zena said after hopping out of the Land Rover. She opened the hamper and handed it to Ningali. Moving under the little humpy, Zena sat down next to Binna. 'My friend,' the old lady murmured.

Zena took Binna's hand. 'Binna, I have something I need to ask you. I know you do this within your own culture but I am asking this of you now.'

'You have da big sorrow in your heart,' the old lady spoke.

'Yes, lots of sorrow, which is why I am here.'

Ningali sat down. 'Sound plenty big serious, missus.'

'My niece, Lisa, whom you met, has suffered terrible abuse to her body by white men. She has a broken soul, and her heart is splintered into many pieces. I'm worried she may never trust anyone fully again, particularly men, and I'm worried about her state of mind. I feel she's been so shattered by her experiences. Horrible things have happened and she is so young.'

The two women started to talk to each other in their native tongue. It was Ningali who spoke. 'Binna, she a powerful elder and spiritual healer. What do you need her to do, missus. She feel dat baby, she bin broken.'

Zena continued. 'I know the spiritual healers treat everything from childhood illnesses to physical and emotional pain, and they restore the spirit balance within the body, treating loss of spirit. My niece is traumatised. Broken. You were right, Binna. How can you help? I mean, are you able to help?'

Zena felt her stomach churn. They began chatting again with each other. It was Ningali who spoke. 'Binna she do smoking ceremony, we have da bush medicine, help her spirit. Binna use her hands. She gonna remove da pain, missus. We hear your cry for help.'

Binna nodded. 'Da white men, dey bring terrible trouble to your baby?

Zena nodded. 'Yes, terrible trouble. I've heard the healers are powerful and do spirit realignment and that your hands remove pain, blockages or obstructions. I know you think the spirit is the core component of a person's body and that you help people to reconnect to their spiritual being. If the spirit is well, the body is well.' Zena felt an aching in her throat and began to sob. She put her head down in her hands.

Binna gently lifted her head back up and touched her face, speaking softly in her native tongue. 'Binna help you, missus. You bin friend to us. I hear big sorrow in your heart. Your girl has same big sorrow, but even worse.' Zena wiped her eyes. 'I so want to help her, Binna. She is such a beautiful girl and these men . . . these disgusting men have done the most vile things.'

'We help you, my friend, take da baby's pain away,' said Binna.

'Thank you, Binna, thank you so much. I'll speak to my niece and see how she feels about coming out here to try these things with you. As I said, her trust in people, particularly men, has been badly damaged.' Zena rose to her feet and hugged both women.

She then walked to the Land Rover and waved as she headed off.

'Her step heavy and angry on da earth. It shaking under her boots,' said Ningali.

As Zena drove back to the house, her mood lightened. She hoped Lisa would say yes to meeting with the two Aboriginal women again. By the time she reached the house, Zena had regained her composure. She was pleased when she saw Alan's ute as she pulled up. Lisa was sitting with Alan when she came into the house.

'Hey, you two. My timing is good,' Zena said as she saw the sandwiches on the plate. Sitting down next to Lisa, she asked 'How's it all going Alan, are we ready for the shearing season?

'All set for the season, and we did the chores together this morning. 'Here,' Alan said as he pushed some sandwiches across the table. 'Lisa is a bit apprehensive about the different people coming on to the property.'

Zena looked at her niece. 'Everything will be fine, Lisa. Alan knows these people, and we wouldn't have anyone on the property that we couldn't trust. But you don't have to go down there if you don't want to. We wouldn't expect you to be there or go anywhere if you feel uncomfortable.

Lisa looked relieved. 'How are Binna and Ningali?'

'They're in good form, and we talked about spiritual healing. Binna is a respected elder. She thought if you wanted to and I agreed . . . you may like to sit with her and talk.'

'I do like them, but what would I talk about?' asked Lisa.

'Be guided by Binna; she's a powerful healer. There's no harm in trying or just sitting and talking with her. I told her today you have suffered major trauma.'

Lisa blushed. 'Does she know what trauma? She took a small bite of her sandwich and chewed slowly.

'No,' said Zena. 'I just told Binna that you had been badly treated and it has affected you in terms of trust. But it's entirely up to you, Lisa. Your decision, darling girl. There is no pressure to do this but if you're in agreement, we can both head out there tomorrow or the day after.'

'It sounds . . . I guess, kind of different, maybe scary, but a little bit exciting in a way. I so love this land, what you have both taught me so far and now these lovely ladies who have this magnetism or an aura. They seem so kind.'

'Indeed, they are, Lisa.' Zena was pleased. 'You have nothing to lose. Yes, it will be different, but they have amazing healing powers. Let me know what you decide. I shall be there to watch and protect you. Always.'

'Um . . . yes, yes, I want to go. Something in my heart is saying this is right. I will sit with Binna and Ningali.'

'Wonderful. Nothing to lose and perhaps more to gain.' Zena paused and then gently asked, 'Do you want to get started on your statements after lunch? Let me know if you're ready or need more time, Lisa.'

Lisa breathed deeply, trying to get a hold of the anxiety that was rising within her. 'It was good being busy with the chores, Aunty, and I did run some things through my head, so yes, please sit with me, and we can make a start.'

Hugging her niece, Zena said, 'You are so brave. I'm so very proud of you. You have the heart of a warrior.' They put their dishes in the sink and headed to the sitting room. It was late afternoon in the peaceful and comfortable room with big windows and views across to the bore. But now these peaceful walls would hear atrocities.

Zena carried a large notebook under her arm and two glasses of water. Lisa could feel her heart pounding. Her aunt held her hand and reassured, 'There is no-one here but us, and you are safe. You are loved under this roof and in this home. Don't be frightened. You're not to blame. Tell me if you're ready.'

Lisa gulped some water and nodded. She began to talk about Lenny. At first her speech was halted and many times she had to stop, but as she continued to tell her story, Lisa bristled with rage and then felt more empowered, wanting to claim her rights and bring justice, not only for herself but for all past and future girls whose lives had been and could be affected by these horrible people.

As Lisa spoke, her aunt tried to stifle her own tears. Lisa could tell that Zena felt sickened by what she had endured. Recalling what had happened, rage filled Lisa's being as she realised how people she should have been able to trust had manipulated all situations. At times, Lisa stopped and cried and sometimes they both cried. It was a cathartic experience for Lisa. She spoke and Zena wrote.

The shadows of the day crept across the plains. The animals drifted in and away from the bore. 'It's early evening. Time to stop.' Zena put her pen down. 'You look exhausted, and I'm ready to drive to Sydney to shoot your brother-in-law. It's enough for today, Lisa.' Putting her arm around Lisa's shoulders, she asked gently, 'How are you feeling?'

'Loads of things, Aunty. Rage, disbelief, disgust, anger, humiliation, loss of faith and trust, lots of those things.'

'Me too, darling girl. Do you need to lie down? I think that may be a good idea. Early shower and then join us on the verandah?'

'Thank you, Aunty. I'll do that.'

◇

Zena watched her niece head to her bedroom. In between tears and revulsion, Zena had managed to write copious amounts of disgusting material. It made her sick to her stomach, and she herself felt violated. That people of this nature had access to power and young girls infuriated her. She ran her hands over her writing. *Monsters that will go to hell!*

◇

It was about 7.00 p.m. when Lisa emerged from her bedroom, carrying another pile of papers that were labelled Parramatta Girls Home. Placing the documents on the kitchen table next to the pile marked Home (Fairfield), Lisa stared at the word Home and tears welled in her eyes as she thought, *Home, my family home, supposed to be a safe place.*

Zena was with Alan as Lisa placed the papers on the table. A look of disbelief crossed her aunt's face. 'You've been writing? When you didn't join us on the verandah, I thought you must have been sleeping,' Zena said, aghast.

Lisa squared her shoulders. 'No, I just wanted to write. It was all in my head, and I wanted to get it out. But now I feel like I can't do anymore, and my energy is sapped.'

'You've been very brave, Lisa, more than brave. You are so courageous. What can I get you, darling girl?' Zena asked soothingly.

'I think I just want to shut my eyes. The writing and talking about the two places has really made me nauseous. My insides are churning inside. It was so sad to write about my friend Julie, who died in the laundry. I always wondered what they told her parents . . . you know, how she died. I hope after all this, Aunty, it puts them away.' Tears were not far from Lisa's eyes. 'I think I'll go to my room and lie down. I really don't feel like eating anything.'

Zena drew Lisa to her gently. 'I've never met anyone as brave as you.' She kissed her cheek and hugged her close before Lisa shuffled back to her room, every bone in her body aching. The emotional and physical terror she had endured would have been visible to anyone who looked at her. Just before Lisa reached her bedroom door, Zena called out, 'May I look, Lisa?' Lisa nodded and closed her door, ready to collapse on her bed from fatigue.

◊

As Zena flicked through and read some of the content, she was shocked to her core. It was sickening, explicit and nothing short of atrocious. Depravity and humiliation at the highest level and from people in a position of power. She felt such intense hatred, more than she'd ever felt in her life. Lisa had suffered so much for her age. These were sickening attacks on a young, defenceless girl. *It's a wonder she's not fucking mad. Please God, don't let her go backwards because of recalling all this.*

It was agonising to read it, let alone live it. Zena grabbed a beer for Alan and went out on the verandah to sit with him. 'How is she?' he asked, taking a swig from his beer.

'Coping, but just. I'll look in on her in about thirty minutes, but right now, I just want to sit and look at this beautiful vista.' Zena put her head on Alan's shoulder and fell asleep.

'Hey, sweet pea,' he said, gently touching her arm. 'You've been asleep for some time now. Best go see how Lisa is doing.'

'Boy, I needed that. Sorry, not much on conversation, was I. Time to make a move and see how my girl is doing.'

Zena opened the door gently. Lisa lay with her back to it. 'Lisa, are you awake?' her aunt whispered.

Lisa rolled over to face her aunt. 'I am, Aunty, just kind of dozing,' she answered groggily. Zena came and sat on the side of the bed. 'I cannot take away or change these atrocities that have happened to you, but what you have done today has been truly unbelievable. I don't know if the powers that be, meaning the police, will want more. I do know they may want to speak to you and perhaps take their own statements from you. There will be lots of questions, but you must be strong. It's the only way to bring justice.'

'That's okay,' said Lisa, 'I'm ready.' Zena felt so helpless, and rage rose throughout her body once again.

'Sleep may be difficult, Lisa. I'll do the usual: leave the lamp on and the door ajar. I'm here if you need me. What I want you to think about before you close your eyes is that you did nothing wrong and what you have done here today has been a herculean effort. You have overcome more mental and physical obstacles than any human being could possibly endure.' She kissed her niece and bade her goodnight.

When Zena lay down next to Alan that night, she wept uncontrollably. He held her tightly and let the tears flow from her like a river. There was no holding back. Sobs racked her body until she fell asleep in his arms.

◊

The following morning, Alan was up early. Zena slept in. It was so unusual for her not to be up with him. He let her sleep. He'd heard her tossing and turning until the early hours of the morning.

Alan moved down the hall and looked in on Lisa. She also slept soundly. No doubt, she'd had the same pervasive dreams. A man not in his right mind would take a gun and shoot those predators, but he had to leave it to his wife and the authorities. He threw on his hat, grabbed some fruit and took off on the motor bike, the dogs barking as he did so.

◊

Lisa roused when she heard the bike and the dogs. Stretching, she remembered the awful thoughts that came to her in her sleep. She had fought the demons desperately through the night. Her stomach still churned, but now she felt a sense of righteousness. She wanted to move forward. Looking across to her aunt's room, she padded in, turned down the bed cover and slid in. Zena rolled over and rubbed her eyes.

'How is my brave girl?' Zena asked softly. They lay looking at each other, the sleepiness still in their eyes. 'Braver,' Lisa replied.

'You're wonderful. How did you sleep? asked Zena.

'Not good. I find the faces come to me at night, and I hear screams. Sometimes I feel like they're touching me, and I try to fight them off. Then I think of home and how that all started, and I so wished Mum had believed me. And then of course, I think of my brother. I so miss him and want to talk to him, but Mum will probably stop him from speaking to me.'

'That's all understandable, Lisa. I had a rough night too. I could see all the things you experienced. My mind was churning until early this morning. We need to do a few things first and cross each bridge as we come to them. I know you miss Mark, but I doubt Agnes will let you speak to him at the moment. But when we prove the things that were done, she may be remorseful and let you unite with Mark again. I truly hope Agnes can do this for everyone's sake.'

Lisa moved over, and her aunt tucked her arm under her neck. She kissed Lisa lightly on the cheek. 'Things will get better, things will change. They may get a little worse when you have to provide information or talk to strangers about the experiences, but I'll be there for you.'

'I want to go out and see Binna today. Is that possible, Aunty?' Lisa asked suddenly.

'Yes, of course we can. The ladies said you are welcome to come any time.' Zena was delighted. 'Let's make a move then. I have some eggs to take to them. The chooks have been churning them out. The women love the eggs and the less work to get them. We'll drive out; it'll be much quicker.'

'That would be great, Aunty.' Lisa felt the excitement mounting.

'Indeed. Off you go to get dressed, and I'll meet you out in the kitchen.'

Lisa was silent for most of the thirty-minute trip. 'Everything alright, Lisa?' Zena squeezed her hand.

'Yes, Aunty. I'm just looking at this beautiful blue sky and breathing in the air, albeit it mixed with red dust. Even though it gets over everything, I love the colour, the red dust colour. It signifies open spaces, freedom. I'm looking forward to seeing the ladies.'

Zena glowed. 'Me too, Lisa.'

As they took the curve in the road, the little humpy came in-to view. The smoke from the women's small fire curled in the air. Ningali stood when the Land Rover came into view, her hand over her eyes from the sun. The women waved. Zena pulled up not far from their humpy.

'Here take these eggs, Lisa. I want to get the big jerry can full of fresh water for them out the back of the Land Rover.' Lisa grabbed the eggs, hopped down out of the Land Rover and walked tentatively towards the women, who were now seated.

'Good morning,' Ningali sang out. 'Da little one, she comes now, Binna. Here, you sit 'em down,' said Ningali. She patted the earth and then Lisa handed the eggs over to her.

'Oooh,' she exclaimed. 'We like 'em, da eggs. Binna's fa-vourite.' The old lady laughed and rubbed her belly. Lisa joined in their laughter.

'Here comes da boss missus,' Ningali said, pointing her fin-ger at Zena. 'Here, ladies, some fresh water,' Zena said as she put the jerry can down.

'You like 'em sit too, missus?' queried Ningali.

'Yes, if I may,' replied Zena, sitting cross-legged in the sandy dirt. Binna nodded and flashed her toothless grin. She reached across to touch Lisa's heart. 'It go up and down, like da butter-fly. Spirit restless.'

Ningali spoke. 'Binna, need 'em panpooni, plenty.'

Lisa asked, 'What's panpooni?' Zena had heard this termi-nology 'panpooni' used before. Jack Pettigrew, their manager for the sheep seasons, had watched a ceremony at another property. It was such an unusual word that she never forgot it or the explanation. She explained to Lisa, 'This is the ceremony where they take away pain, a blockage or some kind of obstruc-tion with their hands. It's where they realign the human spirit.'

Zena continued, 'Binna, you have a healing touch. Can you bring Lisa's spirit back to the right place? If her spirit is not in the right place, she'll keep hurting mentally, physically and emotionally.'

No-one spoke. A light wind with the birds singing was the only sound that was present. Binna sat with her eyes closed, holding Lisa's hands. She finally spoke. 'Dis women's secret business. Da spirits are here.' Binna looked directly at Zena, her tired milky eyes saw everything. Her big heart felt everything.

'Thank you, Binna.' Zena smiled gratefully. Ningali held out her hands, and they all linked hands together in a circle.

'Dis is da healing circle,' said Binna, holding Lisa's hand and chanting softly.

Ningali had started a fire. 'Dis is smoking ceremony,' Binna explained. Ningali had collected various native plants, which were used to produce smoke. 'Dis ward off bad spirits, missus, and make da little one clean.'

Lisa felt energy and a warmth engulfing her entire body. Her eyes were closed, and suddenly she felt an intense love, similar to something a small child would experience with a loving par-ent. Something she had never experienced. Binna kept chanting and singing and felt the girl's pulse slow down. Her eyes never left Lisa.

Binna finally stopped, and Lisa opened her eyes slowly. She looked at her aunt and felt peace.

'We give prayer to our Creator,' said Ningali. Binna spoke in her native tongue.

'She thanks dem spirits,' explained Ningali. 'Give us big strength. Binna tired now. She need plenty rest.'

'Yes, of course, Ningali. Thank you, thank you so much.' Zena reached for their hands and touched both the ladies. Lisa did the same.

'You come sometime next week,' said the old lady. She reached for Lisa's face, tracing it with her fingers. 'Be at peace, no more bad spirits.'

When they got into the Land Rover, Zena looked at her watch and was shocked. they had been there well over two hours. As they drove back to the homestead, the car was once again silent. There was a spiritual presence surrounding Lisa. 'How do you feel, Lisa?' her aunt asked, breaking the silence.

'I lost all sense of where I began and where I ended. I had this extreme feeling of peace and intense love. I felt like I was connected to the earth and the universe. I want to go back, Aunty. It's something they do, how they make me feel. It's like a feeling of cool rain washing over me, taking this weight from me.'

Zena confirmed Lisa's thoughts. 'They are powerful people. They believe that plants, animals and us human beings are all part of this universe. So we have been invited back. I'm so glad that you feel this way, Lisa. I wondered what you would feel. Binna was tired, and no doubt they will be tucking into the eggs right now. But you see what I mean. This spirituality. I know of one ceremony where they paint their faces red. They say it represents the four components of the body, bone, nerve, blood and tissue.'

An overwhelming sense of gratitude washed over Lisa. 'Thank you, Aunty. I feel so much better than I did yesterday—more at peace.'

◊

As they entered the house, the phone was ringing. Zena moved quickly and answered on the fourth ring. 'Hello, this is Zena Smith.'

'Good afternoon, Mrs Smith. This is Jane Fothergill from Child Welfare Authority.' Her voice sounded young and not officious, which was a good sign.

'Good afternoon, Jane. I've been expecting a call from the authorities.' Lisa came to the hallway where the phone was. She had heard the word 'authorities.' Zena smiled at her.

'I've tried calling a few times but you must be often out and about. Anyway, I've read the file and understand Lisa is in your custody.'

'Yes, that's correct.'

'Are you having any problems, Mrs Smith?'

'None whatsoever, Jane. My niece is responding to love and care and has adapted to all the chores and activities around the property. She does her hook up to School Air Australia to continue her education. We adore her, and I think the feeling is mutual,' said Zena as she winked at Lisa.

Lisa smiled and nodded.

'That is wonderful news. The department thought there may be issues with the isolation.'

'On the contrary, Jane. Lisa is a natural bushy, and it may even be her career. I might be able to steer her into agriculture. I've heard Hawkesbury Agricultural College is very good, but that is further down the track. For now, we are happy settling her down, keeping her busy mentally and physically.'

'I've made notes here in her file, Mrs Smith. If there are any concerns, please don't hesitate to call and ask for me. Do you want to get a pen and paper for my direct line?'

'Yes, I have pen and paper next to the phone, so fire away.'

Zena jotted the number down. 'I shall be in touch again, Mrs Smith, just need to follow up.'

'Yes, of course. No problem, Jane. Good day.'

Zena put the phone down and looked at Lisa. 'No problem at all.' She walked towards Lisa and she headed to the kitchen with her arm around her niece. It was a good feeling.

'You're probably wondering why I didn't mention the assaults at the Girls Home?' Zena asked Lisa.

Lisa cocked her eyebrow. 'Yes, I did wonder about that.'

Zena explained, 'I want to inform the police first and I want us to be ready and have as much information as we can possibly write down. We'll continue with this until we can't do anymore. My gut feeling tells me that if I had told Jane what had happened to you, they would be up here crawling all over the place and then of course, alert those bastards to your allegations.'

'Your logic and advice is always the best, Aunty. We both want justice now,' said Lisa.

'I'll do everything in my power, darling girl, to assist that process. I think you know that now,' said Zena.

'Yes, and I'm happy for you to do what you think is right, Aunty.'

'Good, we'll leave it at that, get prepared and then advise the police when everything has been finalised.'

◊

The following week, Lisa and Zena drove out in the Land Rover to see the Aboriginal women. Alan had killed a steer the day before, so Zena took steaks and more eggs. She was so grateful to Binna. Lisa's nightmares had lessened. They had continued writing as Lisa recalled further details. The visits with the women gave her more confidence.

When they arrived, both women were seated. There was a large shell in the healing circle. Zena gave them the basket containing the meat and eggs. Binna nodded, and they all sat cross-legged once again in the dust.

'What's in the shell?' asked Lisa, her curiosity peaked.

'Dat shell have traditional medicines. Sage, sweet grass, cedar and tobacco,' replied Ningali as she began to burn the special herbs.

Binna began to sing. 'Each person must cup da smoke,' Ningali instructed. She cupped her hands to demonstrate. 'Take da smell in.' The shell was then passed over their heads and shoulders. While the ladies held hands, the shell smouldered. Binna was still singing and chanting. It was another ceremony but more like a purification. They all sat silently.

Binna touched Lisa's face again and traced it with her finger, following the line down to her heart. 'No shame,' her voice said softly. Binna prayed again in her own language. When she finished, Ningali passed an eagle feather to Lisa and said, 'Pass dis feather to each person now.' The feather passed between the four women and then they shook hands.

When they stood to leave, Zena saw a serenity and a peaceful aura surrounding Lisa, almost a calmer inner state. Slowly but surely, she was letting go. It was time to make that call.

SIXTEEN

THE INVESTIGATION

Zena dialled the Parramatta Police Station and after speaking to one of the constables, she was put through to Detective Andrew Collette. His voice was strong and well-modulated. 'Detective Collette speaking.'

'Good morning, Detective. My name is Zena Smith. I have my niece Lisa O'Connor staying with me after she was released from the child authorities into my care. She has advised me of horrific sexual assaults that occurred in the family home over a sustained period as well as in the Parramatta Girls Home. Lisa was placed in that home due to a stealing offence but what she was trying to do was get food to escape the family home. It was also unfortunate that while in the Girls Home, Lisa witnessed a murder. One of the other girls there was bashed to death with an iron.'

The detective cut in. 'Mrs Smith, are you able to provide any evidence or statements regarding what you have just said?'

'Yes,' Zena replied. 'My niece has been writing down dates and times, and what occurred. We have just finalised everything. The information is explicit. I can post these down to you. I just need to make a copy in case they get lost.' They spoke for a further hour, and when she hung up, Zena punched the air. *Yes, we are coming to get you, you evil bastards.*

Lisa had finished her chores and had headed in with Alan for morning tea.

'I made that call, Lisa,' her aunt told them as they all sat down. Lisa's eyes widened, and she leaned forward. 'What call?'

'The first call to the police to inform them of what has happened. I have to post the statements you provided. I need to get a copy made of everything we have written down but now I've made that call to the police, it just leaves one more to make, and that is to the child authorities. We've started the process.' Lisa looked numb, and tears welled in her eyes.

'Oh, darling girl, I thought it was time. You have been so different, so confident. I'm sorry if—'

'No apologies, please don't be sorry, Aunty,' Lisa sniffed as she wiped the tears away. 'These are tears of joy.' There was now a light at the end of a tunnel. New beginnings. Justice. Zena came to her niece and wrapped her arms around her. 'We will get these people, Lisa.'

As sleep took over Lisa, her last thought was the same as her aunt's. *I want to get these men.* Her slumber was fitful as feelings of revenge and the misery she had endured haunted her dreams. When she shuffled into the kitchen the following morning, Zena could see the night had been bad.

'Morning, Lisa. Don't forget we are heading into Walgett this Saturday,' said Zena, trying to exude cheeriness. 'Rough night?' Lisa nodded as she reached for the tea her aunt had just made.

What's Walgett like?' asked Lisa, excited at the prospect of venturing into the town. 'It's another country town a bit like Dubbo,' replied Alan. 'And Walgett is another Aboriginal name. It means 'the meeting place of two rivers', which are the Barwon and Namoi. Walgett is sheep country; it was a port in the late nineteenth century for the paddle steamers that moved up and down the Murray–Darling Basin. I think it was about 1860 or 1870 when the first steamer reached Walgett. But the town made the news in the mid-1960s because of a group who called themselves the Freedom Riders.'

'What were they, Alan? Lisa asked curiously. 'Funny name.'

'They were crazy university students that came to Walgett in 1965. They actually protested outside the Walgett RSL, right where we will be playing. They had been told the club was refusing to admit Indigenous ex-servicemen. They also picketed the ladies dress shop because the Indigenous ladies were not allowed to try dresses on. After protesting, the students headed to Narrabri when their bus was forced off the road by a car driven by a local farmer. This brought a lot of media attention to Walgett, the Freedom Riders and the Indigenous people. We need a few more of those blokes about to make people take notice of the racism.' Lisa could only think at that very moment that they were a champion of right over wrong, both of them.

They arrived in Walgett around noon, earlier than their usual arrival time, but Zena wanted to do some shopping and get all the documents photocopied. Leaving Alan to set up at the RSL, Zena and Lisa headed off for some shopping at Mrs Dunphy's haberdashery, agreeing to meet him back at the RSL around 3 p.m.

The haberdashery store was a maze of women's clothing, shoes, hats and handbags as well as cloth to buy. 'Hello, Zena,' said Mrs Dunphy as they entered the store. She was a plump lady with pink cheeks who wore thick black-rimmed glasses. Her flared floral dress barely contained her spreading waist. She looked like she would bust out of the dress any minute. Zena introduced Lisa and left her in the care of Mrs Dunphy.

'Pick what you like, Lisa,' smiled her aunt. 'I'll see you in an hour. Just need to photocopy the documents.'

When Zena returned, Lisa held up the bags and then Zena paid Mrs Dunphy's bill. 'Come on, kiddo, let's get ready. There's a small room with an ensuite attached to the band room, which we shower in before we start to sing. We basically set things up, practise a few songs, get ready and then have dinner.'

Lisa looked around as they entered the RSL. It smelled of old beer and her feet stuck to the carpet in some spots. The carpet was well worn but the space was neatly set up with a parquetry dance floor, tables and chairs. The walls were filled with old shearing photos and outback landscapes. The walls were full of history and photographs of the faces of the stoic men who had worked the land.

'People will start coming in about six o'clock, Lisa, so we have to be ready to go around that time,' said Zena.

When they were all showered and changed, Lisa couldn't help staring at Zena and Alan. It was the first time she'd seen them out of work clothes. They were a handsome couple.

'Gosh, you both look so beautiful,' Lisa said admiringly.

'Thanks, kid,' Alan grinned.

This night would be fun. The dark moments that lay ahead with the police and their investigations could wait.

Zena was explaining, 'So, Lisa, we finish here about 11.00 p.m. We start at 6.00 p.m. and do forty-five minute sessions with fifteen-minute breaks. If you want to come inside, I'll let the doorman know, who will escort you over to our table at the side of where we play. You cannot roam around the club as you are underage, but I'm sure the local constable will not be too harsh. You're welcome to make friends with the local kids. Most play in the street while they wait for their parents, who are usually the RSL clientele.'

It was early evening when Lisa wandered out of the RSL to have a look around. Directly opposite the RSL, she noticed a group of children playing who were all different ages. Lisa crossed the road to join them. An older girl, who was Aboriginal, smiled at Lisa as she approached. She was not very dark; her skin was honey brown with bleached hair that had not seen a brush for some time. She wore no shoes. 'Hello. My name Allira, mean daughter,' the girl said, her grin widening.

'That's a lovely name,' replied Lisa.

'We just playing chasings with dis other white kids. We all have fun. You want join in? What your name?'

'I'm Lisa, and if it's okay with you, I'll just sit on this seat and get to know you and the others playing here. My aunt and uncle are playing musical instruments and singing tonight for the Walgett RSL, so I have to fill in time until they finish.'

Allira suddenly started to wipe the seat down, and Lisa felt humbled by her actions. Allira sat next to her and watched the children squealing and playing, hiding and seeking each other out. Innocent. It made Lisa think of Mark. The kids were all a mixed age from nine years to about sixteen years. Suddenly, everyone stopped playing and looked in the direction of a tall figure looming out of the shadows. His stride was confident and long, and his tall frame showed masculinity and strength. Some of the younger girls squealed and ran towards the figure. As he stepped out of the shadows, Lisa saw that it was a teenage Aboriginal boy. The younger kids ran around him, and he stopped to play with and tease them.

'Dat one Billy, all the girls likum good,' said Allira.

'What does that mean?' asked Lisa.

'Dey all like Billy,' repeated Allira. 'Very good horseman. Strong jackaroo. Everybody knows Billy.' Allira giggled.

When he came into view, he had skin like Allira, creamy light brown. His hair was jet black and curly, which trailed down to his wide shoulders. He waved and smiled at Allira, flashing a cheeky white smile.

Allira fidgeted as he approached. 'See, I tell em straight. Dat Billy make good partner, alright. Billy got powerful elders.' Lisa felt a slight sense of nervousness. Billy now stood towering above them, and Allira poked her finger into his belly button.

'Where youse been, Billy? Gone walkabout? No see for long time.' Billy grabbed Allira's finger and held on tightly to it. 'Bin busy up north, cattle and stations big up there. Youngest jackaroo. Me seventeen years now. Who dis little lady?' His eyes glanced over at Lisa, and she felt herself blush. He had the softest brown eyes, like velvet, and apart from Binna, he had the kindest face she had ever seen.

'Dis one Lisa. She proper good lady. Her folks in RSL playing,' Allira explained quite proudly.

Billy held out his hand to Lisa. It was strong and his long fingers wrapped around her hand, almost pulling her to him. He had an incredible power about him, similar to Binna. As Billy stared into her eyes, Lisa pulled her hand back. The only men she trusted were Alan and her brother. The young man seemed to sense her nervousness. She knew she was acting all jittery.

'You scared of Billy?' he asked, a kind look on his face.

'No, why would I be scared?' retorted Lisa, somewhat taken aback.

'You like da grasshopper. You fidgeting and jumping all round da place, missus, never still, just like dat grasshopper. Twitching and rubbing ya back legs and then dey hop off.' Billy made a hopping motion with his fingers and laughed. Allira giggled at his humour. 'You must be nervous like dem grasshoppers, missus.'

Lisa wanted to laugh with him but she felt edgy around the boy. He seemed to look right through her. *Grasshopper. Is that what I am?* Standing up, she brushed down her clothes. 'Well, I must go. I have to routinely check in with my aunt at the RSL.' Lisa walked towards the RSL door where the doorman was standing. She felt safer. Playing with the girls was okay, but she was not expecting a young man with velvet eyes who seemed to look through her.

Lisa sat and had a cold drink with Zena and Alan during their break and then walked outside again. The group had dispersed, and the only children left were the white kids, now sitting on the seats directly near the RSL front door. Lisa sighed. She should have stayed. The Aboriginal girls were fun. The streets were now almost empty except for a few men having a good yarn.

She went back inside and remained there for the night, marvelling at the dancers on the floor and the entertainment provided. At the end of every set, people whistled and clapped. They were clearly appreciative of her aunt and uncle's music.

As people filtered out into the street, Lisa helped pack the music gear into the Zephyr. When she looked up, she saw a tall figure standing in the shadows watching her. She knew it was Billy. Why did his eyes follow her? Was she that fractured or broken that she emanated something that these people could see? Lisa stared at Billy. She wanted to go over to him. She had that same spiritual feeling she felt with Binna and Ningali. She had not pulled her hand away from his because of lack of trust. She felt something different about him, but couldn't quite figure out what it was. It wasn't bad though.

As they drove home, she sat in the back seat, thinking about the tall Aboriginal boy. He had an aura and a strength about him. Lisa could still feel his hand in hers and although he was only young, there was a power to his presence. She wanted to know more about him. She recalled Allira's words, 'Billy got powerful elders.' Lisa's eyes flew open. *Elders. Spiritual. Like Binna. That's what it was. The same aura.*

SEVENTEEN

THE ARRIVALS

Alan was excited. 'They'll be arriving soon, Lisa. A slow colourful trickle of white and black. Men, boys, lubras, picaninnies, dogs, you name it. I find early spring is the best for sheepshearing as it relieves the sheep of their year-old coats in time to keep them cool and comfortable. This gives them plenty of time to grow a coat that's long and heavy for the winter. Sometimes I shear in March too, unless the weather is particularly mild, in which case I can start end of February.'

'It sounds complicated, Lisa commented. 'I really don't know anything about sheep and shearing, Alan.'

Alan explained. 'You'll know a lot more by the end of the season kid. Producing good lambs and wool is an interesting process. Yep, the shearing season crews are colourful lot, and you'll hear some good yarns in the shearing shed. The whiteys use the shearing men's quarters, and the blacks set up their own camp outside with their lubras. They have their own camps and fires, and a few working dogs.'

'Sounds like organised chaos,' said Lisa.

'Good description, kid. Sure is, a real mixture. Place lights up like a Christmas tree. They all come a few days before, which is good. I call it seasonal bonding. Jack Pettigrew, my manager, keeps them in line . . . you'll like Jack. He's been with me for years. Oversees everything. He should arrive tomorrow, so we'll go down and meet him. He's full of stories and likes a drink, but more important, he doesn't put up with any shit.' Alan hoped that she would like Jack. He could see that she was still feeling a bit uneasy about the prospect of having so many strange men around for the next few months, but he knew these men could be trusted.

The big day had finally arrived. Zena had risen early and packed some scones with butter, jam and cream for Alan to take down to the shed. As Alan and Lisa pulled up in the ute, a large man appeared in the doorway of the men's quarters. He walked towards Alan's ute with a broad grin.

'G'day, Alan! Good to see you, mate,' bellowed Jack as they shook hands. Both men looked at each other respectfully. Jack wore a very old hat that looked like it had belonged to him for years. His face was weathered and deeply lined. His eyebrows were thick and bushy and framed his face like caterpillars. He was barrel-chested, and his hands were the size of a shovel head. These were the hands of a man who had worked hard all his life.

'Jack, this is my niece, Lisa. She's staying with Zena and me for a while. Lisa is like a sponge and wants to learn everything about the bush . . . horses, sheep, pigs, and now the shearing season.'

'Mighty nice to meet you, Lisa. You're nearly as pretty as Zena,' he complimented. Lisa blushed. She was not used to compliments from someone she had just met.

'Lisa, can you fetch those scones for Jack,' Alan asked, Lisa collected the basket of freshly baked scones from the back of the ute and politely gave the basket to Jack.

'These will go down a real treat, Alan', he beamed. 'Thank the little lady for me. I get fatter from her cooking every time I come here.' Both men laughed, and Jack patted his belly. 'Good to be here, Alan.'

'I'll be back tomorrow, Jack. Just settle in and we'll rally the troops when they're all here.' Alan waved as he took off back to the homestead. 'What did you think, Lisa?'

'He's so huge and strong looking. His hands were so big. I think he must have worked hard all his life.'

'Yep, you're right, kid. Some describe him as a big bastard. Jack even likes that description. He likes his tucker and beer but as I said, he's a damn good worker and runs a tight ship when we get going. Saves me a lot of headaches. He started working at age thirteen. Been around horses, sheep cattle and farms all his life. This season will be ten years he's done with me. A bloody decade, so we'll have to have some sort of celebration.'

'What sort of celebration?' Lisa asked.

'Maybe kill a steer, have a few beers around a camp fire, and someone always has a harmonica. A celebration also puts everyone in a good mood and builds up the camaraderie because when they get shearing, these blokes do work real hard.'

Lisa took all this in and nodded. Then she said, 'Is it okay if I take Neddy down to the river and back this morning after chores? I would love to sit with Binna and Ningali and then go and have a swim.'

'Are you confident to go alone?' Alan asked.

'Yep, and when I come back, I want to get in the ute or 'paddock basher' as you call it, and have a go at learning to drive.'

'That's my girl. Take your time, kid. I pity the gear box . . . all that crunching. Most bush kids learn to drive as soon as they can see over the steering wheel. Check with Zena first though about going to the river alone.'

Alan dropped Lisa off at the house and then changed cars. He was taking the Land Rover into town to pick up the fencing equipment and the other things Zena had ordered from the Co-Op. As he jumped into the Land Rover, he heard Lisa squeal. The back door opened and she raced down to the Tack Room. She must have got a yes.

◊

Lisa was breathless with excitement as she mounted Neddy. She was on her own and heading to the river, already imagining the cool river waters around her body. Lisa also wanted to sit with the women again as their spirituality made her float, and it was as if there was more space in her body, her mind. She felt like a caterpillar morphing into a butterfly when near them. It was a sense of pure freedom. The land was huge, the sky above so blue and filled with birdlife. Her spirit and her body felt so alive. She was no longer imprisoned by her thoughts. She felt she could touch the sky.

Since the two ceremonies, Lisa had felt so clear of mind and free of the shame that previously invaded her thoughts. More ceremonies were to follow, or healing circles, as Ningali called them, but only when Binna was ready. Reaching their camp, she waved to the two ladies. Ningali stood to greet her. Lisa tethered Neddy and walked towards them.

'Welcome, missus. We bin waiting for you,' Ningali said warmly.

'Zena said to give this to you.' Lisa handed Ningali the small parcel of food. 'I think it's bacon.'

'She good proper lady that one. Me and Binna likum the boss lady; she like one of our own.'

Lisa smiled and sat down. 'If you have the time, Binna, can you tell me what the Dreamtime is?'

Ningali sat cross-legged with Binna, who drew in the dirt with a stick. 'It's from where our laws come from. Our ancestors, stories of our culture.'

'Can you tell me a story, Binna?' Lisa asked.

Binna cleared her throat. Since the ceremonies, the old lady could feel a difference, a spiritual shift in Lisa. Lisa's voice was light, and it now danced when she spoke.

'Do you know how da sun was made?'

'No, I don't. Please tell me, Binna.'

'Many times ago, there was no sun, only moon and stars. One day, da emu got so angry with another bird, dey was fighting. The other bird threw da emu eggs into the sky, and da yellow yolk burst into flames. Da yolk lit up da whole world, and all da creatures were dazzled by da brightness. Da spirits saw how beautiful da earth looked when it was lit up so dey began to make a fire every day. But dey needed a noise to wake people up, to let dem see da bright light. But what noise? It was da laughter of da kookaburra. His noise rings through da air every morning, and he laughs da loudest to awaken all da sleepy people.'

Lisa beamed. 'What a beautiful story, Binna. Thank you. I look forward to hearing another.' When she sat with the women, it was though her energy was restored. No splintering. Grounded. Lisa felt her emotional wounds healing and tentatively began to trust again. She understood what Binna was trying to do, and she had an acceptance of the greater energies. Lisa felt she was on a spiritual journey, and this resonated soundly in her mind. *Heal. Trust. I'm listening to my body now.*

Binna took Lisa's hand. She pointed to the sky and then moved her arm around her. 'Feel da river, feel da sky, da wind and plants. I call upon dem to do healing. We are one. Open your heart, Lisa, and let da spirits through. Da air we breathe, da waters we drink dat flow over the earth's body, keep these thoughts. Da fire from the sun will warm you. Use all da spirits of nature and Mother Earth.'

Lisa felt a rush of gratitude for Binna. Happy tears began to stream down her face, and she wanted to trust this guiding spirit. Lisa could feel the power, the wisdom, the energy that Binna had spoken of. She wanted to heal, remove the negative energies and clear the blockages that had impeded her in her young life.

Hugging the two women, Lisa was in high spirits, almost a state of exhilaration, when she said goodbye. She headed in the direction of the river and could see it glistening as it came into view. Digging her heels into Neddy, she spurred him to get a move on.

'Come on, you'll soon cool down; the waters beckon us, Neddy.' Lisa dismounted when she got to the riverbank. Neddy drank steadily and then she tethered him to a tree with a longer rope. She looked around and saw no-one. Lisa peeled off her clothes and took out her bathers, quickly changing. She then dived in. It was so refreshing, and the water glided over her young body as she did backstroke up the river. Neddy whinnied, and Lisa suddenly stopped to see if anyone was about.

'Neddy, what's up? There's no-one about.' Lisa relaxed and splashed and kicked, floating on her back. But she felt the presence of something . . . someone. Alarm flooded through her. 'Is anybody there?' she called out.

Suddenly, a tall figure stood up. The sun was in her eyes and she squinted. It was Billy. Lisa gasped. He only wore jeans, which were rolled up. She looked at the hard muscles of his body. He almost looked like a spirit with the sun behind him.

'How long have you been here?' Lisa called out, her voice relaying the anxiety she felt. Billy didn't reply. He merely turned and walked away.

Why did he walk away? Why didn't he speak? Lisa waited until she was sure no-one was around and then walked up the bank, hurriedly drying and putting her clothes back on. On the ride home, she kept turning around to see if he was following, but she rode in silence and alone back to the homestead.

'Well, how was that?' Zena asked as Lisa came into the kitchen.

'Oh, Aunty, it was great. The swim was so refreshing. Binna told me a fantastic Dreamtime story about the making of the sun. I so want to learn more from them. Binna makes me feel like nothing is impossible.' Zena smiled at her niece.

'It's like my mind was so vacant before, and I was so angry I wanted to punch someone, but now there is a stillness like I'm saying goodbye to my old fears, my old thoughts.'

Zena responded, 'I'm so pleased. Alan and I have noticed the difference. Woori has been good for you. By the time the investigation commences, you'll be stronger, my darling girl.' Lisa hoped she was right as that was truly a dark cloud that hung over her happiness.

'I need to get going with my chores now, pigs and chooks, wash Neddy and get into the paddock basher!'

'Be careful with that, Lisa. Just take your time. I know Alan sat with you a couple of times, but mind the gears and just circle the paddocks. There is no hurry out here.' Zena grinned. The girl was happy and planning things. She was healing.

'By the way, I've prepared a formal letter to the police about the Parramatta Girls Home, the sexual abuse from the superintendent, as well as in the family home in relation to Lenny. So we just need to attach the documents. Detective Collette asked me to mark the correspondence personal and to his attention. He'll be in touch when things start moving. I'll keep the statements and information you provided separate, as we have done, Lisa. I also gave him Jane Fothergill's details at the child authorities so they can liaise with her superiors.'

'I don't know what to say, Aunty.' Lisa trembled in shock, and the peace she had been feeling quickly deserted her. She never wanted to face any of these people again. Just seeing their faces would make her ill. Panicking, Lisa suddenly wasn't sure if she could go through with this. Tears filled her eyes.

Zena came over to her immediately. 'I know it will be hard, Lisa. A long and difficult road lies ahead, but Alan and I will be with you all the way. You don't need to do anything at this stage. Let the police begin their investigations and when the time comes, you just need to be ready for their questions. A court room can resemble a battlefield. All parties will vigorously deny your allegations. People may not even believe you. I just hope some of the girls at the home come forward and that fear won't prevent them from speaking. My gut feeling is that once the door is open, they will all come forward, only because of your courage.'

'But why wouldn't people believe me, Aunty?' Lisa asked in a state of disbelief.

'Because it's a man's world and there is the old line: innocent until proven guilty. Your statements are concrete but their barrister will try to tear these down. It's their job. That's what they're paid to do.'

Lisa covered her face with her hands and began to sob. 'No, I don't want to do this.' Zena put her arms around her niece. 'This is when you need to be your bravest. You have done nothing wrong, but they will try to shame you. We have to be strong and be prepared. We'll work with the detectives and the police. They are on our side.'

Rage suddenly coursed through Lisa. 'I hate them, Aunty,' she cried. 'I want them locked away for the rest of their lives, to rot in a cold cell, to feel the despair and loneliness I felt at their hands.'

'Lisa, yes I agree. That's why we remain strong enough to testify and to give the evidence. Those bastards will get put away but we have to focus on providing hard facts and stay in control.' Zena kissed her forehead.

'I'm so sorry to crash your world when you came in so happy but anything involving sexual allegations against men is difficult to prove. Some of them get away with it but my heart tells me not this time. The other girls in the home will come forward and assist in this process, I'm sure of it. But I don't know how in God's name any court could think a thirteen-year-old virgin was enticing men.'

Lisa nodded, her face flushed with anger. 'I want to beat those bastards. People have to believe me, Aunty. Those monsters cannot be free . . . EVER! She thumped her fist on the kitchen table.

EIGHTEEN

BILLY

After a fretful night's sleep, Lisa headed down to the shearing shed with Alan the next morning. 'Come on kid, hop on, can't waste any time.'

'Who will be there?' asked Lisa as she swung her leg over the bike. 'The whole crew should be there by now,' said Alan excitedly. 'If I know Jack, he'll have them all sorted.' He roared down the road and pulled up in a cloud of red dust.

Alan shook Jack's hand and began introducing Lisa to those he knew. Jack was a man mountain with a grin like the Great Dividing Range. Lisa liked him. She also met Cookie, the wiry old chef, and Harry, his best mate. They were an odd-looking pair, but Alan said they'd been friends for years and travelled everywhere together. Ned was another shearer who had terrible bow legs. Alan said you could fit three sheep under them.

'Never trust a skinny chef,' Alan said, looking at Cookie. Harry had more chins than a Chinese phone book from too much food. He had sparkly eyes but seemed to have trouble breathing. 'Too bloody fat, Lisa, that's why,' Harry snorted when he caught her staring at him. She had to stifle a giggle.

Cookie was hanging up his cow bell. 'What's the bell for?' Lisa asked.

'Well, little lady, I clang this bell to let everyone know the grub is on. Ain't got time to pussy foot around and invite them one by one. One good ring of this and they all know. I prepare all the meals, and if they don't come when I ring this, they miss out. They can bugger off because the grub is then gone.'

'I'm glad you and Harry are back here,' stated Alan. 'Can't wait to taste your cocky's joy again and the tea you boil in the billy. It makes me grow a bloody beard overnight!'

'What's cocky's joy, Alan?' Lisa asked curiously.

'Good old Golden Syrup. Cookie makes a great damper, and we splash that syrup all over it. Bloody good stuff. I'm salivating now.' He laughed then pointed to the kelpies. 'You'll soon see why kelpies are so important, Lisa. They do the work of three men and are a valuable part of the team. A bloke has got to have his dogs. The jackaroos do a lot of great work as well. They always help me fix up the fences and a few other things while they are here. Good blokes.'

Alan went on to tell Lisa, 'Jack said old Burnu has brought his son with him this year, and another great bloke is Jimmy. He's done a few seasons with me before. Jimmy is a bloody good horseman but likes a drink, and he has a mean temper. Quick to light up like a fire cracker. Both are only young, but Burnu's son is the better of the two. I think it's all that bloody testosterone. Bit of rivalry in everything they do. You'll get to know them all over the season.'

Alan, Jack and Lisa walked across to some salt bush where a very black man sat. His hair was white. He had a small fire going and sat smoking. Around him were more small tents, humpies Alan called them. The Aboriginal name was gunyah, and they were temporary shelters for the stockmen. Aboriginal women sat in them with their small children. This was the black's camp. The older man stood as they approached him.

'Boss Jack, boss Alan, me ready to work alright,' said Burnu.

'That's good, Burnu. How have you been?' asked Alan as both men shook the old man's hand.

'Bin alright, Boss. My boy keepin' me out of trouble.'

Alan then turned to Lisa and introduced her to Burnu. His brown eyes looked at Lisa intensely. An eagle circled high in the air. All eyes lifted to the sky.

'Spirit bird, a good sign, boss. Maybe good luck sign, your niece.'

'Not in my bloody books, Burnu,' Alan scoffed. 'Those eagles take too many lambs for my liking. Between them and the dingoes, they keep me on my toes. My 303 comes in handy.'

'She fine-looking girl, boss. Strong, plenty strong.' Lisa giggled. She liked Burnu already. He had a sparkle in his big old brown eyes. His hands were leathery, and his fingers were bent and gnarled, thickening at the knuckles, but he also had a presence about him. She felt she could trust him.

'Eagle, powerful bird of prey . . . he circle around here. You bring 'em here, girly. You got the spirits close to you,' Burnu observed. Lisa's eyes widened in fascination.

Jack spoke up. 'Make sure you keep the jackaroos in line, Burnu. There are a few young ones this season, and it looks like we'll have a great shearing season—fat lambs, good wool, so lots of work to do.'

'Yes, boss. Me ready. Me sort dem lazy buggers. Bring my boy to work this year. He plenty good fella, alright. Proper useful. Good stockman. He gone riding, chasing goanna. Be back later but ready for work tomorrow.' Burnu seemed very proud when he spoke of his boy.

'I look forward to seeing him again, Burnu. Heard he went walkabout. You blokes get those young boys sorted quickly into manhood,' Alan grinned.

Burnu nodded. His eyes shone.

'We'll have the usual dinner tonight so tell the boys. I've killed a steer and will bring it down later. Zena has knocked up a few salads and we have cases of beer.' Alan tipped his hat and then walked back to the shearing shed.

'Who's Burnu?' Lisa asked as they got back on the bike, ready to head to the homestead.

'He was a great stockman and could ride a horse blind, still can, but age and grog has slowed him up a bit. He has a cracker of a son who did a couple of seasons with us and then went walkabout. Heard he headed north to work after that, but Burnu said he's here this season. Burnu means warrior, and fifteen years ago, he looked it. Still has a good seat. He's become a friend over the years, and would do anything for you. Good bloke, proper good, as they would say,' Alan chuckled.

'You were right, Alan, I liked them all,' Lisa enthused. 'Yeah, crazy bunch, as I said, it's hard work, but geez a lot of fun during the season. I'll drop you off here, get your chores done and help Zena for the food tonight. I just have a few paperwork things to do.'

Lisa headed out in the paddock basher, feeling confident and very grown up behind the wheel. Mastering the gears was not as difficult as she expected. As she got to the pig shed, she noticed a dust storm in the distance but as she looked closer, she could see a horse doing circles, and the rider seemed to be chasing something. The horse moved quickly, and Lisa could plainly see the agility of the rider. They moved together well, she thought. Must be a stockman. She finished her chores and headed back to the house, only to find her aunt had already finished with all the preparations. After a quick shower, they all headed down in the ute to the shearing shed for a fun afternoon and evening of festivities.

As they pulled up, Alan commented, 'The mob has gathered already. Ready for some good tucker no doubt!' Zena and Lisa went to the back of the ute and carried the salads into the little lean-to, which they covered with a cloth. All the food looked delicious, and Lisa was hungry. Jack rang Cookie's bell and there was silence.

Alan spoke. 'Welcome to Woori and our fifteenth season. I thank you for the good work you will do. Please enjoy our hospitality this day. The sheep are fat and heavy with wool and you have much work ahead of you. But not tonight. Tonight is for fun!' Alan raised his beer and there were cheers.

Lisa could see the respect the workers all had for Jack and Alan. All her life she had heard stories about the laziness of Aborigines and their inability to mix with whites, but this was not apparent today.

'Where's your boy, Burnu?' Jack asked as Burnu wandered over to say hello.

'He comin', boss. Lookem up road there. The cloud of dust. My boy get a goanna. Catch 'em good. He lucky.' Burnu smiled. The rider came closer into view. His black horse was magnificent, and the rider himself was tall and lean and sat firmly in the saddle. Across his broad shoulders was a dead goanna. When he pulled his horse up, near the black's camp, he threw the goanna to the ground.

'Goanna, boss. Taste plenty good.' Burnu carried the goanna towards the open fire and placed it over the hot coals.

Alan and Jack realised it was Billy. Burnu motioned Billy towards the men, and he slid easily off his horse.

'Geez, Billy. Mate, you've grown,' said Alan as he shook his hand. 'Fine-looking lad, Burnu. Welcome back, Billy. Glad to have you here.'

'Yep, me good horseman, boss, nearly a man now, seventeen,' said Billy proudly.

Lisa had come out of the lean-to and she stood still, just staring at the vision of the young Aboriginal man. He was the same one she had met at the RSL. The same one she'd seen at the river, who'd just left without a word.

'That's a fine looking horse, too,' commented Alan.

'My horse, Jed, been working him for two years now. Got him as a colt. Here to work hard, boss.' Alan patted him affectionately on the back. 'Glad to have you here, Billy. Help yourself. Lisa, come over here and meet this special young man.'

Lisa walked slowly towards Billy. He had a mischievous grin on his face, and he took his big black hat off and bowed, holding his hat to his chest. The men roared with laughter, which then set everyone else off.

'Stupid black bastard,' said Cookie affectionately.

'Billy, this is my lovely young niece, Lisa,' introduced Alan as he placed a protective arm around her.

'Proper good lady, boss. Can she ride?' asked Billy, his eyes never leaving Lisa's.

'Just learning, Billy, and not a bad seat, but you're welcome to give her some lessons.'

'Yes, boss fella.' Billy's smile could not get any wider, and Lisa blushed. She heard Jack call out to start playing the harmonica, and Ned, a shearer, had an old guitar, so the music began. Alan carved the meat into chunks and one by one, everyone trooped past the lean-to to help themselves to bread and salads. The fire was big and bright, and it was great to sit on the hay bales and watch the flames flicker. A freshly killed steer on an open fire never tasted so good. Lisa went back for seconds and as she moved, Billy got up and joined her.

'You wanum grub? Me cut for you. Me happy to see you again.' He took her plate and as he did so, his hand brushed against Lisa's wrist. She trembled. She didn't like to be this close. The fear of strangers or men she didn't know was still present. Billy pulled out a large knife and sliced the meat easily.

'How much you want?' he asked, smiling.

'Just a couple of pieces, please, Billy. It does taste good.'

'Sure does,' he winked and followed with his plate to sit next to Lisa.

'You likum try some goanna?' Billy asked.

'Oh, I don't think so. What does it taste like? It might make me sick.'

'No. Goanna taste like chicken. That's why Burnu say find him big goanna.' Lisa laughed. She liked his ease of manner and there was no pretence about him.

'I met your father Burnu today. He is lovely.'

'He clever big pella, slow down now, but still proper good.' Billy got up and began slicing more meat. He then walked over to the humpies. There were about six small children, and they all came running towards him, surrounding him and chattering in their native language. He put the meat on a small table next to their fire. Picking up one little girl, he twirled her around, speaking affectionately to her.

Billy returned and began to slice the goanna. He took a chunk of meat at the end of his knife and handed it to Lisa. She hesitated but then reached out to the meat and placed it in her mouth. Much to her surprise, it was delicious. Lisa smiled at Billy. 'Thank you. I stand corrected but I am so full I can't eat anymore.'

'I cut goanna and more chunks of meat now for the children,' said Billy. 'Don't want no waste, missus.' He moved around the camp with the children, stockmen and shearers. He had an infectious laugh and everyone seemed to have time for Billy. The beer and rum flowed, and the music got louder. It was a wonderful feeling for Lisa to sit under the stars and listen to the tunes the shearers played. It was about 8.00 p.m. when

Alan stood up and said his final goodnight. Zena stood by his side.

'Thank you all, my friends,' Alan exclaimed. 'I shall see you in the morning. It's been a wonderful start to the shearing season.' He turned to Jack. 'Make sure you carve up the steer and throw it in the fridges for whoever wants the leftovers. Let them get a skinful and drink themselves into oblivion. Shitfaced at the beginning of the season and shitfaced at the end of the season. But not during. If anyone gives you any strife, you know how to deal with it.' The two men shook hands.

Lisa looked for Billy, but he was nowhere to be seen. As she turned to follow Alan and Zena to the ute, Billy was suddenly in front of her. *Where did he come from so quickly?* Lisa looked into those soft velvet-brown eyes once again. He had the same presence . . . similar to Binna. She breathed in sharply and stepped back. 'Goodnight, Billy. I may see you tomorrow,' Lisa said shyly.

Billy tipped his hat cheekily. 'Night, missus, big boss, Lisa.'

'And to you,' Alan replied. 'Not too much grog tonight, Billy. Big day ahead.'

'No, boss. Me like to keep proper good.' He watched as the ute drove off into the night.

◊

When Billy walked over to where Burnu was sitting, Jimmy the other stockman sat by the fire, poking the hot coals.

'Bin watching you, Billy. You got da eyes for dat niece. You bring trouble for us blackfellas.'

Billy ignored him and sat next to Burnu. The air crackled. Burnu knew there was rivalry between the two young men. Same age, both good horsemen and plenty strong but Jimmy was quick to light up, and his temper could be ferocious.

'Arsehole, you, Billy . . . you don't speak now? How come? White woman cast her spell?' Jimmy was taunting Billy.

Burnu turned towards Jimmy and pointed his finger. 'No more bad talk. Here to do a proper good job for boss man Alan. Shut up, Jimmy.'

The two young men stared each other down. Jimmy's eyes were blazing. He suddenly stood up and stomped off into the blackness of the night.

'Bastard,' Jimmy yelled as they watched him disappear into the night.

NINETEEN

CLICK GO THE SHEARS

Alan described the rules of the shearing shed to Lisa. 'I know it was a bit of a party yesterday, Lisa, but from now on, it's strictly business with the team,' said Alan. 'The shearing shed really hums with activity during the season. The role of the shearer is to remove the wool effectively without injuring the sheep. The shearers pay for their keep out of their wages. The shed has boundaries and it's usually three areas. The board is the realm of the shearers, the wool room is run by the classers and the yards are run by the head stockperson. The whole operation is then overseen by the station manager or the owner. That's Jack and me. When you've finished your chores, come down and watch.'

'Okay, sounds good,' she replied. 'I think I'll have to learn some pidgin, though. I sometimes have to think hard about what they just said to me.' Alan laughed. 'You'll catch on quickly, let me tell you.'

Alan threw his big Akubra hat on and headed out the door. Lisa could not stop thinking about Billy as she completed her tasks for the day. As she drove towards the shearing shed, Billy came into view. He was herding sheep into pens with the dogs, and his horse Jed seemed to spin on a penny.

Alan saw his niece and waved as she pulled up. 'Come up to the shed, Lisa.' As she came up the steps, she could hear the steady hum of the shearing gear and the men all talking. It was a hive of activity. Alan put his arm around Lisa's shoulder and guided her up the plank into the room where the men were shearing. 'The more sheep they shear, the more money they earn,' said Alan.

Harry looked up as they entered the room. 'Ducks on a pond,' he quipped. The shearers looked up momentarily. Alan laughed. He knew what the message meant.

'What's ducks on a pond?' asked Lisa, confused.

'If a lady enters the shed, it's the saying for all men to take note. It's so they curtail their swearing. Sometimes the air is blue.'

'Oh, I see.' The men were sweating but their agility in moving the big sheep around without damaging them was fascinating to watch. The wool was quickly carried away for classification.

'The wool has to be classed accurately,' explained Alan. 'This takes into account its fineness, strength, colour and condition, and the fleece is put into the appropriate bins and then pressed into a bale.'

'No wonder their hands and knuckles are so big, they never stop,' remarked Lisa. She walked over to where the fleece was being classed. 'It's so soft,' she murmured as she turned the fleece around on the table.

'Darn right,' said old Ben, another shearer. 'Plenty of good jumpers there, missy.'

Lisa wandered back over to Alan. 'I'm off for a ride. Binna promised to tell me another story.' Lisa wanted to sit with Binna and feel the calmness she projected. The news of the pending investigation and the possibility she may not be believed was gnawing at the pit of her stomach. As Lisa came out of the shed, Billy was standing near the ute.

'Hi Billy, how's your day going?' Lisa asked.

'Bin up early, missus, got my part done. Maybe later, I get crackin' again,' said Billy.

'I'm riding down to the river to get more practice. You can join me if you wish and tell me what I'm doing wrong. I'll be heading out in about thirty minutes.'

He smiled that broad grin. 'I'll catch you on the road.'

Lisa was riding for a short time when she heard the sound of hooves behind her. Billy trotted up beside her on Jed and flashed that smile. She felt a little nervous but she had told Alan where she was heading. 'You got good seat, missus. Bin watching you. Just practice now.'

'Thank you, Billy. I've still a way to go, but I want to be as good as my aunt,' said Lisa.

'Yes, she plenty good, that boss missus. I bin seeing her ride. I think she outride me!'

Lisa laughed. His charming personality was very infectious, and she could see why he drew such attention from everyone.

'Why did you walk away from me the other day down at the river or not even speak?' Lisa had to ask.

'I bin for a swim, missus, and was sitting thinkin' when I heard your horse. I had to leave and get back to the sheep, but I thought maybe big trouble for me, being out there.'

'Well, I haven't told anyone, Billy. And anyway, I told Alan I was heading out here today and he even said you could give me a few lessons. So relax.'

Billy nodded. They rode side by side, chatting about the shearing season until Binna's humpy came into view.

'You met Binna and Ningali?' asked Billy.

'Yes, they're wonderful women, and I've already heard one Dreamtime story. I want to hear more.'

'Binna powerful, plenty powerful. She don't look it, little old lady with da white eyes, nearly blind, but she has da spirits inside her. Hey, I can tell you some story too,' said Billy excitedly.

'Really? I thought it was just the elders who could do that.'

'No way. I tell some good talk stories but dem girls got lots more than me,' Billy chuckled.

Ningali stood up, hands on hips as she saw the two riders approaching. She looked down at Binna. 'Little missus is riding towards us, and she has dat jackaroo Billy with her. Not good, white folks being seen out on their own with a black man.' Binna said nothing.

'Morning Ningali, Binna. Um . . . this is Billy,' said Lisa. She wondered why Ningali looked apprehensive.

'Yeah, we know Billy, seen dat Billy before,' said Ningali. She eyed him suspiciously. 'You bin growing, Billy. Like a man now.'

'Yep, me plenty big and doing alright, Ningali.' Billy seemed proud that he was being addressed as a man.

'Where you two heading?' asked Ningali.

'We're going to the river. Billy is giving me more riding instruction,' replied Lisa excitedly.

'Hello, Binna.' Lisa came and squatted down in the dirt opposite her. She took the elderly lady's hand.

'I wondered if you have time to tell me a story. I love your stories. They make me feel energised.'

Binna reached out and touched Lisa's face. The old lady said, 'I tell you story of kangaroo. Why kangaroo got his pouch. Dat one good story.'

Binna started. She sat almost trance-like and closed her eyes. 'Long time ago, mother kangaroo was looking for food with her joey along da river bank when dey came across an old blind wombat. Dat fella, he looked very sick and hungry. Da kangaroo offered to help him find grass but she was worried may lose her joey. He was always getting lost. Mother kangaroo noticed a hunter looking at dat wombat, and da kangaroo, she thumped her tail to scare da hunter away. But da wombat was a true spirit in disguise who come from da skies. His gift to da kangaroo for saving his life was to give her a pouch. So, all da kangaroos have a pouch so dem never lose their joeys.'

Binna stopped and took a deep breath. 'Da spirits and the gods come from the sky,' she proclaimed as she pointed upwards.

Lisa loved listening to these stories. 'That was wonderful, Binna. When I look at the kangaroos, I'll remember your story. I may be back tomorrow or the following day. My aunt said to bring you out some bread she was making. Goodbye, Ningali, Goodbye, Binna. You are my special friends.' The old lady smiled.

◊

Ningali watched them curiously as they rode away. 'I feel trouble, Binna, big trouble. Dat Billy, he a good-looking boy–man now, but those whiteys would not be liking this. Billy has da special gift with people and horses and all da animals. He have da power when he's older, like his father Burnu. But plenty bad, this whitey girl/black boy mix.' Ningali squatted and drew two figures in the dirt with a line down the middle.

Binna looked straight at her daughter. 'Burnu, he liked by da spirits. Dey protect him. Dey protect Billy. Dat boy is good. He love da earth, he is like da nature. Free spirit. He has da same gift as Burnu,' said Binna. 'You worry too much.'

Ningali wasn't so sure. She felt a storm was brewing.

◊

When they got to the river, Billy came around to Lisa and helped her down off Neddy. 'I'm good, Billy. I can do this without help.' He sensed she wanted to avoid his touch.

'I know, but Billy just want to do it for you.' After she dismounted, he stood staring down at her. She was beautiful, but he sensed her panic and fear if he got too close. She was like a grasshopper as he had earlier thought. Twitchy. He compared her to the Aboriginal girls who were fun and easy. He wrestled with them, and they laughed. There was no tension or restraint. With Lisa, he could sense a spirit that had been damaged. She bin smashed . . . Somewhere. But why and when?

'Do you wanna swim?' Billy asked. Lisa looked down at the ground and said shyly, 'Um, no. I'm happy to sit.'

Lisa squatted with her arms around her knees. She wanted to protect herself. After a while, Billy could sense that she was starting to relax a little around him. He was reading her mind and soul. He knew he should sit not too close and avoid touching her. But he wanted her to connect with him. After sitting in silence enjoying the surrounds for a bit, they began to chat easily. Her initial nervousness began to fade.

Lisa ventured, 'Do you ever go to the dances at the RSL, Billy?'

'No, missus. Blacks not allowed. I don't like dem smoky joints anyway. I like to feel da air and stars around me at night. Like to smell da eucalyptus and hear da kookaburra laugh. Feel good here,' he said as he placed his hand on his heart.

'Nature boy,' Lisa giggled. 'Yes, me too. I do love the outdoors. It's the colours, the space, it's so deep in my soul now. Suburbia seems like a zillion miles away. Another lifetime,' Lisa mused. 'Hey, I was sidetracked for a bit then. Sorry. In Walgett they have a cinema that my aunt said shows pictures. Are you allowed there?'

'Yes, missus. I bin there before, plenty good but smoky. Blacks sit in their own spot.'

'What . . . what spot!' she spluttered. 'That's not fair, what do you mean your own spot?'

Billy saw a flash of anger in her, and he paused briefly to meet her gaze. He started to laugh. 'Grasshopper, she has da fire.'

Lisa pushed Billy's shoulder. It was the first time she had touched him. He thought to himself, *She letting go a bit.* But nothing with this girl could be rushed, although he already knew he would fight the stars for her.

'Okay, ha ha, very funny. Well, what I'm trying to say if you will stop laughing for a minute is if we go into town this weekend, would you like to come and watch whatever picture is playing?'

'Yes, missus, but how do I go into town with my horse? Dat very long ride.' Billy was teasing her.

'With us, silly. We wouldn't expect you to ride. I'm sure my aunt won't mind. She likes you. They both do.'

As they began to head back on their horses, Billy talked about the trees and the cockatoos and how he hunted for food. 'Walkabout teach you lots,' he told Lisa.

'Alan said it's like a rite of passage. Is that true? That the young boys go on a journey during adolescence and they live in the bush for a long time to make that spiritual and traditional transition into manhood?' Lisa queried.

'Boss Alan right, Lisa. Da elders teach you all about dem spirits, laws of da land and tradition. We get secrets from da elders about bush tucker and how to survive out there. Some boys, only young, maybe ten, but they can be from ten to sixteen. Walkabout take up to six months. You live and survive on your own. Not easy, missus, and you have to prove you can do it. Da elders decide when boys ready. Maybe sometimes walk 1,000 miles and you have to hunt, make your own shelters, find da healing plants. When you pass, you get da body paint, get decorated. But, it is not about da walk, Lisa. It's about time to think and discover yourself. Dis is when we find da spirits. We are guided by da spirits and some find dat spiritual power. So walkabout is a journey, for up here too.' Billy pointed to his head.

'You mean your mind, Billy?' Lisa was in awe. 'Yes, missus.' Billy pointed to his teeth. 'Lucky I still got 'em all.' He suddenly stopped his horse and dismounted. 'Just stretching the legs, missus, get some water.'

'Good idea, Billy,' Lisa agreed as her legs hit the ground.

'What happens to your teeth then?' asked Lisa, thinking of a teeth-pulling ritual and the pain. She grimaced.

'Sometimes, some boys, dey get their teeth pulled. Elders like to give a symbol. Mmm, maybe like ornament. But on da body. Means we pass through initiation from boy to man. So,' Billy chuckled, 'maybe tooth taken, maybe nose or ear pierced or body cut with sacred markings. I feel da spirits all about me, dey are very strong.' Billy stood and waved an arm across the sky. 'They guide me, follow me.'

Billy looked down at Lisa. 'Does it frighten you grasshopper . . . dem spirits?'

'Oh no Billy, it . . . it's just that you sound so much like Binna . . . and she sees things. Sees into me.'

He sat down next to her and reached out. Lisa flinched. Billy cocked his head to one side. 'You afraid, missus. Billy not hurt you. Never. You twitch and hop, move away. Billy sees. Dat why I call you grasshopper. Moving here and there, twitching your legs. You nervous. Ready to jump.'

Lisa's face flushed as he studied her. 'Uh, I just like to keep a distance from . . . from men, people I don't really know.' Lisa looked down to the ground. Billy noticed she didn't want to make eye contact, but reached out to her very slowly. One finger came under her chin and lifted her face gently, his gaze wandering over her face. He could feel her trembling.

'Billy only a friend. Be like da river, Lisa, be open and flow. I never hurt you. But I feel your pain. Someone hurt you bad?' He drew a deep breath.

'We had best go, Billy.' Lisa said, a bit uncomfortable. They mounted and had a steady canter back to the homestead. As they came closer to the homestead, Lisa saw the ute parked outside the compound. It was late afternoon. They pulled the horses up slowly. An awareness crackled between them. 'I'll say goodbye now, Billy, and I thank you for a lovely day. I'll ask my aunt about the picture show and let you know.' Billy tipped his hat, the humour dancing in his eyes. 'Thank you, grasshopper.'

After hosing Neddy down and giving him a bale of hay, Lisa raced to tell her aunt about her day and to see if she could take Billy to the pictures with her. Her aunt sat with Alan and they were both reading sheet music as she entered the kitchen.

'You look happy, young lady. How was the day?' asked Alan.

'It was the best,' Lisa gushed as she grabbed some cool water from the fridge. 'The time with Binna was special, and Billy is such a good horseman. We chatted all the way down and back about the bush, walkabout, riding, horses and—'

'Whoa, slow down,' laughed Zena. 'Catch your breath, girl. We gather you've had fun.' Lisa sat and took a deep breath. 'I think I'll soon be ready for a gallop. I'm used to Neddy now, and he is probably used to my boots. But Billy said be patient.'

'Billy is right, Lisa,' said Alan.

Lisa knew she was getting ahead of herself. She was rambling about her day, but deep in the pit of her stomach were butterflies about asking her aunt if Billy could come with them to Walgett this Saturday. She suddenly lost her nerve. *I'll ask tomorrow*, she thought. *It will be my birthday wish*. She excused herself and concentrated on her School of Air lessons for the rest of the afternoon.

◊

After Lisa left the kitchen to continue her school lessons, Alan wondered about the bright young girl who was clearly stepping into her own. The air had been crackling around her, and he knew there was a lot more to the day than his niece was letting on. She was clearly enjoying the company of Billy. This was a good thing as she was developing trust, but on the other hand, the racial issues were never going away as far as he could see. He didn't want his niece to get involved with the young black boy. He could only see sorrow and pain if anything developed. The girl had already suffered too much pain in her life. Worry furrowed his brow. It could spell trouble for both or it could be nothing. Alan looked over at Zena. They spoke to each across the table with their eyes. He knew she sensed the danger as well, the danger this interracial friendship could bring to everyone involved.

It was Lisa's birthday tomorrow. Sweet sixteen. It would just be the three of them celebrating. He wondered if her parents would ring. Alan sincerely hoped not.

◊

Lisa rubbed the sleep from her eyes. She could smell the bacon and eggs wafting through the house. *I'm sixteen today,* she thought to herself. *Happy Birthday, Lisa.* She thought of Fairfield and all her previous birthdays. She thought of her brother. *Wish you were here, Mark. You'd love it on the farm.* Putting her thoughts aside for the moment, Lisa bounded out of bed, pulled on some clothes and wandered into the kitchen, her stomach rumbling at the smell of all that food.

'Morning, Lisa,' her aunt and uncle greeted as she stepped into the kitchen. Her aunt had been busy. She must have been up since dawn making the huge breakfast spread that was already laid out on the table.

'Morning, you two,' Lisa replied sheepishly.

Alan and Zena suddenly burst into song with gusto. 'Happy birthday to you, happy birthday to you, happy birthday, dear Lisa, happy birthday to you!' Lisa blushed but was secretly enjoying every minute of it. There had never been a fuss at home, but her aunt and uncle made her feel so very special. She shivered inside.

'Gosh, you sang that so well.' She started to giggle, and then noticed the saddle on the chair in the corner.

'Oh, what's that!' she squealed, pointing to the saddle.

'All yours, kid. The new horse will come later,' smiled Alan.

Lisa jumped out of her chair and ran towards the saddle. 'It's so beautiful,' she admired, running her hands across the brown leather. 'I love it!' She hugged Zena and Alan. 'It's the best birthday ever, and the best birthday present too.'

Zena opened the fridge and pulled out the cake. Alan lit the candle and another happy birthday song flowed. 'Come on, blow out the candle and make a wish. You cannot tell us though, bad luck,' said Zena.

Lisa blew hard and then smiled, her whole face lit up thinking of Billy and the possibility of him coming to Walgett with them. *I wonder if she knows what I just wished for?*

TWENTY

THE RSL

After a busy day with chores and School of Air, they all sat down to Lisa's birthday dinner. Zena had set the table beautifully with her best white tablecloth and cutlery, and candles were lit, capturing a soft gentle mood. Bunches of eucalyptus were in large vases and the smell wafted through the air. It was magical. Over dinner, Lisa chatted about the walkabout rituals.

'Yes, it's quite unique,' Alan remarked. 'In turning them from boys to men, the elders basically leave the youngsters out in the desert to survive. Not many white boys could do that.'

'Are we going into Walgett this Saturday? Lisa asked. 'I would love to go to the picture show and I wondered . . . um, if Billy could come. He said it's smoky inside the cinema, but that's okay. I don't mind the smoke, but it would be nice to sit in the cinema and wait for you instead of wandering the streets. What do you think, Aunty?'

Zena smiled at her enthusiasm. She knew Lisa had progressed but still had a long way to go regarding the mental trauma and sexual abuse she had sustained. However, this was a girl now asking questions, getting on with life and healing.

Zena also knew the pending police investigation was never far from Lisa's mind. She didn't want to deny her anything at this stage.

'Well, as a matter of fact, we are heading to Walgett. I don't see Billy coming along as a problem,' said Zena. 'What are your thoughts, Alan?'

He lit a cigarette and took a long deep drag. 'No problem, but Lisa, you need to know the boundaries between blacks and whites. You may experience issues with some people. You cannot retaliate. It's just the way things are at this stage. Promise me you'll make a mental note of that.'

Lisa frowned. 'What sort of issues?'

Alan sighed. 'Some people just don't like blacks. You sitting or just being with Billy may cause some people to say, well, say things that aren't nice, but rather offensive and cruel, actually.'

'Oh,' Lisa's face saddened. 'Is that a no, Alan?'

'Nope, but just making you aware.'

'So that means Billy can come?'

'You get a yes on both fronts, Lisa.'

'Yippee, that's great! Lisa exclaimed. 'I'll let Billy know. Thank you for making my birthday so special . . . for making me feel so special and for this beautiful night. It's been the best birthday ever.'

'Darling girl, it was our pleasure,' smiled Zena.

'May I be excused? I want to read the book Alan gave me about the early settlers of the Dubbo and Walgett areas.' Zena nodded and Lisa left the room. It was the first book her niece had wanted to read in a long time.

◊

'Looks like they're forming a good friendship,' said Alan, rubbing his chin. 'Billy's a kind boy and very respected for his horsemanship. Good worker too, just like Burnu. But I worry about the consequences of them forming a relationship, albeit as friends. It does look odd—a very attractive white girl and a young dark boy.'

'Yes, I know what you mean, Alan, but I don't want to pull the reins in. He's the first boy she's trusted since everything she's been through. I never thought that even possible.'

'I know that, Zena. But there's also an issue of the rivalry between him and Jimmy. I've noticed Jimmy watches Lisa too, when she comes down to the sheds. Jealousy can be a dangerous thing, and Jimmy has a foul temper. We're lucky that Jack keeps him in line.'

'Testosterone and rivalry, what a combination. Anyway, as you said, you have Jack down there, and he'll sort them. As for my girl, she's just young, as is Billy. I want them to be friends, but nothing further, if you know what I mean,' Zena added.

Alan nodded. 'I think I do, but the heart wants what the heart wants. And the heart is not worried about the colour of the skin. I know Billy is not that dark, but he is Aboriginal. A lot of people don't like the races mixing, although some don't give a rats and just get on with liking a person for who they are. One day it will be accepted, but not in our time. I think for now, this would be a dangerous boundary to cross, for both of them. But we may be reading too much into it and getting ahead of ourselves. They can just be good mates, and anyway, he leaves at the end of the season.'

'Yes, you're right. They are only young, and when shearing season is over, he'll go off in the bush again and that will be the end of it. He'll probably drift off somewhere, roaming the earth, like a lot of them do. She may never see him again.'

Alan stood up and grabbed a beer out of the fridge. 'Do you want one, my darling?'

Zena nodded, and they slipped outside onto the verandah. The inkiness of the night crept over the wide open plains and the moon rose higher and higher. They sat in companionable silence until it was time for bed.

◊

When Lisa woke the next morning, it was barely dawn. She was so excited that she took off without breakfast. It seemed that she was the first one up. She drove the ute to the sheds to catch Billy before he disappeared into the back paddocks to bring in the sheep. It was very hot with the rising sun, and some of the shearers were already starting work for the day.

Lisa waved to Harry and Cookie, having grown very fond of them. They seemed to be inseparable and 'always yakking' as Alan put it. She pulled the ute up in front of the black's camp. 'Burnu, have you seen, Billy?' she asked. He pointed his finger to an area in the distance where she could see the dust swirling.

'Thanks, Burnu.' The old man watched as she drove away.

As Lisa came to a stop, Billy rode up to the ute. He took off his black hat and held it to his chest. Lisa started to giggle. Those big brown eyes and long lashes. He was food for the eyes. 'Billy, good morning.'

'Morning, grasshopper. You up early.'

'Yes, I wanted to catch you. I have some good news. My aunt and uncle are heading into town tonight and they said you can come with us so we can catch the picture show. I don't know what's playing but I'm sure it will be good.'

Billy frowned. 'You sure it's alright?'

'Yes, I've checked, and you'll be with me, so it'll be fine.' She watched the smile spread across his face.

'Anyway, you can help with those blasted gates. So, be ready in your finest clobber, and we'll come past about 4.00 p.m.'

Billy nodded. 'Yes, missus. Now I have to keep moving before dem shearers get angry. Have to keep da sheep coming.'

'Okay. I have my chores too. See you later, Billy.' Lisa swung the wheel of the ute and headed back to the homestead, the smile never leaving her face. *Got my birthday wish.*

After breakfast, she disappeared with a list of things to do. Her aunt was keeping her busy. There was a note on the kitchen table. 'Dear Lisa, please take the two cakes down to the shearing shed just after lunch. We're off doing fencing. Love, Us.'

After she'd done her chores and fixed herself a sandwich for lunch, Lisa pulled out the cakes from the fridge. Yum. Chocolate and passionfruit. She ran her finger across each cake and then licked her finger. They tasted so good, the shearers would love them!

Lisa put them into a small open basket and then drove the ute down. There was a group of men outside the living quarters. Maybe they had stopped for lunch and a smoko. When she poked her head inside the shed, there were more men inside, which was unusual. She saw old Harry lying down, and his breathing appeared laboured.

'Is Harry okay?' she asked anxiously.

Cookie replied, 'He's getting old. Just catching his breath, Lisa. He'll be right, just having a breather.'

Lisa thought Harry looked pale, and he was sweating profusely. 'Can I do anything?' she enquired as she placed the cakes on a nearby table.

'Nah,' said Cookie. 'The old fart is getting on, that's all, and it don't help he's the size of a house. Blame myself though. He loves my cooking. Well, at least someone does. He'll be up and about in no time. Don't worry your pretty little head.'

Cookie reassured her again, and she left the shed. She had to let her aunt and Alan know about Harry. She didn't know which fences they would be fixing, but her aunt had mentioned they were a long way out, so she thought it best to wait for them in the house. Lisa headed back and hoped Harry would be alright.

Later that afternoon, she heard Alan's bike and the dogs barking. As they came into the kitchen, Lisa told them about Harry. 'What was wrong?' asked Alan, his concern showing.

'They just said he was an old fat fart and that Harry was catching his breath.' Alan laughed. 'Sounds like Cookie, but if it was serious, I'm sure they wouldn't stay. He's getting on and has been with me for years and is no doubt slowing down too, dear Lord, like all of us, but Harry is like a rock and has a few more years left in him.'

'I really like Harry and Cookie,' said Lisa. 'Are you sure Harry will be okay, Alan?'

'Stop stressing, Lisa. They're a pigeon pair. Cookie will settle him.'

'Where's home for them?' Lisa wanted to know.

'They have an old shack at Lightning Ridge, which they head back to after the shearing season. They fossick around for opals. Harry loves his opals. Better than diamonds, he says. It's a strange friendship between him and Cookie, and there is some talk.'

'What sort of talk?'

'Never you mind.' Alan looked at his watch. 'We have about two hours before we head off, so let's start getting organised. I'll load up the Zephyr. You two be off now and get yourselves ready.'

Alan sat patiently sipping a cold beer. *Why do women take so long to get ready?* he wondered.

'Aaaah, finally. You both look lovely. Worth the wait.'

Without any further ado, they headed out to the Zephyr. Alan had already packed the car with all the instruments and sheet music.

'Billy will be waiting down at the first gate at 4.00 p.m.' said Lisa looking at her watch. As they drove towards the first gate, Billy waved. 'There he is, Aunty!'

'Yes, I see, Lisa. Calm down,' smiled Zena. She looked at the tall, lean boy as they approached. *Handsome*, Zena inwardly acknowledged.

Alan chuckled. Billy wore a white shirt and clean jeans, with the trademark black hat shadowing his face. 'Hi Billy, welcome aboard,' said Zena.

'I'll open the gates, missus,' Billy offered.

'Good on you, boy,' Alan commented. 'Have to keep the princess in the back clean. New white dress. Not the best colour for all this red dust. You don't scrub up too bad either with the dirt off you.'

After closing the first gate, Billy slid in next to Lisa. She flinched sitting so close to him in the back seat. He looked sideways at her. 'Grasshopper,' he murmured.

'Smells nice in here, boss,' remarked Billy as he sniffed the air. Alan looked in the rear vision mirror.

'That's me, Billy,' said Alan. 'Not the ladies. I dabbed a bit of cologne on behind the ears, just for you.' They all laughed as they headed to Walgett. When they finally drove into town, it was quiet, and Billy helped them unpack their music equipment. Once everything was unloaded, Lisa and Billy headed over to see what picture was playing.

The billboard poster showed *Tarzan's Greatest Adventure*. 'This should be good, Billy!' exclaimed Lisa.

They crossed over the road, and Lisa went inside the RSL to let her aunt know what picture they'd be seeing. 'Wait here, Billy, I won't be long.'

Alan dug into his pocket and pulled out a note. 'Here's a quid. It'll be enough to get you both into the picture show and buy some popcorn. What time does it start?'

'Thanks so much, Alan. It starts at 7.00 p.m,' Lisa said.

'Well, you have a little under an hour to fill in. Grab a lemon squash and then head outside. You know where we are if the movie finishes and we're still playing. Don't forget that Billy is not allowed in the RSL. They won't even let the black ex-servicemen become members. It's bloody wrong. They served our country and they can't come in. Makes my blood boil,' Alan seethed.

Lisa remembered the story about the Freedom Riders, those university students who came up to protest about the treatment of Indigenous serviceman and Indigenous women not being allowed in dress shops. 'Why do they hate the blacks? They're great people. They're so strong and tell so many wonderful stories. If anyone is rude to Billy or Burnu or my friends Ningali and Binna, I will . . . well, I'll have something to say.'

'You're going to see more discrimination, Lisa, with the passage of time. I'm not saying turn a blind eye, but be careful,' cautioned Alan.

Her face was pinkish with anger. 'Well, I'll stand up for them. Colour shouldn't make a difference.' Lisa walked over to the bar and asked for a lemon squash. The nosy barmaid eyed her over. 'You're under age,' she snapped.

Lisa was taken aback at her rudeness. She raised her voice and retorted, 'Yes, I know, but I just wanted a lemon squash. I'm with my aunt and uncle. What's the problem?' The old barmaid's mouth flew open.

'I don't care who you're with, now nick off. Savvy.' Lisa stood her ground. Zena heard the loud voices and could see the animosity at the bar. She quickly walked over and addressed the woman. 'I see you've met my niece, Elaine. Where is John the Publican? Please tell him I want to see him.'

'She's a feisty little thing. Lucky I didn't tip the drink over her,' shot back Elaine.

Lisa fumed. The barmaid disappeared and Big John the publican appeared. He was a large man who ambled along like a bear. 'Hello, Zena, looking ravishing as always. Who's this lovely young thing?' John gestured to Lisa.

'Lisa, this is John, who runs the Walgett RSL.'

'Happy to meet you,' Lisa said as she extended her hand.

'What can I do you for?' John asked cheerily.

'My niece just wanted a lemon squash, John. She's with us until we get going tonight, before she heads to the pictures.'

'Sure, no problem. By the way, Mrs Dunphy from the haberdashery brought over the mail today. She heard you may be coming this weekend and asked the postie for your mail. Saves you waiting another week. The letters are in my office, I'll go get them.'

By the time he reappeared with the letters, Lisa was sipping on her lemon squash while the barmaid Elaine glared at her. She must have been ticked off by John as he passed by her to his office. Another person who thinks she has power!

When he returned, John handed Zena the mail and apologised. 'Sorry about Elaine's manner. Just doing her job. Not seen Lisa before.'

'No problems, John. Thank you so much. Lisa may be a regular with us.'

'Good eye candy, Zena, two beauties from the bush,' John said cheekily.

Zena turned to her niece as John ambled off. 'Well then, you go on your way, Lisa. We have to get ready, clean off the dust and freshen up. Keep your head down and remember Billy is Aboriginal. You may find there is a separate door for him to enter or even a partition. He may even be herded into a group to sit up the front.' Zena was trying to prepare her niece and soften the blow.

'You mean we'll have to sit separately?' Lisa pulled a face. 'That's not fair.'

'Lisa, it's just the law. People are frightened of things they don't understand. Since white people arrived in Australia it has

always been difficult for them to understand Aboriginal culture. Ignorance led to many thousands of Aboriginal people
being killed by white settlers. They even tried to breed out their
culture through assimilation.'

Lisa looked horrified. 'That is so bad, Aunty.'

'I know, I know and I agree, Lisa, but their justification was
that they were doing it "for their own good". I don't know how
any sane, intelligent person can agree with that. Aboriginals are
still denied their basic rights. The white man's policies stopped
access to education, receiving award wages, marrying without
permission, eating in restaurants, entering a pub, swimming in
a public pool or having the right to vote.'

'That is so racist and unfair!' said Lisa angrily.

'I'm just trying to explain the whole picture to you. There is
talk of things being amended, so both Alan and I are hoping
this gets passed through the government.'

'So I really will have to be separated from Billy at the cinema?'

'Yes, probably, my dear. Unfortunately, everyone does not
think like us. Just be aware. The Aboriginal kids are not even
allowed to use the public swimming pools here, attend the
Town Hall or even local football matches. I can remember a
sign when I was in Dubbo last year at their local pub. It said
Aborigines not allowed in the lounge without the licensee's
permission.'

Lisa just shook her head, disbelief on her face.

Zena added, 'I even had a disagreement with Mrs Dunphy.'

'Mrs Dunphy, from haberdashery? What for? She seemed so
nice?' Lisa looked puzzled.

'She wouldn't let the Aboriginal girls come in and try on
some dresses one day in her store. I ended up buying a couple
of dresses for the girls and handing them out. Gave Mrs Dun-

phy a piece of my mind. I was the talk of the town there for a while but at least I said my piece.'

Lisa laughed. She suddenly had a vision of her aunt giving Mrs Dunphy a serve. 'I love you, Aunty.'

'I love you, too. But be careful. If you get angry and cause any trouble, it will only bounce back on Billy. You'll be seen as a troublemaker, but he'll bear the repercussions.' Lisa froze, she thought of the isolation cell and Billy being put in one.

Lisa took a deep breath and hugged her aunt. *My rock, my anchor.* Walking over to the bar, she placed her glass down with a thud. 'Savvy,' she said as she glared at the barmaid and then left to find Billy.

When she got outside, Lisa's eyes searched for Billy. She didn't have to look far. He sat opposite the RSL, his eyes focused on the front door, waiting for her appearance. Lisa walked over to him, and the things her aunt had just told her rushed through her head. She would heed her advice as she wanted no trouble for her or Billy. How could they do this to him or his people? She thought of Binna and Ningali and even Burnu. Proud, good people. Billy stood up and they headed over to the picture show.

'I think da picture going to be real good,' said Billy, his brown eyes sparkling.

The elderly woman in the box office had grey hair pulled up tightly in a bun. Her face looked like she hadn't laughed in a long time. 'Two tickets, please,' said Lisa. The old woman peered at Billy for several seconds. 'That black has to sit down the front in a group on the floor.' Her mouth twitched.

'No, he's not, he's sitting with me. He's my friend.' Lisa's eyes narrowed. She was trying her luck.

'Friend!' the woman snorted. 'He's a darky and he sits down the front away from the white fellas. If you don't like it, you can piss off, the pair of you.'

Lisa looked at Billy, her anger rising. She wanted to throw something at the woman, who clearly displayed her dislike for Aborigines.

'He's not a darky. Don't call him that.' Lisa was on the attack.

Billy interjected. 'It's alright, missus. Don't want no trouble. I can sit down da front.'

This seemed to pacify the old lady. She slapped two tickets down. 'You go in this door, and he goes in that far door. Do I make myself clear?'

'Yes, very clear. It's pretty crappy, and you are just rude. You're a rude woman.' Lisa was defiant in her response and wanted to say more but kept tight lipped in case she took the tickets back. Billy sauntered off and waved as he went through the far door.

When she got inside, Lisa looked for him and smiled. He sat so tall amongst the smaller children.

The smoke curled around the lights that shone from the projection room. Billy was right. It was smoky and had a bad smell. She saw his head turn and she waved. Then the picture started.

Lisa loved the naturalness of where Tarzan lived. The movie was basically about good against evil. Four British villains raided a settlement to obtain explosives for use in a diamond mine and in doing so they nearly destroyed the settlement, so Tarzan pursued them to their mine. The children down the front clapped and cheered. It was wonderful to see the action on such a big screen. When it finished, Lisa headed to her exit door where she found Billy waiting.

'What did you think of that, Billy?'

'Pretty good, missus. Me Tarzan.' He thumped his chest.

'You are so funny,' she laughed, and they began to walk back to the RSL.

'Here, I saved you some popcorn.' They sat on the seat opposite the RSL. 'This is the seat I sat on when I first met you, Billy.'

'I remember.' She watched his long fingers take a few pieces of popcorn and pop them into his mouth. 'Salty but good.' He looked at her in the darkness. Admiration transformed his face.

'I wish you could come in to the RSL, Billy, but my aunt said you're not allowed.'

'It's alright, missus. I get used to it. We all do.' But there was a sadness about him when he said it.

'My aunt said things will hopefully be better for your people soon.' Lisa was eager to offer empathy.

Billy changed the subject, having noticed her feistiness when discussing the differences between blacks and whites and how she had challenged the lady selling the tickets.

'Popcorn is good, missus,' he said, trying to make small talk. Lisa dragged her eyes away from his strong brown hands, and her mind wandered. His mere presence made her pulse race, and his eyes seem to hold hers with a frightening intensity. He was powerful, potent and taboo.

'Hey, where did you go, grasshopper?'

'Sorry, Billy. I was just thinking. It's so hot, I was wishing it was the daytime so I could go for a swim. How come you can swim if you've never been allowed in the pool?'

'I teach myself in da rivers. Some of my friends have been allowed in to some pools, but dey get hosed down before dey allowed to swim.'

'Hosed down? Are you joking!' Lisa sighed, her voice trailing off. 'I hate it. I hate it so much. Those white people should get hosed, see how they like it.' They were interrupted by the appearance of her aunt and uncle walking out of the RSL.

'We go help dem,' said Billy.

After loading the music equipment into the Zephyr, Zena asked how the picture was.

'We loved it, but you were right, Aunty. Billy had to sit down the front.'

'Billy, I'm sorry,' apologised Zena, 'But there are some of us who hope things will change.' They all loaded into the car and began the journey home. Lisa felt sleepy in the back and her head rested on Billy's shoulder. At every gate, he gently laid her head back against the seat and when he hopped back into the car, he let her head slip back on to his shoulder. It did not go unnoticed.

'We'll be home soon, Billy. Thanks for your help, mate,' said Alan. 'Sorry about the situation at the cinema.'

'Okay, boss, all good,' Billy replied as he opened the last gate.

'See you in the morning, Billy,' said Zena as he stood watching the Zephyr head to the homestead.

Zena gently woke Lisa. 'We're home.'

'Where's Billy?' she asked sleepily.

'Heading home to bed,' said Alan, 'Big day tomorrow for the lad.'

Lisa said her good nights and closed her bedroom door. Leaving the bedside table light on, she undressed and hopped into bed. Her thoughts turned to the evening, the segregation and the treatment of Billy. Her thoughts then went to the Girls Home. People in power. Men in power who make stupid rules and treat people like shit. They do what they want. They ruin lives. She had a fitful sleep that night.

Lisa woke to the sound of the cockatoos. She stretched like a cat and looked at her crumpled white dress on the floor. *It was a good night,* she thought as a lazy smile crept across her face. *Billy is so lovely. I feel safe with him.* Rubbing her eyes, she dressed in her jeans and t-shirt and headed to the kitchen, where she could hear voices.

'Sleep well?' asked Alan.

'Yes, I did, but I did toss and turn initially when my thoughts turned to the unfairness of the black people.' She sat down and poured herself a cup of tea.

'You know your aunt's thoughts as well as mine on the subject. The wheels turn slowly, but at least they are turning. If you go back in time, Lisa, the explorer William Dampier described in his books that the Aborigines were primitive, even likening them to monkeys and the most wretched people on the earth. He would eat his words now. The Australian Aboriginals are one of the proudest, majestic people I know. They have cures for everything. But that fool's comments were made around 1690 or thereabouts. They knew no better then.'

'We can learn so much from the Aboriginal people though, Alan,' said Lisa wistfully.

'Indeed. I've seen an oil the old girls make up from leaves. They use it on blisters for the feet. It's bloody magic and works a treat. Anyway, we have about two weeks left of shearing and then they'll move to the next property or go where they need to be,' added Alan.

'Does that mean everyone goes?' asked Lisa.

'Usually. Maybe a few roustabouts remain to clean up, but basically they all move on.' Lisa felt an inner sadness. She wouldn't see Billy again after he left. Her mind went into turmoil.

'Everything alright?' Zena queried.

'Yes, fine, Aunty.' Although a thousand thoughts raced through her mind.

'By the way, we got an official letter in the mail from the New South Wales Police Force,' Zena confided.

'Why didn't you tell me!'

'I only received it last night. It was in the mail John handed me at the RSL.'

'What did they say, Aunty?' asked Lisa, frowning and fearing the worst.

'There's not a lot in it, just basically informing us of their actions. There will be an official investigation into the Parramatta Girls Home and Superintendent Ash. Maybe even a Royal Commission. They will also investigate and question Lenny. So those two vile men will be getting a visit. It may have occurred already.'

Lisa put her cup down. The Girls Home, Lenny. Her heart beat faster and her stomach churned. 'That . . . is good news.' She gritted her teeth as the words flashed in her mind, *They may not believe you.* 'I hope justice will prevail. I want them locked up forever.'

Zena reached out and took her hand. 'This will be just the start of it, Lisa. As I said before, it's going to be difficult and you'll have to re-live and speak about those sickening atrocities. We will have to be brave as they try to tear your evidence down.'

'I'm ready,' she vowed with a steely determination. She felt an inner strength that she'd not noticed before. Maybe the time in the bush and in a loving environment had made her stronger. 'I'm not letting them get away, Aunty. I'm sick of the rotten and unfair treatment people in power dish out, just because they want to. They should not have power to control or the power to inflict pain or misery.' Her voice rose with anger.

Alan looked across the table. 'Well said, Lisa, and hold that thought. Zena and I both want them behind bars. Don't let them unhinge you when the time comes. Keep that anger and remember what you just said.'

It felt good to have an opinion and to voice that opinion without being slapped or punished, unlike when she had voiced opinions at home. *I have a voice. I will use it*, she promised herself.

TWENTY-ONE

AN UNEXPECTED TURN OF EVENTS

It was early afternoon when Detective Collette called. Zena answered the phone.

'Hello, Mrs Smith, it's Detective Collette. I'm just following up my recent correspondence to you.'

Zena greeted him warmly. 'Thank you, Detective. Yes, I have received your letter and look forward to the progression of this matter.'

Detective Collette continued, 'The police have more information about Superintendent Ash, which confirms what Lisa has said in your documents. They have requested a Royal Commission into the Girls Home due to the allegations. I have also had discussions with the child authorities, so we will be liaising with them. We also want to come out and see Lisa and make our own official statements. We record these during the interview process. I'm thinking early November if that suits you?'

'Yes, that would be fine. My husband Alan and I will be here to support Lisa through this process. It will be harrowing for her, especially sitting with strange male police officers and telling them about the atrocities that have occurred.'

'That's understandable, Mrs Smith. We do have female police officers that can come with us if you like?' the detective said comfortingly.

'Under the circumstances, a female police officer would be most preferable. I know Lisa would feel more comfortable,' Zena said anxiously.

'Not a problem, I'll get on to that now for you, Mrs Smith. I'll be in touch with the exact date in November. I'll come with another male police officer, but will check which female can be present and let you know in due course.'

'Thank you so much, Detective Collette. I'm very appreciative.' Zena bade him goodbye as she hung up the phone, nervous for Lisa about the journey ahead but also pleased at the thought of justice being served.

'Well,' Alan said, having overheard the conversation, 'you gave them all that information, so they should know which way to head with their investigation, particularly about that monster of a superintendent, and Lenny.

'Yes, I know, Alan,' Zena began, 'but I'm worried about further traumatising Lisa. She has really developed and matured over the past six months. I know Binna has been partly responsible for this as well as Billy, and us. But I wonder if we should seek professional help for her. John Raby from the Walgett police said there's a very good female psychiatrist in Dubbo who specialises in sexual abuse.' Alan agreed that this may be a wise course of action, especially to help her through the court appearances. He knew how much the barristers could wear a person down.

'It's a stupid system. That the perpetrators could get away with this just because of a good barrister,' complained Zena.

'It's a sad fact. But it happens,' Alan said, rising from his chair. 'You're fretting and worrying and it's only early stages.

We have to have a plan and a strong plan at that. My thoughts would be to discuss this openly with Lisa about the police officers coming to the farm, to have all notes prepared and statements, and be the buffer zone she will so desperately require. Getting her professional counselling is a good idea, probably the sooner the better.'

'Where's Lisa now?' queried Zena.

'She's with Billy. He wanted to show her the boundaries of the property and how far the fencing goes. Just company for Billy, I guess, but surprisingly, she wanted to learn about fencing. The dingoes have her intrigued. In fact, everything has the kid intrigued. She seems to love it all.'

'I know, it's a wonderful thing,' said Zena. 'But Lisa is now asking about the shearers and when they're all leaving. So, I'm guessing she's thinking about Billy.'

'Well, he's an itinerant worker and moves around, especially as he'll still probably go on walkabout. He's still a boy at seventeen, although nearly a man. We can't keep him here, and she'll have to learn that. Shearing season will be over in a week's time.'

'Will we still have the end of season bash?' Zena asked.

'Yes, of course. The lads have worked hard and we always have a few beers at the end of the season. It's been a great year, so we'll go out with a bang and no problems whatsoever with the crew. I want them all back next year. Not sure about two of them though.'

'Oh . . . enlighten me; you've never said that before,' said Zena.

'Old Harry is one. He's had a few bad spells,' explained Alan. 'And Jimmy, there is a clear jealousy there. Harry said just quietly they came close to a punch up. Got a lot to do with Lisa I think and the fact that Billy is moving around with her. Seems to rattle Jimmy, and he's a hot head as we know.'

Alan looked at his watch. 'I best get a move on. Need to discuss a few things with Jack, including that rivalry between Billy and Jimmy, but nothing that the older blokes are not handling. I'll see you later.'

Zena followed Alan down the back steps when the ute pulled up. Lisa hopped out, her face glowing.

'Hi, darling girl, you saved me a trip. I was about to come and look for you but realised you had the ute and Alan is taking the bike.' They waved him off in a cloud of dust.

'What's up, Aunty?'

'The detective called. They'll be here in November to talk things through with you. They have all your statements, so the investigation has basically commenced. When they come here, they'll record your official interviews.'

'They won't take me away, will they?' Lisa steadied her breath and tried to calm her rising panic.

'No, not at all, it's just part of their investigation. Don't be fearful. Alan and I will be here. Come and sit down. We need a quiet space to talk this through so you understand what is coming and all the possible consequences.'

They headed to the big open sitting room and when they sat, Zena hugged her niece. 'I won't let anyone hurt you, so just relax and we'll face everything together.'

'Yes, Aunty, it's still very embarrassing. I feel so ashamed.' Those old feelings of dread and humiliation began to rise in Lisa's stomach.

'You know this will be traumatic and harrowing, and you'll have to re-live all the horrible things that happened to you. It may bring flashbacks and nightmares. I know Binna has been good for you, but there is something else I'd like to suggest.'

'What?' Lisa's voice was soft, almost childlike.

'There's a woman in Dubbo, a psychiatrist who specialises in sexual abuse. She comes to Walgett once a month. I think it would be a good idea if we make an appointment and talk to her about what has happened to you, and about what's coming in terms of the investigation. The counselling and insight she can provide will be invaluable and give you resources you never knew you had. How do you feel about this?'

There was a long silence. Zena continued, 'If we go once, and you feel okay about it, we can go again. There's no harm in trying and certainly no harm in being stronger for this investigation. I have mentioned this to you before but in court, they will try to make you look and feel bad. They'll try to make out you are lying. This is what the barristers do and they are paid handsomely to do it well.'

Zena could see that Lisa felt very vulnerable, as if the shields that protected her at Woori were being stripped away. Her voice tremored, 'I will try, Aunty. I know you're only doing what is best for me but I don't want to see their horrible faces.' Lisa began to sob, and Zena placed an arm around her.

'It's okay, darling. You're allowed to cry and there will be many more tears before this is over. But you have nothing to be ashamed of. You did nothing wrong. They will not take you away, and Alan and I are here to support you. Facing them will be shocking but there is no other way, unless they confess, and that is unlikely.'

Zena could feel Lisa shaking. She felt the girl had taken two steps back already. 'Let me make a call to John Raby at Walgett Police Station. I'll get this lady's name. Do you want to stay here or can I get you anything?'

Lisa wiped her tears. 'No, I feel like some fresh air. Billy and I are heading to the river in about thirty minutes. Taking the ute. We wanted to cool off. Hot work that fencing but it gave me a perspective on how big Woori is and all the work you and Alan do. I'd like to help if I can.'

'Yes, you wonder what we do all day when shearing is over. Now you can see that the maintenance never stops.'

'I also want to say hello to Binna and Ningali. The last time we travelled past, they weren't there.'

'They are often out foraging for bush tucker, berries and plants, so they're not always there, Lisa.'

'Also, after the season, Billy wants to take me to his secret spot as he calls it. It's a bit further than the river, but he said it's a magical and spiritual place. It's a two-day ride there and a two-day ride back, so it means we would camp out, Aunty.'

'I'm not too sure about that, Lisa. I'll have to think about it and discuss it with Alan. You do understand that all the workers will go shortly, and that includes Billy.'

'Yes, I know, Aunty. But please, I would love to see this special place. I may never see it if Billy goes.'

'As I said, Lisa, I'll discuss it with Alan. I'm worried letting you two go out by yourself. It's not the proper thing, especially in view of what has happened to you. Billy is a young man and things often happen when you are out of sight, especially way out bush. So I know you really want to go and no doubt will be disappointed if I say no, but I would only be making the best decision for you.'

Lisa hung her head. 'Okay, we'll just head out for a swim then.' Her voice was filled with sadness as she headed to her room to get her swimmers, but Zena had to make her understand that remoteness and camping out with a young Aboriginal boy may be dangerous.

Zena sensed her niece's disappointment. 'Lisa,' she called out. 'I know it sounds hard but you are both young. I always have your best interest at heart. Now on your way before the day escapes you.'

She followed her niece as she hurried down the back steps and wondered what secret place Billy was talking about. No doubt all the Aboriginals had sacred sites or special places. But Zena knew in her heart that she could not let Lisa go alone with Billy. If the barrister had this knowledge or anyone told the defence she had camped out with a black boy, her reputation would be shot. They would tear her to shreds. Sleeping out under the stars with a black boy. There was no doubting Billy was a good looking boy who was very charismatic. There was an aura, an inner strength to him but also a softness. The chemistry between them was obvious.

Billy pulled up his horse in front of the homestead, pulling her out of her reverie. Lisa stood waiting for him, sitting on the back step. Zena came down to join her. 'Afternoon, boss missus, Lisa,' said Billy, taking off his hat.

'Heading down to the river to swim?' Zena asked politely.

'Yes, missus, cool off. Bin hot today.'

'Yes, it has, Billy. Lisa was telling me about your special place that you want to visit,' said Zena.

'Yes, missus, bin there lots. My place, feel my spirits there.'

'Where exactly is it, Billy?' enquired Zena.

'Can't tell you, missus. Billy's secret.'

'Well, I need to know where it is if you intend to take my niece there,' replied Zena.

Billy hesitated and looked at Lisa, who had a sadness in her eyes, but Zena could see he understood why she was asking.

'Goobang, missus.'

'Ah, yes, I've heard of this place before. I'm not too sure, Billy, if taking Lisa there is the right thing to do. I'm sure you would understand that. But I will discuss this with Alan and let you both know.'

'Sure, missus,' Billy said.

Zena kissed her niece goodbye and watched as Billy started the ute.

'Thanks, Aunty. We won't be long, just a quick swim.' Lisa did look drained. Her mind was no doubt churning in relation to the police and the investigation, and also the fact that Billy was leaving. Zena waved goodbye and watched the ute disappear down the dusty road. Should she say yes and let Lisa go with him to Goobang and then worry herself to death, or say no, and see her girl even more despondent. Billy would probably take off after the season and wouldn't be seen again. But the thought of them out there alone. Her gut feeling was no and no.

Zena headed inside. She had to plan the end of season shearer's do and was pleased at the distraction. She heard Alan's motorbike approaching. He looked worried when he came inside. 'What's wrong, Alan?'

'It's old Harry, he's had another funny turn. Cookie has him resting on his bunk down there. I don't like the look of him; he's a funny colour, almost greyish, and his breathing is quite laboured. Told him he has to give up the durries. As if! I think he goes to sleep with a fag still in his mouth.'

'Should we call the Royal Flying Doctor?' asked Zena, sounding concerned.

'No, not just yet. See how he goes. The heat knocks him about, with all that weight and smoking. Let him rest up a bit. Where's our girl?'

'The usual—off with Billy. They took the ute so they could go for a swim. But she asked me if she could ride with him to a special place. Goobang. It's a two-day ride there and back. They would camp out for the three nights. Your thoughts?'

'He's a good boy, Billy, and well aware of the black and white issue. Interracial relationships are just not accepted. Burnu has drummed that into him. I would trust the lad, but I understand emotions and the heat of the moment. Two good-looking kids. I really don't like the sound of it, especially after everything Lisa has been through. Not one bit. I'm worried when they're around together out here, let alone camping and staying overnight! My answer would be no, Zena.'

'Oh, God, I knew you'd say that. She's going to miss him so much after the season, and she really wants to go. I don't like to say no to her or let her down.'

Alan was firm. 'Sometimes no is a good thing. You cannot say yes all the time, even though I know you're trying to please her and make up for all the shit she's gone through. I think we really need to focus on the investigation and how that will affect her. And although perceptions have progressed, it's only marginally with the different cultures, and racism is still rampant as you well know. I even heard the other day from one of the shearers a story about a whitefella in Narrandera. The shearer said he was taken by his father and uncle on a hunting party one Sunday morning to shoot Aboriginal people. So it's not a good idea, Zena.'

'Oh, Alan, that's awful. When did this happen? It should be reported.'

'Who knows, it's just the gossip in the shed. But it scares the shit out of the jackaroos. Billy would have heard that too. He may be back next year or we may never see him again. Anyway, I'm off. If Harry is worse, I'll be back to radio the Flying Doctor. You'll only see me in the next hour if he deteriorates

After some time had passed, Zena looked at her watch. It was well over an hour and Alan had not shown. Old Harry must have rallied again, but she was worried like Alan. He had been a great worker and was getting on in age. He was overweight and smoked heavily. She had noticed this season that breathing was not easy for him.

When Alan returned, his face said it all. 'I'm going into the office. I'll call the Royal Flying Doctor Service. I'm really worried about Harry.' Alan disappeared, and Zena started to prepare dinner. She heard the ute pull up a short time later.

◊

'Thanks Billy, the water was so refreshing. It's great to spend time out there. So peaceful. Shame Binna and Ningali weren't there. I really wanted to see them.'

Billy fumbled into the pocket of his jeans and pulled out a small white cloth. 'Here, dis is for you.'

'What is it?' Lisa was smiling.

'It's wrapped up, just open it.' Billy flashed a big grin.

As Lisa opened the layers of white cloth, she saw a mixture of feathers, grasses, reeds and colourful rocks, intertwined on a piece of leather. It was a necklace. 'Means you belong to my people, my family. You connect to da land now.'

'It's lovely, Billy,' gushed Lisa, holding the necklace up.

'This is tradition. My people wear dis during ceremonies. For decoration, and to help with new growth and babies. Has special meaning. My gift to you,' Billy said proudly.

'Put it on for me, Billy. I want to wear it now, please.' He carefully undid the ends and then placed it around Lisa's neck, tying it tightly.

'I love it, Billy, thank you.' Lisa beamed. He touched her face lightly with his finger. 'Grasshopper. I see you tomorrow.' He kissed her forehead tenderly and stepped away.

Lisa watched him leave and then headed inside. 'There you are, have a good swim?' asked Zena. She then noticed the necklace. 'That's lovely, where did you get that, Lisa?'

'Billy made it for me, Aunty. My birthday present.' She touched the necklace lovingly. 'It's all things from the earth. He said I'm now connected to his family, his people.'

'That is very soulful, and it's really special when something is made just for you.'

'Hey kiddo,' said Alan as he sat down. He directed his gaze at Zena. 'I spoke to Derek Burns at the Royal Flying Doctor and just put him on notice. Harry said not to make a fuss but I'd rather he go and get help or something rather than lying down there in a hot shed. Doesn't want to leave Cookie. Stubborn old bastard but I can't force him if he doesn't want to go.'

'What's going on?' asked Lisa.

'Old Harry. He's not doing so well,' replied Alan.

'Oh no, I feel so sad for him.' Lisa looked distraught.

'If he gets any worse, I'll make him go,' said Alan.

After dinner, Alan went to his study, and Zena cleared the table with Lisa. 'You wash, Lisa, and I'll wipe while we talk.' Lisa knew they had made a decision about her going to Goobang with Billy.

'Have you made up your mind about Goobang? asked Lisa as she passed a plate.

'Yes and no,' her aunt replied.

'What does that mean?'

'Well, of course it would be great for you to experience such a spiritual place with Billy. That's the yes part. But the no part is that it's not right for a young girl who has had your traumatic experiences to be travelling with a young Aboriginal boy and camping out in a remote area.'

The sadness crept over Lisa's face. 'There is only one other solution if you really want to see this place: Alan and I go with you. Instead of riding, we can take the Land Rover. We'd be there and back in a day. We could have lunch at Goobang but you have to understand my decision. I don't want you to be alone out there. You can hike around with Billy to see the place he loves. We won't get in your way. I really think this is a better solution.'

'Thank you, Aunty.' It wasn't panning out exactly like Lisa had hoped, but it was better than not going at all. 'It does sound like a good idea,' she relented, 'and I know you're looking out for me. I'll mention this to Billy.'

'We can go after the shearing season has finished, Lisa. We can get up early and head out there.'

Lisa kissed her aunt on the cheek. 'I'm turning in; I feel tired after today.'

'See you in the morning, Lisa. Goodnight sweetheart.'

Lisa thought about Goobang and Billy. She felt the softness of his kiss on her forehead. She understood her aunt's decision but was disappointed. She wanted to explore the special place with her special boy. Alone.

When she woke the next morning, the house was empty, which was nothing unusual. She dressed quickly and headed for the ute. As the shearing shed came into view, there were men crowding at the door to the men's quarters. She saw her aunt running towards her. Something was wrong for all the men to be at the entrance door of the living quarters.

Lisa hit the brakes. 'What is it, Aunty?'

Zena swung the passenger's door open and hopped in. 'Quick! Get me back to the homestead. Harry has had a very bad turn. I need to call the Royal Flying Doctor.'

Lisa waited while her aunt made the desperate call. She re-appeared some five minutes later, and they headed back down. Ned and a few other shearers were standing at the door. The shearers parted and Zena stepped in. 'I just called them, Alan. They're out on another call. Who knows when they will be here.'

'Ned, what happened?' asked Lisa, standing in the doorway.

'Old Harry, he just had this funny turn. Wasn't doing noth-ing, just seemed to go pale and pass out. Says he's got the chest pains again.' Lisa made her way into the shed. Alan looked up as she stepped inside. Harry was a terrible grey colour. Cookie stood at the end of the bed, so Lisa made her way up to him. She placed her arm around his waist. Harry was speaking in a fairly wheezy manner, and it sounded like the death rattles.

'Alan, you've been a great mate and I never paid you for helping me and Cookie back in Lightning Ridge a few years back' he wheezed. Just talking seemed to take all his strength. 'Here I am, not working at the shed and not paying my way again. I want you to have my stones. They're under my pillow. Me and Cookie got these out of a good rock. Been carrying them around with me for years. Please take 'em.'

Alan pulled out the jar from under Harry's pillow. There were brightly coloured green-blue stones swirling around in a jar of water. Opals. 'I can't take these, Harry. You and Cookie have worked hard for them.' Alan was solemn in his response.

'Nah, you take them, Alan,' said Cookie. 'He wants you to have 'em, and you and Zena have been so good to us both over the years.' Alan looked at the small jar. The opals were a beautiful colour. Lisa could see the tears welling in Cookie's eyes. She was not far off, pools slowly filling her eyes.

'Just hold on, Harry. You ain't going anywhere. Need you around here just for good luck,' said Jack, who was also standing by the bed. Harry gave a faint smile but was having trouble breathing as he clutched his chest, his face contorting with the pain.

'You're a good man, Alan, and a good mate. Jack, you been the best boss to work with too. Where is my Cookie?' His chest wheezed and rattled.

'I'm right here, cobber.' Cookie came and sat at his bedside. He took Harry's hand. Harry gave a final gasp, and his head fell to the side. The only sound to be heard was the laughter from the kookaburras, and the flies buzzing in the shed. Cookie looked desolate. He closed Harry's eyes and covered him with a sheet. His best mate had gone. Lisa felt the sadness swamp the room.

Alan took control. 'Okay, everyone out. Over by the tree where Burnu has his camp. We'll say a few words for Harry.' It was a sombre crowd that marshalled around the tree. Lisa walked with Cookie, who just shuffled along, tears falling down his cheeks. Lisa couldn't stop crying either. Zena came over to Cookie and flanked him with Lisa.

The workers stood with their heads bowed. All of them had removed their hats. Some stood in a state of disbelief. They seemed to be tongue-tied and looked to Alan. 'Harry was a good and decent bloke, a friend to all who knew him. A hard worker who loved the land. He will be missed.'

'Here, here,' said Jack, and the same words were uttered from the other men.

Nobody moved, and for hardened men who had only known physical labour all their lives, their sensitivity was apparent. A few of them wiped their eyes, and everyone came past Cookie and touched his shoulder. The camaraderie was clearly evident.

'We'll have a special dinner for him tonight, and a quiet beer. Please head back to work. Could everyone be back here around 6.00 p.m.'

Lisa knew Billy would be upset. He was out herding sheep. They both liked old Harry and his mate Cookie. Howling noises started coming from the black's camp.

'What's that noise?' Lisa asked.

'It's the blacks,' Jack said. 'They know when a spirit has departed. Who knows what they're saying with those sounds, but it's about the spirit leaving this earth. Sometimes they go on for a day or so, and sometimes well into the night. The sounds travel, so you may hear it through the night, Lisa. Don't be alarmed. Remember, they have their own laws and customs.'

Alan came over to Jack. 'Mate, give me a hand with Harry's body. We'll take him up to the Tack Room and wrap him up until the Flying Doctor arrives.'

Alan looked at Zena and informed her, 'No urgency now, if you know what I mean. You just need to make that final call and advise that Harry has passed away.' Zena nodded and grasped hold of Lisa's hand.

Harry was loaded into the back of the ute. Alan got on the bike. Zena and Lisa drove silently back to the house. 'Go and put the kettle on, Lisa. We'll join you in a few minutes,' said Alan.

After they had taken Harry's body to the Tack Room, the three of them sat solemnly in the kitchen. Alan had the jar of opals on the dining room table. He twirled the bottle around, and the beautiful blue and green colours of the opals shimmered in the light. Alan recalled when he travelled to Lightning Ridge to help them fence their property. He told Zena and Lisa that they'd had no money to pay but Harry had said he was always good at eventually paying his debts. He did not expect the debt to be paid like this though, he told them.

At 5.00 p.m., they had finished for the day, and Alan suggested they have a drink on the verandah. 'Let's gather a bit of strength before we head down. What about a gin and tonic, Zena?'

'Sounds perfect,' she said.

'You sit right there. I'll get it and a soda water for our girl. I'm having a Scotch, and a bloody double at that.'

Alan carried the tray of drinks out and then sat, taking a decent sip of the Scotch. 'Well needed. What a day. Hey, Harry,' he toasted as he raised his glass to the sky. They sat quietly and watched the animals come to the bore.

'It's a sad time for Cookie and us, with Harry no longer being in the land of the living, but time heals. Life goes on, Lisa,' Alan said, raising his glass. 'To Harry. In shearer's heaven.' The women followed suit. Lisa looked to the sky and smiled. Harry had joined the spirits.

After finishing their drinks, they loaded the food and beer into the ute. Lisa saw Billy galloping Jed down the road. 'He's been gone all day up in the back paddocks, working the sheep,' said Alan. 'He's a natural roamer. Gawd knows where he goes or what he gets up to, but all I know is he gets things done.'

When they pulled up to the shed, everyone was waiting. The shearers helped unload, and Cookie had the table set with a nice cloth. Lisa saw Billy sitting with Burnu, who was obviously letting Billy know what had happened.

Jack spoke. 'I guess this is what they call a wake. I know there's been no funeral or burial yet, but most of us here won't be around for that, so with respect to Harry, we'll celebrate his life now. Please help yourself and tell a few yarns, good or bad, about Harry. I'm sure he's listening and will be pleased to hear what you think.' There was a chuckle and a few discussions amongst the men, and then Ned began to play his harmonica. The sun was setting, and the blistering heat began to fade.

Billy came and sat next to Lisa. 'Are you okay?' he asked her gently. She nodded. 'Yes, I'm fine, sad though. He was so lovely. I feel sadness for Cookie too.'

'Harry go to da Big Sky, Lisa. He see you. He happy. This is sorry business for da ones left behind,' said Billy.

Lisa suddenly changed the subject, all of a sudden remembering something. 'Guess what, Billy. I'm allowed to go to your special place, but my aunt and Alan are also curious about this place, so I cannot go with you on our own, but they suggested we all drive out in the Land Rover and have lunch and a wander around. What do you think? Could you share your special place with three other special people?'

A big smile crept across Billy's face. 'Sound proper good.' They finished their meal, listened to Ned's tunes and one last speech from Jack. It was time to say goodnight. Lisa watched the beautiful sunset, the big blue sky turning orange and pink as it began to greet the night.

'Let's go, kid. It's been a long day. Bed awaits.' They drove back to the homestead in silence, the stars twinkling as they made their appearance.

When Lisa lay down that night she whispered 'Goodnight, Harry. I hope the spirits are looking after you.' She listened to the sound of the howls that carried across the night air and closed her eyes. The Flying Doctor would arrive tomorrow to collect Harry's body. Cookie was leaving with them. Everything was going to change now that it was the end of the season.

Splintered Heart

TWENTY-TWO

END OF SEASON

Dawn broke and the beauty of the sunrise unfolded. Alan heard the plane land. 'I had best move and get these old bones out of bed, Zena. He's earlier than I thought.'

'Do you want a hand, Alan,' asked Zena, wiping sleep from her eyes.

'No, it'll be fine. Cookie and the good doctor are on hand. Cookie would have no doubt heard the plane.' Alan made his way to the gate leading out of the compound as Derek, from the Royal Flying Doctor, approached.

'Morning, Derek,' Alan greeted him, 'Thanks for coming so soon. Bloody sad moment for all of us.' The men shook hands. 'I'll go get Cookie, but Harry's body is in the Tack Room, just opposite the house. We've got him wrapped up so the flies don't carry him away.'

Alan jumped into the ute and headed down to the sheds. Cookie sat waiting on the small wooden bench just outside the shearer's quarters. He looked a solemn figure, his packed tote by his feet. Alan felt sorry for the old fellow; sadness marked his weathered face. *Loss and grief, we all have to face it.*

'The doctor's here, Cookie. We can go now if you like.' Cookie drew a deep breath. 'That's fine, Alan. I'm ready, been ready since before sunup.'

The two men headed to the homestead and then around to the Tack Room, where the doctor sat waiting with Zena. 'Derek, this is Cookie, best mate of old Harry. He'll be going with you.'

'Sorry for your loss, Cookie,' Derek said as he shook his hand.

'It's okay, mate. We all got to go some time. Taxes and death, right?' Cookie never seemed to be lost for words or his sense of humour, even in his darkest hour. Alan and Derek carried Harry's body to the ute. Zena handed the men a basket containing a thermos of tea and some fruit cake for Derek and Cookie. 'Thanks, Zena' said Derek. 'Cookie and I sure will enjoy that fruit cake along the way.'

'Goodbye, Cookie,' Zena said, hugging the old man. 'Come back next year; we'd love to see you here.'

'Not sure, missus, but we'll see.' Cookie hopped into the back of the ute and waved as they headed to the plane. His arm was draped over his mate's body. After loading Harry's body into the plane, Alan shook Cookie's hand. 'Thanks Cookie, goodbye old friend. Come back next year.'

Alan watched the small plane take off and saluted the air. 'Goodbye, Harry old mate. I'm sure you'll be fossicking up there somewhere for opals.'

◊

With Cookie gone, Zena was kept busy cooking for the crew until the end of the week. It kept her mind off the investigation. The crew made no complaints. Sometimes they said Cookie's food was bloody disgusting. End of season was always fun but it would be tinged with sadness this time. As she boiled the potatoes and prepared the food on platters on the dining table, the jar of opals caught the light. 'You're with us aren't you, Harry?' she whispered.

It was now the last night of the shearing season. When they got down to the sheds, the fire was roaring, and men were sitting on the bales of hay, scattered in groups, yakking and holding a beer. Ned began to play his harmonica.

'Hey, grasshopper, let me give you a hand.' It was Billy.

'Thanks, Billy,' said Lisa, appreciative of the help. 'Just grab those plastic tubs. They have all the plates and cutlery. If you could place them at the end of the table that would be great.' Lisa carried the food with her aunt to the long white tables and covered them with the nets. They were set to go.

Alan banged one of Zena's pots. 'Last speech for the season. Thank you everyone for a great job. You've all worked very hard, and you're a wonderful team. There's a small bonus in each of your pay packets and there's no work tomorrow, so I'm sure Jack the boss will let you kick on to the early hours of the morning tonight. Let's raise our glasses to us and old Harry.'

Hats were thrown into the air, and the shearers and crew began to move around and celebrate another good year. Woori was always a good place to work. They would return. God willing.

Alan took Zena into his arms, and they did a waltz around the camp fire. Billy watched. He stood up and extended his hand to Lisa. She jumped up and joined her aunt and uncle. They fumbled about on the red dirt. Neither could dance.

'Ouch, Billy, you have two left feet,' Lisa giggled. There was applause and much laughter at Billy's attempts to dance. 'You are way out of time, Billy,' Lisa said, laughing out loud. 'You go one way and I go the other!'

Jimmy, who stood menacingly against a tree, walked towards the couple. Jack watched, as did all the crew.

'My turn, Billy,' he said as he tried to take Lisa's hand.

'Bugger off, Jimmy,' said Billy, and they began to push and shove until Jack strode over and pulled them apart like wet paper.

'Hey, you two, knock it off!' His big hands held both of them back separately. Lisa stepped back. Jimmy made her feel very unsafe.

'Jimmy, you've had too much grog. A bloody skinful. You can either go to the men's quarters and sleep it off or I'll lock you up in the shearing shed. Make up your bloody mind, but it stops here.'

Ned put down his harmonica. Only the crackle of the fire and sounds of the night could now be heard.

Jimmy pulled Jack's arm away, anger burning in his eyes. 'You bastard, Billy,' he yelled and strode off towards the men's quarters. Ned began to play his harmonica and the jovial mood returned.

The night wore on and many stories were passed around about Harry and Cookie and the past seasons.

'It's getting late, Lisa. Do you want to come home with us,' asked Zena.

'Is it alright if I stay awhile, Aunty? I'm having so much fun, despite what just happened, and I'll clean up and stack plates before I leave. Billy will get me up to the homestead safely.'

'Okay, darling, but not too late.' Lisa waved them off and returned to sit by the fire.

Jack came over and sat with them. 'So how are you two going? Been doing lots together, I hear.'

'Yes, Jack, I wanted to learn more about the bush and riding, and Billy has been very helpful. I'll be sad to see him go, but I'll just have to keep practising so I can outride him when he comes back!'

'You'll need a lot of practice, young lady. Billy is the best horseman I've seen in a long time.' Jack slapped Billy's back and went off for another beer. Lisa turned to Billy and said, 'I have to ask my aunt which day we can go to Goobang. But she did say after the season, so maybe tomorrow or the day after. I can't wait to see your special place.'

Billy slapped his knee. He was jubilant as he'd really been expecting a no. 'I can't wait to show it to you. Such a special place and good spirits,' he said as he gazed into her lovely face.

They then loaded the plates and cutlery into the tubs Alan had provided and put the food leftovers in the fridge in the men's quarters.

Jimmy sat in the far corner watching them like a hawk, his face glowering with rage. Lisa was very aware of his presence so she moved quickly. She didn't like his menacing eyes. She'd seen eyes like that before.

'You get away this time, brudder,' Jimmy snarled at Billy. 'But you got to get on the road sometime. I be waiting. Be waiting for you! No Jack to protect you then.'

'Get lost, Jimmy. You're pissed.' Billy rolled his eyes, shrugging off Jimmy's threats. But he pulled Lisa quickly out of the shed and walked towards the yards where the blacks and shearers kept their horses.

'Come on, this way. You can ride bareback with me to the homestead.' Billy swung his long legs over Jed. 'Get on behind me.' He grabbed Lisa's arm, and she swung up as he pulled her close behind him. Her arms encircled Billy's waist as they galloped towards the homestead. She looked up and saw the stars. She breathed in Billy's scent. His smell was of the land. She wanted the moment to last forever.

Lisa slid off the horse when they reached the homestead.

'Goodnight, Billy.'

'Goodnight, grasshopper.'

Lisa grinned. 'I'll see you tomorrow and let you know what day.'

◊

Billy watched her walk away. He felt a lot of emotion for the girl. Too much for a whitey. He wanted more, but he knew she was still young, and that some whitefellas had smashed her spirit proper good. He shuddered at the thought of anyone hurting this girl. She still had lots of healing to do. That was okay, he was a patient fella. He would wait for her. He didn't care how long it would take but he wanted to heal her spirit, teach her more about the land and his tribe. Billy hoped one day there would be more and that her heart would one day belong to him.

TWENTY-THREE

UNTIL WE MEET AGAIN

'Morning,' said Zena as Lisa came out into the kitchen, yawning and stretching. 'There's a bit of tidying up to do today down there, but I think tomorrow is a good day to head out to Goobang with the Land Rover.

What say you, Alan?' asked Zena. He nodded in agreement. 'Sounds good.'

'What time can I tell Billy we'll be leaving for Goobang?' she asked excitedly.

Alan picked up his hat. 'Tell Billy to be here at 6.30 a.m., and we'll have lunch out there. But I'm heading down to the shearer's shed shortly to help Jack, so I can mention it.'

Alan drove to the main shed and saw Billy helping load bales of wool onto a truck. 'Are the crew packing up?'

'Yes, boss. Big Jack has dem organised. He said he had shitloads to do. Burnu said stay until we get back from Goobang.'

'Very good. We can head out there early tomorrow morning. Say about 6.30 a.m. Have your breakfast. Zena will bring lunch and a few other things, so we won't starve, knowing my wife.'

'Yep, alright boss, look forward to it. Lots to see at Goobang. Special place. We see boobook owls, big eagles, wallaby, kangaroo. Lots of lizards and goannas. Small pools of water, big paperbark trees. Lots of nature. No-one but us in Goobang.'

Alan slapped the boy's back. He was a good hard worker, like his father Burnu in his youth. He really liked the boy and was glad they were all going to Goobang. It would be a special day and a good day for Lisa to remember.

◊

The house was now empty. Lisa was off doing her chores, so Zena made a follow up call to John Raby at Walgett Police Station.

'Constable Raby speaking.'

'Hi John, it's Zena Smith. Have I got you at a good time?'

'Yes, Zena. Sorry I haven't got back to you quicker, just so many things to do here at the station. I have that name and number for you. She's apparently very good and goes to Walgett monthly. Good luck, and if there are any problems, let me know.'

'Thanks, John.' Zena looked at the name and number she had scribbled down. Dr Helen Tyler. Zena dialled the number, and a young girl answered.

'Dr Tyler's rooms, this is Sandra, how can I help you?'

'Yes, good morning. My name is Zena Smith. I wanted to make an appointment for Dr Tyler to see my niece in Walgett. She has not seen Dr Tyler previously and she has suffered rather traumatic sexual abuse for which there will be a police investigation.'

'I'm so very sorry to hear that. I'll fit your niece in. Dr Tyler is there Thursday of next week. Would 1.00 p.m. suit you? It's usually her lunch period but if there's anything urgent such as this, she asks me to get the client in quickly.'

'I'm very grateful, thank you. My niece's name is Lisa O'Connor. She's aged sixteen years. I can bring statements and information that will help Dr Tyler. Because of the investigation, we have documented the details of the assaults.'

'That would be very helpful,' Sandra agreed.

Zena jotted down the address. 'We'll see you next week. Thank you, Sandra. You have been most helpful.'

Zena quickly dialled Detective Collette. He picked up on the first ring. 'Thanks for calling, Mrs Smith. We were actually going to call you. We'll be there on the 5th November to start the investigation. Does that suit you and Lisa?'

'Yes, no problem, that will be fine. Why I'm ringing though is to confirm whether a female police officer will be present.' Zena took a deep breath.

'Yes, Mrs Smith. As I mentioned, this is a common request, and having daughters of my own, this is understandable. I believe, looking at your file, Lynette Harrison, one of our senior detectives will be coming with us.'

She sighed with relief. 'Thanks, Detective, I'll let Lisa know. She'll be very grateful. See you on the 5th November. We have accommodation for you, so that isn't a problem. Stay as long as you like. No need to go back and forth into town. We just want to get this right.'

'So do we, Mrs Smith, so do we. It's also a matter of bringing justice for Lisa and all the other girls.'

She hung up the phone and breathed deeply. Now she had to tell Lisa. She hoped it wouldn't dampen the girl's spirits before they headed to Goobang.

Alan and Lisa appeared late in the afternoon. 'All done?' Zena asked. 'What does it look like down there?'

'Yep, it was all hands on deck for the clean-up. We brought this up from the fridges down there. Some of it was from last night. May make your job lighter for lunch tomorrow,' said Alan, placing the food down. 'We gave some food to the shearers and the lubras for their trip out. Who knows where they're all heading to.'

'Who's left down there?' queried Zena.

'Jack, but as usual he's the last to leave. Makes sure everyone and everything is off the property, but Jimmy was still lurking about. I told Jack to keep an eye on him. Billy was loading bales of wool onto the trucks, but I'll be glad to see Jimmy go. Too much tension between the boys. I need a cold beer.'

'I need a shower. I'll go wash, up. I smell and I'm dirty,' Lisa piped up, kicking off her boots.

After Lisa left the kitchen, Zena said, 'I've got some news too, but I'll let her know over dinner.'

'What's that?' asked Alan, his brows drawing together.

'Tell you over dinner. Which is not far away. So finish that pale brew and we can discuss it with Lisa.'

◊

'That's better,' said Lisa, sitting down. 'The red dust seems to cover me from head to toe.'

Zena took Lisa's hand and said gently, 'I spoke to the detectives who will handle the investigation, and they are bringing a female police officer with them.' Lisa looked relieved and let out a sigh.

'I feel so much more comfortable with that, Aunty. I've been churning over and over about telling men about what other men have done to me.' A pink flush crept over Lisa's face.

'Detective Collette is very easy to talk to. Said he had daughters of his own. They are arriving here on the 5th November and will stay for as long as it takes.'

'Stay here?' Alan asked.

'Yes. We cannot have them going back and forth to Carinda. They would have to stay at the pub and so many hours would be lost in travelling there and back every day.' Zena continued, 'The other thing I have to tell you is about the female psychiatrist I told you about. Her name is Dr Helen Tyler, and she has an appointment for you next Thursday at 1.00 p.m. in Walgett.' Lisa looked apprehensive.

'Lisa, your face just dropped. Are you okay with this?'

Lisa nodded but could feel a wave of nausea. She put her fork down and swallowed hard. 'It's just that this will be the first time I've spoken to a complete stranger about what happened.'

'Yes, I know, darling, but she is a doctor and a professional and that is all she does. She specialises in sexual abuse and the resultant trauma. I really think this will help you. Dr Tyler will teach you behavioural therapies and coping strategies. You'll be able to draw upon these things as we move through the investigation. I think you need her help at this time.'

Lisa was quiet over dinner. They washed up and there was more silence than usual. 'I'm heading to bed, Aunty. I need an early night for the big day tomorrow.'

'It's going to be an amazing day, Lisa. Billy has so much to show you, and us, for that matter. We can't wait either.' She kissed her niece goodnight.

The sun shone through her window. It was about 5.30 a.m. Lisa's mind was swirling with so many different thoughts. She moved slowly off her bed and dressed. She could hear noises in the kitchen.

'Morning, kid,' Alan said cheerily as passed some toast across.

'Thanks,' Lisa yawned.

'You had better wake up, kid. That boy will be here shortly to give us the Goobang tour.' Lisa laughed and nodded. Alan always put her at ease.

The clock ticked towards 6.30 a.m., and there was a knock at the door.

'Come in, Billy,' said Alan. 'She's been up early, our girl, and is keen to get going.' Lisa met Billy's eyes. She felt a tingling sensation.

Zena appeared with a large picnic basket and some blankets. 'Okay, everyone set to go?' They loaded up the Land Rover and Alan took off. Billy chatted in the car about the beauty of the place and how he would swim in the billabongs and hunt and fish. The conversation flowed about the shearing season, Harry, horses and the spirits of the land. It was going to be a great day.

When they arrived at the bottom of the ridge, the sun was high. The scenery along the way was breathtaking. The big open plains and wildlife were in abundance. Billy pointed to the top ridge. 'We can walk up there. The view out to da land is good, boss. You can reach to da spirits up there. We can take a small track, not far from here. Take you way to da top.'

'Lead the way, Billy. I'm just as excited as my girl here. We'll grab some water and a blanket and head up there.'

Lisa sighed and said, 'This is just the most tranquil and beautiful place, Billy. No wonder you think it's special. I would love to swim in a billabong one day.' They found the track and started to climb. It was an easy walk, and they arrived at the highest peak in just under an hour. The view before them stretched out forever. Eagles soared above them. 'Spirit bird,' Billy pointed. 'They follow you, Lisa.'

'It's spectacular up here, Billy. It's so different being higher up to being on the flat,' said Zena.

'Yeah,' Billy agreed. 'At night, me lay up here and look at da stars, at da Southern Cross. Milky Way stretch out across da sky like a big white veil.' She would love to lie on a blanket, here at this place, under the stars and looking at the Southern Cross. Maybe one day, she thought.

'Nothing can hurt us up here,' said Lisa aloud. Billy looked at her and across to Zena.

'She bin hurt, your Lisa?' Billy asked Zena tentatively. Zena nodded.

Lisa looked at him as he spoke. She wanted to tell him everything. She had only hinted at what had happened to her. Would he reject her if he knew everything?

Billy sat cross-legged and looked out across the plains and up to the sky. He tapped the ground with a stick and spoke in an almost sing-song fashion in his native tongue.

'What did you say, Billy?' Zena asked. He looked directly at Lisa.

'I ask da spirits to look after Lisa. No-one will hurt her now. Da spirits mend your broken soul, heal you. Bad dreams go. Flow like a river, da eagle he follows you.'

Lisa was visibly moved, and she squatted down next to Billy. To Zena, it was plain to see the boy was good for her and was opening her up, just like Binna. He had the power to see inside her. The power to heal her.

Alan nodded in Zena's direction. He could also see the special affinity Billy and Lisa had for each other. The silence washed over them in waves. They drank in the views and the special atmosphere.

It was Zena who spoke. 'This is the spirit country, Billy. We thank you for sharing your sacred place. But I think we best make a move now.'

Billy helped Lisa to her feet but held her hand tightly. He lightly brushed his lips over the back of her hand. 'Be still, let your heart be quiet. You safe grasshopper.' Lisa followed Billy down to the Land Rover. She lay her head on his shoulder on the journey home. She finally felt trust in a man.

They dropped Billy off, and he headed over to where Burnu's fire was going. It was just Jack, Burnu and Billy. The others had all left.

◊

In bed that evening, Zena turned to Alan. 'Interesting day. That boy has a spiritual effect on Lisa. She looks the same as how she does when she sits with Binna. They heal her, they see through her.'

'Yep, I was there too remember,' Alan said.

'He travels into her mind, and she trusts him. I think we have a long way to go, but she is healing. These people have amazing skills. What did he say . . . spirit country? I think it's the perfect description,' said Zena.

◊

Lisa woke up as the sun rose. She was dreading this day. Billy's last day. She was teary at the thought. *I'll be lost without him.* She threw some clothes on and jumped into the ute. *I have to hurry. I can't let him go without saying goodbye.*

Jack was leaning against his own ute, talking to Billy. 'Someone is in a hurry,' he smiled as Lisa pulled up and jumped out of the vehicle.

Billy smiled. 'It's my grasshopper.'

'I thought you would all leave without saying goodbye.' She was breathless as she exited the ute.

'No, I was heading off to the house shortly to let Alan know I'd finished. These two blackfellas, well they usually just take off.'

Lisa looked at Billy. 'I wondered if you wanted to have one more ride with me, Billy, before you go. It's still early,' she asked shyly.

Billy called out to Burnu. 'One more ride. Is dat alright, Burnu?' The old man nodded.

Lisa clapped her hands together. 'We can go past Binna and Ningali. I'll have some breakfast, and we can meet at 9.00 a.m. Does that suit you?

Billy's eyes flashed. He would miss her. 'Sounds good, missus. I ride Jed up and see you then.'

When Lisa got back to the homestead, Jack was there chatting to Alan. 'Jack is heading off now, Lisa.' She stopped to shake his hand. 'It's been really nice getting to know you, Jack. I hope to see you next year.'

Jack tipped his hat. 'I will see you next year, little lady. What did Billy call you . . . grasshopper?' He laughed and shook Alan's hand. Zena appeared at the back door. 'Take care, Zena. The perfect hostess as usual. You're a lucky bastard, Alan Smith,' Jack called out as he hopped in his ute and sped off, dust flying everywhere.

Zena turned to Lisa. She looked a bit down. 'I went down to see if Billy wanted one more ride before he and Burnu leave.'

'I know this is hard for you, Lisa, saying goodbye to Billy. Alan and I saw it yesterday, the connection you two have. He is soothing to you, like Binna, I guess. But please remember they have their own customs. Yes, one last ride. Go and have fun and take Noir.'

Lisa nodded her thanks. She loved riding Noir. 'We'll go out past Binna and Ningali. Do you need me to take anything?'

'Yes, I have a lot of greens from the vegetable patch and some potatoes. I shall throw them in a sack, and you can hang it over Noir. Don't be away all day. Billy will have to get on his way, they will now be on the move.' Lisa bit her cheek. The reality was all too real.

Lisa had saddled Noir and was in the yard when Billy rode up.

'Hey,' she said softly.

'Hey back, grasshopper. You ready to go?'

They rode out along the dusty road chatting about Goobang and when Billy might return. It was close to noon when the black women's little humpy came into view. Ningali saw them first. 'Binna, I can see Lisa. Dat Billy, he riding with her.' She scowled.

The smoke from their fire curled into the air. Ningali called out. 'Hey, Lisa, good to see you. Bin thinking where you bin.' She looked at Billy.

Lisa dismounted and pulled the bag of vegetables off her horse. She gave Ningali a hug and went over to Binna. Sitting down, she put her arm around the old lady. 'It's so good to see you both. I'm sorry I've not been out here but I've been busy with school and learning to ride, and generally helping out for the season. We came by a couple of times and there was no fire. You weren't here.'

'I go into da bush for tucker. Binna just sleeping. So no fire. We heard someone had died from da shearing crew,' Ningali said. 'That sorry business.'

Lisa looked amazed. *How did they know?* 'Yes, very sad. It was old Harry.'

'Aaaah. We knew old Harry. Good bloke. He treat us black women good and proper. We don't mention his name anymore now.'

'I've heard of this custom about not mentioning names of the dead. Billy explained it to me. It's a mark of respect to the deceased and also because it's too painful for the grieving family.' Binna and Ningali nodded. They seemed proud of her interest in their culture.

Lisa added, 'We're just going for a ride, but I'll come out in a few more days. Is there anything that you need, Binna?'

'No, me alright. Ningali, she good at da bush tucker.' Binna held out her hand to Lisa.

'Of that I'm sure, but I just know my aunt will give me something to bring. She always worries about you two women out here. I'll have more time with the season over, and when Billy leaves.' Binna heard the sadness in her voice. There was something more here.

'Binna, I wanted to thank you. Your smoking ceremony and cleansing ceremony made me feel like I was protected, and the bad spirits were moved away. It was like I was suddenly released from my body and the spirit gave me this knowledge. Everything that had been confused was clear and everything that perplexed me was explained. I struggled with some bad stuff for a long time, but you helped me to let go of it.'

Binna nodded knowingly. 'Keeping da good spirits important. I have another ceremony for you. I bin waiting to see you. I feel in your body now, you are well. You get better. I feel things running smoothly, like a river.' Be like a river, Billy had said. Be open and flow.

Lisa smiled. 'We'll be off then, Ningali. Billy is leaving maybe today or early tomorrow, so there's not much time left in the day. I'll catch you as soon as I can. Lovely to see you both. Keep well.'

◊

As they rode away, Ningali spoke. 'She like Billy. Dat plain to see, Binna. Dey lookem' good together but she is young and white, and he black man. No good, big trouble. I see it.'

Binna drew in the dirt but this time the two figures were connected. She looked up to the sky. 'Destiny. Great spirits brought dem together. Dem souls dey meant to meet. Dey bring her to me and to Billy. She was broken. Now she mending. Spirits don't care about da colour of skin.'

◊

When they rode into Woori, Lisa felt a great sadness. This was their last ride together.

'I'll take Noir around the back of the Tack Room.' Billy followed Lisa and helped her unsaddle Noir, rinse her down and hay up.

The dogs were barking across the bore, and Lisa knew they would alert her aunt and Alan. Billy carried the saddle into the Tack Room and began to wipe it down while Lisa cleaned the bridle.

'I'll be saying goodbye now, grasshopper.' Lisa turned to face him. Here was the first man she could trust, who made her feel clean and decent. Now he was leaving. There was a lump in her throat. Billy tipped his hat. He pulled her gently towards him and lightly brushed her lips.

There was no repulsion. It was sweet as she felt the softness of his lips. 'Thank you, Billy, for the best time. You taught me so much. I'll miss you so much. I don't know how to be here without you.'

'Me miss you too. You like da air I breathe. Your voice like da summer rain to my ears.' Lisa's heart pounded and she felt the emptiness inside her already, and he hadn't even left yet. Billy mounted Jed, tipped his hat once more, dug his heels into Jed's flanks and cantered down the road towards Burnu.

Lisa watched the cloud of dust as he disappeared out of sight. Her heart felt heavy. She wanted to run after him. 'Hey,' came her aunt's voice. 'Heard the dogs barking, so we knew you weren't far. Where's Billy?' asked Zena.

'He headed back to see Burnu. It's too late to leave now, so it's an early start tomorrow for them.' Lisa's sadness was evident.

'Come on, Lisa' said Zena, her arm gently coming around Lisa's shoulder. 'Billy has things to do, like you, and he'll be back next year. We have a lot of things to cover in terms of the investigation, and Dr Tyler's appointment is next week, so we need to prepare. In no time, the police will arrive, so I'm hoping you'll have a few sessions with Dr Tyler before that.'

'Binna wants me to have another ceremony. She said something about how she could feel better flow in me. I thanked her and told her how I felt. I feel great when she works with me, Aunty. Like I've been cleansed. I'll go out in a couple of days.'

'It's getting towards evening. Wash up. Alan is cooking tonight. A good old fashioned barbeque. If you get up early enough, you can head down to say goodbye to Billy and Burnu tomorrow.'

Lisa's face brightened. 'What a great idea, Aunty.' She finished dinner quickly, packed up the dishes and excused herself from the table. She just wanted to escape into her bedroom with her own thoughts and feelings. Like how good Billy made her feel. Would he be back and when? How would she ever find him if he didn't? She just wanted him near her, to feel his warmth. She touched her lips. His lips were so soft, and she loved his softness. She wanted more. Her head was spinning and she closed her eyes. *Billy, come back to me.*

She flopped down on her bed and imagined she was laying under a canopy of stars in the bush, looking at the moon and the Southern Cross. A blanket of diamonds. *He is my diamond,* she thought.

Lisa closed her eyes and whispered 'Billy.' In her sleep, she saw the tall dark boy riding towards her. She was not frightened; there was no fear. Her spirits were high, and the eagles flew above her. His stride was long, and his arms reached for her, softly kissing her mouth. He was beginning to make love to her, slowly, with no force, with no pain. He tenderly touched her, and she ached for more. She could hear him breathing and feel the strength in him. The vision was strong. She felt his light feathery fingers tracing her body. He whispered, 'I love you, grasshopper.' She opened her eyes and the vision was gone. But she'd felt him.

Lisa rose early. Billy saw the ute heading towards them and smiled at her.

'Good morning, missus,' he shouted as the ute came to a halt. She could tell he was happy to see her. Lisa's heart thumped as she slowly got out of the ute and stood before the young black boy who made her feel safe. 'I've come to say goodbye to you and Burnu.' Lisa felt the sadness wash over her and the tears welling in her eyes.

Billy held up her hand and kissed it, moving her hand to touch his cheek. 'Don't be sad. I be back, grasshopper. Wait for me. I promise I come back for you. Let's walk.'

Lisa sensed that Billy wanted to be away from his father's gaze. They headed around the back of the shearing sheds. He was eager to kiss her but was aware of the gentleness needed. Lisa loved that about him. He was so respectful of her. She looked up at him as she felt the softness of his lips once more.

'I don't want to let you go, Billy.' Lisa clutched at his shirt, not wanting to release him.

'I promise I be back, grasshopper. Wait for me. Say you will. Wait for me.'

Lisa nodded, and as her head lay against his chest, his strong arms came around her. She began to cry.

'Please don't cry, grasshopper. I be back next year. I be a man then. Come on. Burnu waiting.' He wiped her tears away with his shirt.

When they reappeared, Burnu could see Lisa had been crying. This was more than a friendship. He looked to the sky and out across the land. *The spirits, dey draw dem together. Powerful.*

'We be back, Lisa. My boy Billy like working at Woori, now more dan ever. I take good care of him. You don't worry now.'

'Thank you, Burnu. I'll try not to.'

'We join our people soon, do things, go walkabout, maybe work, maybe rest. Time go quickly.'

'Take me with you,' Lisa blurted. Burnu's eyes widened in surprise as he looked at Lisa.

'Can't take white girl. Big trouble for us.' The sound of a motorbike approaching stopped the conversation. It was Alan, who had come to say goodbye.

'All packed up, Burnu?' he asked as his long legs slipped over the bike.

'Yes, boss. Me and Billy heading west. Join our people. Stay awhile,' Burnu said proudly.

'Thank you, Burnu. You too, Billy. You're a great team. You are both welcome here always,' Alan said.

'Thanks, boss. He be head stockman soon, den take over from Jack. We be on our way now.' Alan shook their hands, and Billy mounted Jed.

The old man turned to Lisa and gazed into her eyes. He did a full circle around her face with his bony finger and then produced some quartz from his pocket.

'Dreamtime is da past, and it moves with da flow of time. Like a river. It can take us to what will come. Good energy for all creatures. We use da quartz and da crystals.'

Burnu opened her hand and placed them in her palm. His eyes burned brightly as he stared into her soul. Lisa closed her fingers.

'Long ago, da spirits rose up from underground and come down from da sky. As dey walked da earth, dey called out da names of animals and things. As each word was spoken for da first time, dat tree or bird or mineral, it come to life. Da spirits, dey returned underground or dey fly back to da Big Sky. Dis is quartz from around Uluru. Special giant land, dat Uluru. Give you energy and da strength. Dis energy help you step into your spiritual power. When you want to cleanse, smudge your body with dis quartz.'

He said something in his own language and brought his hand up to touch her face. Lisa trembled. *I so want to go with you, Burnu. Please take me with you.*

Burnu waved to Alan and then walked towards his son who had his horse ready.

Lisa began to sob. The thud of her heart matched her short breaths, and anxiety ripped through her, thinking she may never see Billy again. Alan put his arm around her shoulder. 'Now then, young lady, time to get busy and take your mind off things. These blokes need to do their own thing now. They will be back. Season after season. Trust me. Come on, kid, let's head home.'

Lisa stood rigid, and her gaze never left Billy. It was though he knew she was looking, and he turned. His heart was the same as hers. She could feel it. Emptiness ebbed into her body, and her heart collided with the sadness of his departure. She felt the quartz in her hand. She waved, and then Billy turned to face the road with his father by his side.

Lisa knew her fate was somehow intertwined with Billy's. *I need you like the air I breathe. You put the darkness away.* She would pine for him until he returned. She wanted more of him, not just seasonal. *I don't care about the colour of your skin. I see the person beneath.* She sensed they would love each other, but until then, the road ahead for her would be grievous and uncertain. 'I will wait for you, Billy,' *she whispered.*

What do the spirits have in store for Lisa and Billy?

Will justice prevail for her in the New South Wales court of
law?

Will the monsters who stole her innocence and splintered her
heart be locked away for good?

Does Lisa ever reconcile with her parents and see her brother
Mark again?

**Find out in Book Two of the Red Dust series, due to be
released in 2020.**

ACKNOWLEDGEMENTS

Thank you to Juliette (my wonderful editor), my brother Mark who supports me so unconditionally, Willo, (my gorgeous farmer), my Maianbar friends who are just so special, especially Shirley Anne, Doris & Lindy, Eddy, and all those who have listened to and supported me.

ABOUT THE AUTHOR

Linda Dowling grew up in the western suburbs of Sydney, Australia. During her childhood, she spent most of her time in rural areas and has continued to enjoy life in the bush or in areas with natural surrounds. Her aunt, a wonderful horse-woman, lived in Carinda, New South Wales and taught her a great deal about horses, riding and the outback. It was during her vacations with her aunt that Linda herself fell in love with the vast outback plains and the Aboriginal culture, their stories and their unique but simple way of living. Linda has a natural affinity with Indigenous peoples and was the only white girl selected to play for the Papua New Guinea softball teams at the Pan Pacific Masters.

In her professional life, Linda has established and managed four medico-legal firms, including her own. During the course of her career, she has been involved in reporting on coronial matters and inquests. She has also worked with the New South Wales Police State Crime Command Centre and in various Royal Commissions where she was exposed to the worst of human nature. Linda has drawn upon her professional and personal experiences while writing her Red Dust novel series, but the stories are a work of fiction and do not depict any person, living or dead.

Enjoyed the book? You can follow the author at:

Email: lsd777@bigpond.com

Facebook: facebook.com/authorreddustnovels

LinkedIn: linkedin.com/in/linda-dowling-10bb0635/